RENEGADE'S
PRIDE

B.J. DANIELS

RENEGADE'S PRIDE

HQN™

ISBN-13: 978-0-373-78926-9

Renegade's Pride

Copyright © 2017 by Barbara Heinlein

This edition published by arrangement with Harlequin Books S.A.

For questions and comments about the quality of this book, please contact us at CustomerService@Harlequin.com.

This summer I rode behind the boat on a tube called Big Mable with one of my granddaughters who has no fear. As we were flying over the waves, mostly airborne, laughing, screaming and hanging on for our lives, I thought this is what keeps me writing. So this one is for Hayden, the teenager who I first rode with when she was five—and just as fast. Thanks for keeping me young and reminding me always that life is an adventure.

CHAPTER ONE

A SLIVER OF moon hung high in Montana's immense night sky as Ely Cahill made his way out of the mountains. In the distance, he could see the ranch with its huge barn and, past it, the sprawling house where he'd once lived with his wife, Mary, which meant he didn't have that much farther to go.

He stopped at the edge of the dark pines to shift the heavy pack on his back. It had been easier making this trek when he was younger. Now at almost seventy his gold panning in the mountains took a lot more out of him. He couldn't bear the thought of the day he might not be able to make this trip.

Moving again, he licked his lips, anxious for that first drink he'd have once he reached town. He'd been prospecting in the mountains for over a month now and had found enough gold that it was weighing down his pocket, begging to be traded for cash.

A cloud passed over the moon, pitching the Western landscape into shadow. As if a spider had raced along his bare skin, Ely shuddered and shifted the pack again. He stopped to sniff the wind, alert to danger. At first he thought it might be a bear ahead in the shadowed darkness. He'd cleared the pine trees that blanketed the mountain and now looked down on the pasture. Nothing moved that he could see.

The moonlight glinted off the chain-link fence enclosure in the middle of the pasture. He felt his pulse bump up as his stomach did a slow, sickening roll. He had lived with the horror of what was buried inside that fence for years.

Now he listened, his ears attuned to trouble. As if what was buried there wasn't frightening enough, it was what the enclosure attracted that made his blood run cold. Goose bumps rippled over his skin, an eerie chill in the night air.

After all these years, Ely knew every sound the night made in this part of Montana, from an owl hoot to a hawk's cry to the snap of a twig under the weight of a predator's paw. It was one reason he'd survived in the wilds all these years alone, which was the way he liked it.

Over the next rise, the lights of town beckoned. He licked his lips again, needing that drink more than ever. Boots heavy, he pushed on through the tall grass as he searched the horizon for whatever had spooked him. It wasn't the first time he'd felt his skin prickle at this particular spot. He suspected it wouldn't be the last.

His hand went to the back of his neck. He rubbed his nape under his long, curly graying hair and considered taking a detour around this particular spot. But it would take him a lot longer, and he was anxious now for noise and lights and food he hadn't had to cook himself. Also, he could almost taste that first shot of hooch.

He'd been in the mountains too long. His stomach rumbled at the thought of hot cooked food. Cloud cover blocked the silver moonlight, deepening the darkness over the pasture that stood between him and civilization. He took a step, then another, the tall grass whickering against his filth-crusted canvas pants as he moved. He said the words like a mantra: whiskey and a bath in a tub with hot water and real soap. It propelled him forward a few more steps before he stopped again.

Nothing moved. Even the wind had stopped as if holding its breath. He might have thought he'd gone deaf if not for the tremulous thump of his heart.

It was on a night like this in 1967 that he'd first seen them. The memory was too fresh. He cursed himself for letting his thoughts take that particular path.

"Don't be a damned fool," he said out loud, needing to hear something, even his own voice. "They aren't out there."

And yet every fiber of his being knew better. They were here again. It was his only thought as he turned and tried to run, knowing it was a fool thing to do in the dark in a pasture full of gopher holes.

He'd taken only a few strides when his foot dropped into a gap. He fell face-first, the weight of his heavy pack slamming him down hard into the earth. The fall knocked the wind out of him.

Sprawled in the dirt, he gasped for air as he heard them coming. It was the same swishing sound as before, but this time there were two of them. He sucked in a ragged breath and tried to hold it.

Telling himself that maybe they wouldn't see him if he stayed down, he waited. The waiting was too painful. He lifted his head just enough to peer over the tall grass. They looked larger than he remembered, their bodies hidden beneath the huge blinding-white space suits they wore. He could hear their breathing systems swishing in and out as they labored through the tall spring grass.

Ely thought he might be able to outrun them. He tried to slip off his backpack. It caught on his coat sleeve. Maybe if he could get to his pistol, but there wasn't time.

He put his face against the cold ground and prayed they wouldn't take him this time.

CHAPTER TWO

Sheriff Flint Cahill didn't even bother to look up as the door to his office banged open first thing the next morning.

"Seriously?" his sister, Lillie, demanded as she strode to his desk. "You arrested our father *again*?" Hands on her hips, she glared at him with narrowed gray eyes from a face that could only be described as adorable—even when furious.

He sighed. "What would you have me do? Ely was drunk and disorderly. *Again*. Anyone else who behaves the way he does gets thrown in the slammer."

"He's not just anyone else."

"No, he's not. Did I fail to mention he resisted arrest? Deputy Harper is sporting a shiner this morning."

"I've wanted to slug Harp a few times myself," Lillie said, looking toward the cell block as if the deputy was the last person she wanted to see this morning.

"I hope you brought Ely some clean clothes. He… soiled himself."

"You'd piss yourself too if you saw what I did," his father called from his cell down the hallway.

"Nothing's wrong with his hearing, anyway," Flint muttered under his breath as Lillie set a large brown paper bag with the clothing in it on his desk.

"Nothing's wrong with his mind, either!" Ely called back.

Flint shook his head and lowered his voice. "You know, Lillie, you don't have to be the one to bail him out all the time. You could send one of our brothers to do the dirty work."

She said nothing as Deputy Harper Cole came in as if on cue. She gave him a disinterested nod. He eyed her with his one good eye, the one that wasn't swollen shut. Lillie, clad in a pink T-shirt, worn jeans and sandals, had her long, curly dark hair pulled up in a ponytail. "Mornin', Lillie. You're looking *fine*."

"Harp, please take these to Ely and make sure he changes," Flint said, holding out the bag to his deputy before Lillie gave the man another black eye. Messing with this particular Cahill would be a huge mistake. Lillie had grown up with five older brothers. She could hold her own and Flint didn't want to have to arrest her too.

He could tell his sister was fired up and wondered if it was only about Ely's arrest or if there was more going on with her. He would have asked, but when she was in this mood, questioning her would be like poking a porcupine with a short stick.

He could hear Ely arguing with the deputy from his cell down the hallway. "I'm telling you something has to be done about him," Flint said quietly to his sister. This was a matter they were going to have to deal with.

"He's *fine*."

"He's not fine. We can't keep putting our heads in the sand and pretending that he isn't getting worse."

She shook her head. "How about you stop arresting him?"

"You know I can't do that. Fortunately, he spends most of his time up in the mountains. But every time he comes out…" He sighed and ran a hand through his hair. The thick dark hair was something all of the Cahills shared, along with the gray eyes.

"You need to cut him some slack. What would be wrong with that? He's an old man. He's *your* old man."

Flint shook his head as their father came out grumbling, but wearing clean clothes. He still looked wild from his full gray beard to those piercing light gray eyes so like his own. But he wasn't the worse for wear given how much he had to drink last night.

"You're going to regret not listenin' to me," Ely said to his son. "I'm stone-cold sober this morning. I told you what I seen last night. I ain't crazy. It's them from outer space agin. They're back and they're hangin' around our missile silo. Any fool knows no good'll come from that. I'm tellin' you. Them devils is up to somethin'. Somethin' bad."

Flint shot his sister a see-what-I-mean look. Back in the late 1950s, their grandfather had signed over a two-acre plot of land in the middle of his ranch so the US government could bury missiles in perpetuity for national defense.

The US Air Force had buried a thousand Minuteman missiles three stories deep in ranch land just like theirs. A missile on constant alert and capable of delivering a 1.2 megaton nuclear warhead to a target in thirty minutes was still buried in their backyard. The program was called MAD, Mutually Assured Destruction.

Ely believed it was that missile that had brought a UFO to their land back in 1967. He swore it landed and aliens had taken him aboard their spaceship and did medical experiments on him. And that had made him known as the biggest crackpot in the county.

"Come on, Dad," Lillie said, sending a scowl at Flint. "You must be hungry. Let's get you to my place—"

"I want to go home," Ely said as they headed for the door. "Home to my cabin."

She glanced back at Flint, no doubt knowing what he thought about that idea.

"He shouldn't be alone," Flint said to their retreating backs.

"Don't pay him no never mind, Lillie Girl. Flint always did have a stick stuck—"

"Dad, maybe we should stop at the grocery store first and get you some food," she said, cutting him off.

"Got plenty of food at home," their father argued. "Put up a nice buck into jerky last fall. But I could use a little whiskey, so maybe we should stop by your bar."

LILLIE WAS STILL fuming as she drove her father out of town toward the bar she and her twin brother, Darby, owned, the Stagecoach Saloon. Darby was eight minutes older and never let her forget it.

They'd opened the place in an old two-story stone stage stop not far from the ranch. She'd wanted a way to preserve the building and Darby had suggested a bar and café.

"Don't you be listening to Flint, my Lillie Girl," her father said again as they were driving out of town. "You know how he is."

She nodded and smiled over at him, even though her bad temper was still flaring inside her. She'd never understand her brother. Flint was the black sheep of the family. The one who had followed every rule from the time he was young, while the rest of them disliked rules and seldom followed them, especially when the Cahill clan banded together.

True, it had always been Flint who bailed them out of trouble before their parents got wind of what they'd been up to. But he'd also had to lecture them at length, which never went over well.

"Flint's worried about you," she said now to her father. "So am I."

Ely shook his head. "No reason to worry."

He sounded so unconvincing that she shot him a glance, surprised how old he looked. She often didn't see him for weeks or sometimes months at a time. He would disappear into the mountains. Then she'd get a call that he'd been arrested and she always took it upon herself to get him out of jail.

"What happened last night?" she asked as she'd done so many times before.

He was quiet for long enough that she thought he either hadn't heard her or wasn't going to answer. "In the mountains I can hold the memories at bay. But once I come down…" He cleared his throat and looked over at her. "I swear on your mother's grave that I saw 'em last night. They was in the same pasture as where I was took. I feared they'd come back for me. They was almost on me when I smelled whatever gas they use to knock people out. When I come to, I was lying in the pasture and they was gone." He shuddered. "I don't think they took me this time, though."

Lillie didn't know what to say. She'd first heard about her father's abduction by aliens in the school yard from Ronnie Eckert. He'd taunted her until she'd slugged him and bloodied his nose. "Take it back!" she had yelled at him. "Take it back or I'll hit you again."

A teacher had broken them up. Lillie had run home fast as the wind to tell her mother what had happened before the school called home. One look at her mother's face and she'd known it hadn't just been Ronnie making up stories.

"Your father claims he was abducted by aliens near the missile silo on our ranch," she'd said. "It's old news."

"But is it *true*?" she'd demanded.

"Your father believes it was."

Of course, Lillie had questioned him, both fascinated and horrified by the idea that it might actually have happened. Often she had lain in the tall grass at night and stared up at the stars wondering if there were other beings out there.

His story about his abduction was a little disappointing, though. Men in white space suits, their faces obscured by their helmets, had grabbed him. He'd thought they communicated telepathically, but he also remembered them talking to each other. He'd seen their lips moving but hadn't been able to hear them because of their huge helmets and the swishing sound of the breathing systems.

"What did they do to you?" she'd asked, holding her breath.

"They conked me out with some kinda gas. I woke up in the pasture starin' up at the stars. But I remember being in a small cramped place before that. I still taste somethin' metallic when I think about it."

She'd known then why everyone in the county believed that Ely Cahill no longer had all his ducks, let alone had them in a row. He'd always been part mountain man, disappearing into the mountains in search of gold or wild animals he could kill for meat for his family, even though they raised beef.

His father had been a rancher, but Ely had never taken to it and was glad when two of his sons had taken the place over. "Rather have a nice whitetail buck any day over a slab of beef," he often said. "Lost my taste for beef after them aliens took me."

"He's made our family a laughingstock," her brother Tuck had said not long before he'd left for good. That had been right after high school. Tucker said Gilt Edge was just too small for him, gave him claustrophobia. But she'd always suspected something had happened to make him leave.

Lillie forced those thoughts back into a dark corner along with others she kept locked up there as she parked in front of the Stagecoach Saloon.

"Home sweet home," she said as she admired the historic two-story rock building. She never tired of looking at it. It had been a stagecoach stop back in the 1800s when gold had been coming out of the mine at Gilt Edge. Each stone, like the old wooden floorboards inside, had a story, she thought with pride. If only this building could talk.

With her twin brother, they'd restored it. The lower floor had been turned into a bar and café, while the upstairs had been remodeled into a home for herself. She'd furnished it with restored pieces she'd picked up at garage sales and junk shops and loved every one of them.

She also had the best view in the county. From her living room window she could see three of the four mountain ranges surrounding the area. She loved this old building and the life she and Darby had built with it. But deep in her heart there was always that feeling of something missing. Someone. Even when she didn't say his name or imagine his face, there was always that ache of something lost, something she feared she would never have again.

"Come on, let's see what we can cook up for you," she said to her father.

He smiled over at her. "Could use some breakfast now that you mention it."

She laughed. His appetite was legend. "What do you say to chicken fried venison steak, eggs, hash browns and biscuits and milk gravy?"

"That's my girl," Ely said.

But as she started to open her door, she saw something...*someone* move along the side of the building. Her brother Darby wasn't here yet or his pickup would have been parked in the spot next to the big old pine tree. She'd gotten only a glimpse of what she thought was a man hiding in the trees.

She handed the keys to the place to her father. "Here, you go on in and I'll be right with you." She waited for him to climb out before she reached under the pickup seat and pulled out the .45 pistol she kept wrapped in a piece of an old blanket.

Slipping from behind the wheel, she unwrapped the gun, tucked it into the waist of her jeans and covered the weapon with the hem of her T-shirt.

Her father had made it as far as the front door. He turned and looked back at her. "Everything all right, Lillie Girl?" he called.

"Fine, Dad. Just need to check something."

He nodded, hesitating as if worried about her. Say

what you will about Ely Cahill, he wasn't as far gone as her brother wanted her to believe, she thought.

"I'm fine. You make yourself at home. I'll join you in a minute."

As he unlocked the front door of the bar and disappeared inside, she moved to the pine trees that flanked the stone building on three sides.

Stepping to the edge of the building, she began to work her way carefully along the side, keeping to the shadows. Even as she did, she told herself she had imagined the broad shoulders, the slim hips, the glimpse of dark wavy hair under the Western straw hat as she had so many times over the years.

She'd gone only a dozen yards when she saw him. She felt a tremor move through her. With shaking fingers, she reached under her T-shirt and pulled the gun to level it on the broad back of the man standing only feet away.

"Don't move!" she ordered, surprised that her voice sounded so unruffled when her heart had taken off like a wild horse in the wind at the sight of him.

"You wouldn't shoot a man in the back."

The deep resonance of his voice sent her pulse thundering in her ears. She'd heard that voice only in her dreams for the past nine years. The ache she felt was laced with hurt and anger, not to mention the hit her pride had taken.

"In your case, I'll make an exception," she said, easing her finger onto the trigger. Her thoughts whirled like tumbleweeds in the wind. Trask Beaumont had the nerve to show his face around her after all this time? After all that he'd done?

He raised both hands in the air and turned slowly as if he hadn't lost all of his good sense during those years away. He'd known her like no other man, like no other man ever would because she'd never let another get that close again.

Staring at him, she couldn't believe it. How many times had she told herself that she would never see that face again, a face so handsome it had to be crafted by the Devil himself.

Her finger twitched on the trigger of the pistol as she reached into her jeans pocket for her cell phone.

"Easy, darlin'," he said, taking a step toward her. "You don't want to shoot me. You don't want to call your sheriff brother on me, either."

"You sure about that?" She thought of the night she'd waited for him until the sun rose and she'd realized he wasn't coming back for her.

Trask Beaumont's lips curved into the grin that had haunted her sleepless nights for years. That grin had not just let this man into her jeans but into her heart. "Damn, Lillie. I can't tell you how I've missed you."

"What are you doing here?" She hated the tremor she heard in her voice. She had her cell phone out. All she had to do was hit 9-1-1. Her brother would be there in a heartbeat. "I asked what you're doing here."

Before he could answer, a vehicle roared up on the other side of the building. She recognized the sound of the engine. Engine cut, the driver's-side door opened and slammed. She listened as her brother Darby entered the bar, then yelled her name.

She glanced over her shoulder, afraid he'd come looking for her and catch the two of them out there. Knowing how her brothers' felt about Trask, she hated to think what would happen. It was one thing to have him arrested. It was another to let one of her other brothers at him.

When she turned back, Trask was gone. Lillie blinked. It was as if he hadn't been there at all. And yet her heart still thundered in her chest. If she dialed 9-1-1, Flint would come running.

She stood, the gun in her hand growing heavy, the phone just one keystroke away from the sheriff's department dispatcher. Trask. He'd come back.

And now he was gone. Again. Had she not been sane, she might have believed that she'd conjured up his image from a desire she'd spent years trying hard to bury. But she hadn't dreamed him. He'd left behind his boot prints in the dirt, and even if her eyes had deceived her, her heart had not.

Trask was back. Conflicting emotions warred inside her. Trask, after all these years. She pocketed her phone and slowly lowered the gun as she began to shake all over. Tears burned her eyes. Why would he come back now? How could he come back, knowing how dangerous it was for him?

"Lillie?"

Tucking the gun into the waistband of her jeans

and covering it with her shirt again, she turned to find her brother standing a few yards away. Had he seen Trask?

"Have you lost your mind?" Darby demanded, making her fear she had. Before she could respond, he continued, "You leave Dad alone in the bar? Alone in a bar stocked with bright shiny bottles of booze? Didn't you just get him out of jail?" He stopped his rant to frown. "What are you doing out here, anyway?"

She said the first thing that came to mind that might make sense. "Thought I saw a bear. Didn't want it getting in the trash again."

"We have worse problems in the bar. Come take care of your father," he said only half-jokingly.

"He's your father too," she pretended to remind him as she followed him. Inside, she found Ely behind the bar with a bottle of whiskey clutched in his hand and a big grin on his face.

"I'll be in the back," Darby said with a disgusted shake of his head. "Apparently, you promised him a Johnson breakfast." It had been their mother's specialty named after her family.

The moment Darby disappeared in the back, her father asked, "Find what you was lookin' for out there?" He was no longer grinning. Nor it seemed had he indulged in the whiskey. Darby'd had no reason to worry. Their father had only been pretending to start the day with whiskey.

Ely put the bottle down and poured them both a

cup of coffee from the automatic coffeemaker that Darby had set last night.

"She thought she saw a bear," Darby called from the back over the clatter of pots and pans.

"A bear?" her father repeated as he studied her over the rim of his coffee cup. He'd definitely seen Trask, she realized, but he was going to keep her secret, since he was the only one in the family who'd ever liked the man his daughter had fallen for at a tender age.

She swallowed the lump in her throat, touched that her father would understand why she wasn't going to call the law on the only man she'd ever truly loved.

"Ya got to watch them bears, Lillie Girl," her father said, looking worried, "'specially the renegade ones. They'll turn you every way but loose."

CHAPTER THREE

"YOUR FATHER GETS crazier every year," Deputy Harper Cole said from where he lounged against the wall at the entrance to the cell block.

"Nothing wrong with his right hook, though, huh, Harp." Flint had inherited the deputy when he'd taken the sheriff job with the understanding that the mayor's son would be kept on.

The deputy straightened, anger marring his handsome features. "He should have to do time for slugging an officer of the law."

"If you'd cuffed the prisoner last night, you wouldn't have that black eye," Flint said. Earlier he'd noticed the deputy admiring his wound in the side mirror. Harp was good-looking and spent way too much time taking selfies. Flint would bet he'd put one up on Facebook last night.

"He nailed me before I could get the cuffs on him. If it had been any of the other deputies, you would have charged him with assault," Harp whined.

"The other deputies wouldn't have taunted him."

"What?" he asked as if incredulous. "Is that what he told you?"

"He didn't have to. I know you."

"Well, it's my word against his and he's a liar."

Flint looked over at the deputy. "Be careful, Harp. You're hanging on by the skin of your teeth as it is because of complaints against you. I would tread lightly. Even your father, the mayor, won't be able to save you next time." He rose to his feet. "Let's take a ride."

As Flint drove out of town, his deputy said, "Heard the old Chandler ranch just sold to some corporation called L.T. Enterprises. Like we don't know who's buying up the whole damned valley. Wayne Duma."

Flint said nothing, knowing that Harp was needling him. Wayne Duma was married to Flint's ex-wife, Celeste, and his deputy knew it was a sore point with him.

"That's a nice ranch. Maybe Duma plans to move up there and sell that big old house he has in town," Harp said, shooting him a look no doubt to see if he was getting to him.

Ignoring him, Flint turned onto the road into the south forty acres of his family's ranch.

Harp let out an oath. "Don't tell me you're going out to the missile silo."

"Ely saw something out there last night," the sheriff said.

Harp shook his head. "He's a crazy old coot. No offense," he added.

"Crazy or not, whatever he saw last night scared

him, and I can tell you right now, there is little out there that scares my old man."

"Except for flying saucers and little green men," the deputy said under his breath.

Flint didn't take the bait. Ely Cahill was one of a group of people around the world who swore they had been abducted by aliens. It had happened, according to Ely, back in 1967—the same time an unidentified flying object had been seen by the air force stationed in the area. The disk-shaped object had hovered in the air over more than a half dozen of the missile sites—disabling them. It caused a panic with the military.

According to the military's records, at one missile sight, an officer on duty reported that lights streaked directly above them, stopped, changed directions at high speed and returned overhead again. He described it as glowing red and saucer-shaped, hovering silently.

That information had been classified for years – even though numerous civilians had also seen the flying object. Of course, no one but the US Air Force had known about this until years later when the information was declassified. By then everyone was convinced that Ely Cahill was a nut-job.

All that aside, they still lived knowing what they had out in their pasture—a bomb capable of destroying everything for miles should something go wrong. The night of the UFO sighting, things had definitely gone wrong.

Not that anyone believed it had been a spaceship filled with aliens—except for their father.

Flint drove out of Gilt Edge toward the missile silo, where his father had claimed he'd seen something last night. Most people drove past the silos without even knowing they were there. The only indication that one of them was there was an eight-foot-high chain-link fence around a small area of land in the middle of the pasture. At the center of it was a concrete pad, a few wires and antennae sticking up, but nothing that gave away the fact that a nuclear missile was resting below ground waiting for someone to push a button.

"Wait here. I'm going to take a look around," Flint said and got out. He knew better than to get too close. Alarms would go off at the command center and within minutes a military vehicle would come flying up with armed officers inside.

Instead, he walked away from the missile silo, his gaze on the ground ahead of him. The air was crisp this morning. Only a few puffy clouds floated on the breeze. Snow still capped the mountaintops that surrounded the valley. Flint breathed in the rich spring scents and studied the Western landscape.

The grasses had started to green up in the pastures and alongside the highway. Summer was coming, a busy time because of the tourists who traveled through the state. Not that the locals weren't a handful all year long, especially his father.

He thought of Ely with affection and aggravation. No man was more stubborn or independent. He hoped Lillie was right and that the old man wasn't losing his mind. He couldn't imagine him locked up in some nursing home, let alone any of them trying to corral him if he moved in with them.

He hadn't gone far when he picked up the huge footprints. Flint stopped to glance back at his patrol SUV. Harp was watching him. Anything he did would get back to the mayor and his friends. He took another step, then another as he dropped over a rise, careful not to disturb the tracks he'd found.

Once out of sight, he pulled out his cell phone and took several photographs of the oversize footprints—and the man-size boot prints where there'd clearly been a scuffle.

Before he could pocket his cell phone, it rang. A glance at caller ID showed the call was from his office. "Cahill," he said into the phone, turning back toward his patrol SUV and the waiting Harp. In the distance, he could see dust as a military vehicle roared toward them.

"Sheriff, I have Anvil Holloway on the line. He says his wife is missing."

BACK AT THE Stagecoach Saloon, Darby made enough breakfast for the three of them, but Lillie had lost her appetite. She kept thinking of Trask in the days before he'd left nine years ago. Something had been bothering him for several weeks. A darkness had taken hold of him. Her usually cheerful, laid-back

lover was moody and irritable. She'd often found
him scowling and he'd definitely been distracted.

"Is it your job?" she had asked.

"What?"

"This mood you're in."

"Sorry, I've just had things on my mind."

"Things you want to talk about?"

He'd pulled her to him, kissed her and said, "It's
nothing to do with you. I'll handle it, okay? Just give
me a little time."

She'd had no idea what that meant. He'd even been
at odds with his best friend, Johnny Burrows. She'd
seen the two of them having a heated argument one
day when she'd went by the Lazy G Bar Q Ranch,
where Trask worked. When Trask had seen her, he'd
quickly stepped away and pretended it was nothing.

"I'm not a fool. What's going on between you
and Johnny?"

"Just a difference of opinion. It's nothing."

She suspected that all of it had been leading up to
the fight with his boss, Gordon Quinn, and him getting fired. But did she really believe that Trask had
come back that night and killed Gordon?

Now she half listened distractedly as her father
and Darby talked about the weather, the price of
gold and the decline of elk in Yellowstone Park and
the rest of Montana because of the reintroduction of
wolves. She'd been pushing her food around on her
plate until her brother finally took her plate along
with his own and her father's, and headed for the

kitchen. She followed him, wanting to talk to him alone.

"Flint thinks we need to do something about Dad," she told him, making sure their father was out of earshot.

"What do *you* think?" Darby asked as he began stacking the rinsed dishes in the commercial dishwasher, then looked at her.

"I don't know. One minute he seems so like his old self, and then he starts talking about aliens and abductions. He swears they came after him again last night. Apparently, that's why he got so drunk and so…'disorderly,' as Flint put it." She smiled, feeling almost ashamed as she did. "He punched Harp in the eye." She winced. "His eye was swollen shut when I saw him at the jail this morning."

Darby chuckled. "You can bet that Harp asked for it. As for Dad, it doesn't sound like anything new to me. But you shouldn't always be the one to take care of him. Call Cyrus or Hawk next time. They aren't that busy on the ranch that they can't get Dad out of jail once in a while. And you know you can always call me."

"I know, but I didn't mind going," she said with a shrug. Her brother's smile was thanks enough. "I'd better get him home. He's determined to stay there alone. At least until he can't take it anymore and heads for the hills."

"You want me to come with you? Billie Dee should be here soon." Billie Dee was their cook, a large, older Texas woman with a belly laugh and twinkle in her eye. "She can hold down the fort until we get back."

"No, I could use the drive. Wouldn't mind a little time to myself on the way back."

Darby caught her hand before she could turn away. "Everything all right, sis?" That was the problem with being twins. They sensed when something was wrong with their former womb-mate.

She gave him her best everything-is-all-right smile. He didn't look as if it fooled him, but then their cook came in the back door singing at the top of her lungs, and Lillie hurried to see what trouble her father had gotten into in the bar.

FLINT DROPPED HARP off at the sheriff's department. But as the deputy got out of the patrol SUV, the sheriff told him, "If you happen by the mayor's office today and your father calls me later to ask me how you got a black eye, I'm going to tell him the truth."

"It's my word against your crazy old man's," Harp said, scowling.

"Which do you think your father is going to believe? That not-quite-seventy-year-old Ely Cahill, drunk on his ass, got you, a trained deputy, before you could cuff him? Or that you were giving him a hard time, enjoying making fun of him, and he dropped you with one punch? Either way, I got the whole story from some of the patrons who were watching from the bar window. If you don't believe it, they took videos with their phones."

Harp clamped his mouth shut. "Is that all?"

"For now," Flint said and drove north out of town on a dirt road toward Anvil Holloway's farm. It was a good twenty miles of rolling hills. Turning onto an even narrower dirt road, he saw the farm ahead.

In the field next to the house, decades of old cars, pickups and farm equipment rusted in the morning sun. A few clouds scudded across a robin's-egg-blue sky. The mountains around the wide valley were still snowcapped and the air had a crispness to it that warned summer was still months off.

Flint parked, shut off his engine and started to climb out when Anvil rushed from the house to stop on the dilapidated porch. The house needed paint and didn't look much better than the porch.

"Have you heard from her?" Flint asked as he walked toward the house and the man anxiously waiting for him.

Anvil shook his head as if unable to draw the words. He looked older than fifty-seven. His brown hair needed cutting. It framed a once handsome face now weathered from years of working outdoors. He still looked strong from his days playing football at the University of Montana in Missoula, his only claim to fame. His large body was clad in faded overalls over a clean white T-shirt. He'd obviously dressed up for Flint's visit, since he'd recently shaved. He still had a dollop of shaving cream congealing on one ear.

"Why don't we go inside and sit down. You can tell me what happened," Flint said.

Anvil nodded nervously, practically wringing his hands before he wiped both down the sides of his overalls. "It's just not like her to take off and not call and let me know she's all right."

Flint followed the farmer into the kitchen of the ranch house. The room was neat and clean, dishes done, floor recently mopped, he noticed with concern. In this part of the country, men worked in the fields, barns and pastures. Women worked in the house. That Anvil had mopped the floor sent up a red flag that Flint hadn't been expecting.

If Jenna had been gone since yesterday evening, she hadn't been the one to mop the floor. It seemed a strange thing for Anvil to do unless he had something he needed to clean up.

They took a seat at the 1950s metal-and-Formica blue table. Anvil had inherited the farm along with the house and furnishings from his father after he graduated from college. His parents had moved down to Arkansas to be near his sister and her family.

Flint noticed that, like the floor, the table too had been wiped down recently.

"So tell me what happened," he said as he took out his notebook and pen.

"We had an argument," Anvil admitted as he

wiped a hand over his face. His voice broke as he said, "She left."

Flint saw with growing concern that the knuckles of Anvil's right hand were scraped and bruised. "She leave in her own car?" Anvil nodded. "She take anything with her?"

"A suitcase and her purse."

"She packed *after* the argument?" Flint asked.

Anvil shook his head. "She'd already packed. Said she needed some time to think."

"Think about what?"

Anvil looked at the floor.

"She leave because you hit her?"

The farmer's head bobbed up, shock and guilt on his face. "It wasn't like that."

"It wasn't the first time you'd hit her?"

"I'd never laid a hand on her before. I swear to God." The words came out in a strangled cry. Tears had filled the man's eyes. Remorse making him appear even older. "It was the first time I raised a hand to her. I swear on my grandmother's grave. I…I slapped her."

Flint reached across the table to lift Anvil's ham-sized right hand. "Looks like you did more than slap her."

ELY CAHILL PERKED up a lot after his Johnson breakfast. Lillie had studied him as he'd eaten every bite on his plate. He was still a strong man in so many ways. Stubborn as a stump that refused to be pulled from the ground. Weathered by life and the outdoors. Tough as the proverbial nail. She envied him that he knew what he wanted and didn't wait around for life to give it to him.

The drive up the canyon to his cabin was a beautiful one. Spring in Montana couldn't be any more delightful. The sky was a clear blinding blue dotted with puffy white clouds over a sea of new bright green grasses and dark pines. She took it in as she drove, thinking how nine years ago she would have given all of this up for Trask.

Ely Cahill lived within sight of an old ghost town. Only a few shells of buildings still stood in the middle of the tall spring grass. His cabin fit right in.

He'd built it years ago out of hewn logs with his sons helping him. It was small and apparently all he needed.

The logs had weathered from the sun and snow and thunderstorms that passed over. Vegetation had grown up around it in his absence. From a distance, a person would think it was abandoned.

Ely spent little time here and even less in the ranch house down the road, where he'd lived with their mother and helped raise the six of them. *I'm done ranching*, he'd announced after their mother had died. *You all can have the ranch. I want that hill overlooking this valley. That's where I plan to die.*

That had been almost twenty years ago. Lillie's older brothers Cyrus and Hawk had taken over the ranch. She and her twin, Darby, had wanted nothing to do with it. Tuck, the oldest of her brothers, had struck out on his own at eighteen, not to be heard from again.

Tuck was the smart one to get out of here, Darby had said recently after mentioning that he should probably sell his share of the Stagecoach Saloon and take off to find his fortune.

Lillie hoped he was just talking. She couldn't run the bar and café alone and she didn't want to sell out or take on another partner. It wasn't just a business. It was her home. She loved the old stagecoach stop, could feel its history in the stone walls and marred wooden floorboards, and she was determined to preserve it. Making money was the least of the reasons she had bought the building. The bar and café had been a way of hanging on to it—and put a roof over her head.

"Thank you, Lillie Girl," her father said as she pulled up in front of his cabin. "No need to see me in. The pack rats probably carried off most everythin' and left a mess ta boot."

She shuddered to think what the inside of the cabin looked like as she watched him lift his pack and the bag of groceries she'd insisted on. "How long will you be staying out of the mountains?"

He looked up toward the Judiths, still snowcapped. "As long as I can stand it." Lewis and Clark had discovered the mountains on their expedition to find the Northwest Passage. Clark named them after his soon-to-be wife, Judith.

"You'll let me know before you leave." What if Flint was right about their father? What might happen to him up there alone, let alone in the mountains?

Ely met her gaze. "Don't worry about me," he said as if reading her mind. "Your brother doesn't know what he's talking about."

She didn't need to ask which brother. Flint was the second oldest and the one who went into law enforcement after generations of Cahills who had teetered on the edge of the law. He was also the one who seemed to think it was his job to run the family with Tuck gone. She hated how reasonable he always was when just once she'd love to see him lose his cool like the rest of them. The only stupid thing her brother had ever done was marry Celeste York.

"You sure Flint wasn't adopted?" she joked. "Or maybe you found him on your doorstep, where someone dumped him when he was a baby?"

"He's well-meaning," Ely said, surprising her.

"He *arrested* you."

"He did that." Her father laughed good-heartedly. "But I wasn't myself last night. I understand why he had to."

Lillie shook her head. "Always by the letter of the law."

"Yep, that's our Flint. He'd arrest his own grandmother if she was alive." Ely laughed at the family joke. "But that's only if the fool woman broke the law. It's his job. Don't forget that, Lillie." He turned those gray eyes on her. "He takes bein' sheriff seriously, no matter the cost to hisself."

Her father was trying to warn her, as if he needed to remind her, what would happen if Flint found out Trask was back in town. She tried to swallow the lump in her throat, touched by her father's attempt to protect her. It filled her with fear of what the future held.

Trask was back, and when Flint found out, he'd have every resource available out looking for him. This time, Trask wouldn't get away.

Hopefully, the cowboy had come to his senses and left town again. She preferred that over seeing him behind bars. But the thought that she wouldn't see him again for another nine years or possibly ever was like a clenched fist around her heart.

"Take care, Lillie Girl," her father said as he slung his pack over his shoulder and started to close the pickup door.

She nodded, her thoughts on Trask, a dangerous place for even her thoughts to be.

CHAPTER FOUR

TRASK BEAUMONT WAS no fool. Not anymore at least. He knew how dangerous coming back there was— let alone going near Lillie. If one of her brothers had seen him—

As it was, her father had. Ely Cahill wouldn't tell, though. Trask had always liked the old man and thought Ely liked him, as well. It was Lillie's brothers he had to worry about—especially Flint, the sheriff.

He knew he was taking one devil of a chance by being back in the state, not to mention what he planned to do now that he was.

As he drove the back roads he knew so well— even after nine long years of being away—he felt happy just to be home again. He'd missed all of this, but nothing like he'd missed Lillie. She was more beautiful than she'd been nine years ago, as if that was possible. She'd grown into the amazing woman he'd always known she would become. He couldn't have been more proud of her for what she'd accomplished with the old stagecoach stop.

Leaving Lillie had been the hardest thing he'd ever done. Now he feared he'd come back too late.

If he'd lost Lillie, then all his plans would have been for nothing.

He reached the turnoff that would take him up in the mountains and drove through thick pines as the narrow dirt road snaked upward. The day was incredible from the blue of Montana's big sky to the white puffy clouds riding on the breeze to the jewel green of the pines against the snowcapped mountaintops. He'd forgotten how breathtaking it could be.

Or how much he would miss it. But he'd had no choice but to leave all those years ago. He was facing a murder rap for a crime he hadn't committed. The law was looking for him, and Lillie... Just the thought of her made his heart ache. He should have stayed and tried to find out the truth. But he'd been young. And scared.

He'd left here a young arrogant rodeo cowboy with a chip on his shoulder and a temper. Now he'd come back a changed man determined to set things right—not just with the law, but with Lillie.

Trask worried that the latter would be the hardest one to right.

The road turned into a Jeep trail. He shifted into four-wheel drive and drove a little farther up the mountainside before pulling over in the pines and walking the rest of the way.

This spot on the mountain had been a favorite of his when he was a boy. He used to come here when life got too tough even for him. The view alone buoyed his spirit. As a boy, he'd pretended that all of this would be his one day, as far as the eye could see.

He'd definitely been a fool in so many ways, he thought now as he reached his campsite. Back in his youth, he hadn't known what the real cost would be and not just in money.

Now, though, he knew. He'd come home determined to fix the mess he'd made—or die trying.

ANVIL HOLLOWAY LOOKED shocked that the sheriff would suggest he had beaten his wife, let alone killed her. He looked guiltily at his bruised and bloodied knuckles. "That's not from hitting my wife. I…I… After she left…" He pointed to the hallway.

Flint got up to inspect a spot where the Sheetrock had been smashed repeatedly. There was still blood-stains where it had soaked into the ruined Sheetrock, although it was clear Anvil had also tried to clean it up as well as the rest of the kitchen.

When he turned back to the man, it was with growing dread. "That wall shows a lot of anger, Anvil."

The farmer nodded and hung his head.

"It must have been some argument."

Anvil said nothing.

"You need to tell me. If there is any hope of my finding Jenna…"

Slowly, the farmer lifted his head. "She told me she…had met someone else."

Flint had expected the complaints most wives of farmers and ranchers who lived out of town often aired. Too much work, no comforts, too far from town and other people, a hard existence with little thanks, let alone money.

But Jenna had never seemed like the complaining type. A plain, big-boned, solemn, conservative woman, she'd appeared to be the perfect wife for Anvil despite their decade difference in age. Jenna was only forty-seven.

"She *met* someone?" Flint repeated. "You mean she had an affair?"

Anvil buried his face in his hands and began to cry in huge body-shuddering sobs.

He waited until the farmer got control of himself again. "Do you know who?" Flint asked, thinking that was probably where Jenna had gone. That is, if Anvil was telling the truth and she'd actually left under her own power last night.

The recently mopped floor still bothered him, now more than before. Just as the destroyed Sheetrock in the hallway did. He feared the wall could have been busted *before* Anvil turned that rage on his wife.

Anvil wiped his face with his sleeve and took a few choked breaths. "She wouldn't tell me."

Flint let that sink in, hearing not just frustration in the farmer's voice, but anger. "Did she say why she wouldn't tell you who he was?"

He swallowed again and looked at his worn work boots. "She said she was afraid I would kill him."

Great. So Jenna had already been aware of her husband's temper.

Flint closed his notebook. "Here's what we're going to do. We're going to give Jenna a little time to think. I'm betting she will call pretty soon or maybe even show up. If that happens, you call me right away, okay?"

Anvil nodded, looking relieved.

"She say how long she'd been...seeing this other man?"

He shook his head. "I got the feeling it had been going on for a while."

"So you'd been suspicious?"

Anvil emitted a bitter laugh. "Hit me like a bolt of lightning out of the blue. Never saw it coming. Not in a million years."

Flint had had the same reaction. Jenna Holloway just didn't seem the type. Whatever type that was. He thought of his ex. Right, *that* type.

"How long have you been married?" he asked.

"Twenty-four years. She's quite a bit younger than me." Anvil seemed to grind his teeth. "I reckon the man is younger than me, as well."

"I'm going to need the clothing you were wearing when Jenna left."

Anvil looked up at him. "You still think I did something to her."

"It's protocol in a situation like this. I'm sure Jenna will call today and we can put all this behind us."

The farmer rose slowly from his chair and disappeared into the other room. He came back with a pair of overalls and a T-shirt. "This is what I was wearing, but I washed them…since they were soiled."

Flint met the man's eyes. "How often have you washed your own clothes, Anvil?"

The man looked confused. "It isn't how it looks."

"It looks like you cleaned up after she left to hide something."

"I did. When I slapped her, it made her nose bleed. There was blood on the kitchen floor." He broke down. "I was so ashamed for losing my temper. I didn't want anyone to see the place the way it was. I was going to fix the Sheetrock today, but the lumberyard was closed."

"Anvil, I shouldn't have to tell you how bad this looks."

The man dropped his head. "I was just so ashamed."

Flint waited a few moments before he said, "Anvil, if you did something worse that you regret, now is the time to tell me."

The farmer raised his head. "I didn't kill her. She drove away. I swear."

"All right. Here's what you do. Go about your usual daily work until you hear from her," Flint said. "I know that's a hard thing to ask. But these things often work themselves out. In the meantime, I'll keep an eye out for her. If she just went to town, checked into a motel…"

Again Anvil looked relieved to think that was all she'd done last night as they stepped out on the porch.

"Give me the make, model and color of the car she was driving," Flint said and pulled out his notebook again. He hoped he was right and Jenna was in some cheap motel in town deciding what she was going to do next.

"By the way, how much money did she have on her when she left?"

Anvil looked surprised by the question. "I don't know. We live on a pretty tight budget. I suppose she could have saved back some from the grocery money, but it wouldn't be much." Clearly, this had never crossed his mind.

"She doesn't have a checkbook or credit cards she could use to get a motel?"

The farmer scratched the back of his neck. "Don't believe in credit cards. The checkbook's only for the farm business. I always gave Jenna whatever she needed. Like if she wanted a new dress or had to get her hair done for some special occasion."

Flint nodded. He figured a lot of the farmers and ranchers operated much the same, especially the older ones. The women seldom left the place except to go into town for groceries or church.

"What is her cell phone number?"

Anvil looked confused. "She doesn't have a cell phone. We have the landline here at the house. That's all we've ever needed."

Flint thought it probably wasn't that unusual given

that they seldom left the ranch. And cell phone service in these parts was scattered at best. It was the way everyone had lived not that many years ago, back when people didn't need to be on call 24/7.

Still, no cell phone in this day and age? No credit cards? It meant no way of tracking her.

"What about a computer?" Flint asked, thinking that might be where Jenna had met this other man. But Anvil again shook his head.

"Never saw the need for one. Accountant takes care of the farm books. I want to buy somethin' I can drive into town. Sure as the devil don't need to be telling the world what I had for lunch on some blamed thing like Face Chat."

Facebook. "Jenna spend any time at the library in town?"

"You're thinking she met this man there?"

"They have computers and Wi-Fi service you can use at the library."

Anvil frowned as if confused.

"Often people meet other people by chatting via computer. They get to talking, seem to have a lot in common, even fall in love without ever meeting each other in person."

The farmer was staring at him. "That's the craziest thing I ever heard."

"Unfortunately, often the person on the other end of the chat isn't telling the truth about themselves. Jenna could have been lured by one of these people. They call it catfishing."

Anvil looked both horrified and completely out of touch with the world beyond this farm. Was Jenna more worldly?

"I'll check at the library," Flint said. "It's a long shot, but you never know. She ever show any interest in learning to use a computer?"

"I thought her only interest was in old recipe books. She loved to bake. She was happiest in the kitchen. At least that's what I thought."

"I'll get back to you if I hear something," the sheriff told him. "Try not to worry."

Anvil walked him out as far as the top porch step. "This isn't like her. She's always so sensible. She never asked for anything. Never seemed…unhappy."

A thought struck Flint as he reached his patrol SUV. He turned back to the farmer. "You notice any change in her recently?"

Anvil seemed to think about it. After a moment, his expression changed. "Well, there was one thing, now that I think about it. I'm sure it's not important. I feel foolish even mentioning it."

"What's that?" the sheriff asked when the man didn't continue for a moment. He seemed embarrassed.

"Lately, she's been wearing…makeup."

TRASK WATCHED THE last of the day's light dissolve behind the mountain. Darkness came quickly in the pines. He breathed in the cold sweet scent and thought of Lillie—as if she was ever far from his mind. At first he'd told himself that she could do better than him. That he was doing her a favor by staying away.

But getting over her had been impossible. A day hadn't gone by that he hadn't thought of her, yearned for her. Sometimes he felt as if he couldn't breathe if he didn't see her again. He'd had to come back to make things right no matter how it ended.

Trask threw another log on the campfire. Smoke rose into the twilight. Sparks flickered for a moment, then died off. Seeing her today had left him shaken. He'd expected Lillie to be angry. He'd practiced what he was going to say to her. He'd thought he'd been ready to face her.

What he hadn't been ready for was her cool demeanor. This wasn't the Lillie he'd left that night nine years ago. His Lillie was all fire and shooting rockets. His Lillie wasn't like any woman he'd ever known. His Lillie…wasn't his anymore.

He pushed that thought away, determination burning inside him. He'd get back what he lost. Lillie was at the bar tonight working. Tomorrow…

Trask tried not to get too far ahead of himself. Coming back here wasn't just about facing Lillie. It meant facing his childhood and the man this town thought he was. Thought he would always be.

He'd grown up on the wrong side of everything. It wasn't just that he lived out in the sticks in a dilapidated old house, that his father was never home because he was on the road with a traveling carnival doing cowboy rope tricks or that his birth mother had taken off when he was ten, leaving him with his father's mother.

His grandmother had been nice enough, though too old to discipline him. He'd run wild. That hadn't changed when his grandmother died and his father brought home Shirley Perkins to be his stepmother. Shirley had a son, Emery, younger than Trask, wilder than him too.

Fortunately, they hadn't stayed around long, either. By fifteen, he found himself on his own. No one even knew that his father had died in a vehicle accident while caravanning with the carnival in the Southern states. Trask certainly didn't tell anyone for fear of where the authorities might decide to put him. The owner of the carnival had contacted Trask and had Wild Bill Beaumont cremated, the ashes sent to Trask in a cardboard box, which he'd buried up here on the mountain, not far from where he had spent most of last night and today.

Feeling like life just kept kicking him down, he'd developed a bad attitude that went well with his bad temper. The only good thing in his life had been Lillie. Not that most of her family wanted him anywhere near her.

It was easy to look back and understand why when he'd gotten in trouble nine years ago, everyone thought he was guilty. Also why he'd done the only thing he knew. He'd run.

But in those years he'd changed, he'd grown up, he'd come to terms with his earlier life, and now he was back. Back to show everyone, especially Lillie, that he'd changed.

That meant proving first that he hadn't killed Gordon Quinn.

He looked out over the valley. This spot on the side of the mountain provided a great view. He could see if anyone was coming up the trail below him. Not that he expected anyone to come looking for him. He knew in his heart, in his soul, that Lillie wouldn't have called Flint on him. At least that hadn't changed about her.

Night was coming on fast now. A cold blackness puddled under the pines around him. Montana's big sky deepened under a blanket of cloud cover.

He threw another log on the campfire and watched the sparks rise like fireflies into the night sky. He'd had years to think about who might have murdered Gordon. What he didn't know was whether he was an easy scapegoat or if he had been purposely framed.

At the sound of a twig breaking, he picked up the rifle lying next to his bedroll.

"It's just me," came a voice from the darkness.

He relaxed but still held the rifle until his friend topped the rise. It was going to be a dark night, clouds hiding the stars and moon. There was just enough light to make out his friend Johnny Burrows's silhouette as he walked toward the fire. He carried a heavy bag over his shoulder, which he laid down with a grunt.

"I forgot how far it was back in here on foot. I'm

not as young as I used to be," Johnny said. "I brought you groceries."

"You're sure you weren't followed?"

"No one knows you're back in town, right? So no one has any reason to tail me, but I took the usual precautions."

When they were boys, they often took off for the mountains rather than go to school. Looking back, Trask knew that it was his fault that Johnny was in trouble with his father a lot of the time. He was the one who talked his friend into skipping school. Johnny was always afraid he would get caught—and often did.

It was only one of the reasons Johnny's father, John Thomas "J.T." Burrows, didn't like Trask and didn't want his son associating with him.

But Johnny had remained a good friend all these years despite some problems nine years ago.

Johnny stepped to the fire to warm his hands. "You sure this is a good idea?"

"The fire?"

"Coming back here like this." Johnny had stayed in town after graduating from college and ended up working with his father in the construction company where he'd worked in high school. Gordon Quinn had been one of the original partners, along with J.T. and Skip Fairchild.

Thanks to Johnny, Trask had been able to keep in touch and had known what had been going on in Gilt Edge—and especially with Lillie.

"You have a better suggestion?" Trask asked, now surprised Johnny hadn't been happy to hear that he'd come back to clear his name.

"Maybe you should go to the sheriff and turn yourself in."

"Turn myself in to Flint Cahill? The hanging sheriff? Right. Just throw myself on his mercy. I don't think so. Especially since we all knew how he felt about me dating his sister."

"It was more serious than that with Lillie, wasn't it?"

Trask said nothing for a few minutes as he picked up a stick and poked at the fire. "I've never been able to forget her. It's the main reason I came back." When his friend didn't comment, he looked up at him. "What?"

Still Johnny hesitated.

"You aren't going to tell me that she's now seeing someone."

"No, but Junior Wainwright has been trying to get her to go out with him for the past few years."

A fist closed on his heart. "But she hasn't gone."

"No. She's dated a little, not much, just like I've told you."

Trask's first thought was to find Wainwright and set him straight. But that was the old Trask. "She can date anyone she wants."

Johnny laughed. "When you told me that you'd changed, I didn't believe it." His friend eyed him. "Maybe you *have* changed. The old Trask—"

"Would have gone after him," Trask said "I know. That's one reason that the sheriff thinks I killed Gordon."

"I had to put up with him at the construction company, so I can understand why you got into it with him." Trask had been working for Gordon on his ranch when he'd caught him beating a horse with a two-by-four. He'd pulled the man off, taken the board away from him and warned him if he ever saw him treating an animal like that again, he'd kill him.

It had been a stupid threat, but he'd been so angry, so horrified by what Gordon was doing. Unfortunately, several of the other workers had overheard his threat to kill the man. Worse, when Gordon told him to mind his own business and fired him, Trask had told him what he could do with his job. Gordon called him a few names and Trask slugged the man and knocked him down.

He'd regretted it at once, but it was too late. Gordon threatened to have him arrested for assault and things went downhill from there.

"I would think things are better at the construction company with Gordon gone," he said now. Johnny's father had insisted his son learn the business from the ground up after college.

Johnny looked past the fire for a moment. "You know I never thought you killed him."

"I appreciate that. Unfortunately, you were one of the few."

"It was just bad timing. If you hadn't gotten into it with him that day…"

"And run," Trask said with a groan. "At the time, it seemed the only thing to do. Lillie had told me that Flint was looking for me. Even though I swore I didn't do it, I didn't even think she believed me. I was afraid I would get railroaded. Flint would have loved nothing better than to see me locked up in Deer Lodge. Anywhere away from his sister."

"I just don't understand what you hope to find out after all these years. If there was any evidence of someone else killing him…"

They'd had this discussion before over the years. But then it had just been talk. He realized now that Johnny hadn't expected him to ever come back to try to find the real killer.

"I have to find out who killed Gordon. I wasn't the only one who couldn't stand Gordon or to have a motive for wanting him dead."

"But enough to *kill* him?"

He knew what Johnny was saying. "Obviously, someone did hate him enough. I figure once I start digging into it, the killer is going to get nervous and then…"

"And then you're going to get yourself killed. Trask, I really wish you weren't doing this. If you left again, maybe—"

"I'm not leaving. I can't keep running from this."

Johnny looked worried. "I heard the sheriff has an eyewitness who swore they saw you leaving the stables that night right before Gordon's body was found."

"Since it wasn't me, someone is either mistaken or lying. I'm going to look into Gordon's friends, family, associates. Someone killed him and let me take the blame." Gordon had been one of the original partners in Pyramid Peak Construction Company along with being a local rancher. "You were working at the construction company back when Gordon was killed. You would know if there were problems between the partners."

Johnny shook his head. "Remember, I was just a grunt helping build the houses. I was hardly ever in the office."

Trask nodded, knowing that this was a touchy subject given that Johnny was now one of the partners along with his father and Skip.

"When I got your call today, I was shocked. I wish you'd told me you were planning to come back."

"So you could try to talk me out of it?"

His friend met his gaze over the glow of the campfire. "I guess I don't have to tell you how dangerous this is. I don't want to see you get yourself killed."

Trask was touched. He hoped that was the reason Johnny was upset about his return. He and Johnny had had their problems nine years ago, but they'd been best friends for too many years to let one incident change that. "I have no choice. I have to clear my name. It's the only way to get Lillie back. And right now it doesn't look good."

"You've seen her!" Johnny guessed, sounding both shocked and worried. "What makes you think she didn't call the sheriff on you?"

"My charm?"

"Good luck with that. You are taking a hell of a chance. What if she's already notified her brother?"

"She wouldn't do that."

"I don't know, Trask. If I were you, I'd either get out of town or turn myself in. Better than Flint finding out you're back and coming after you."

"I just need a little time to follow a couple of leads." He saw Johnny look at his watch. "You should get back to your fiancée. I'm looking forward to meeting her one day."

His friend nodded. He didn't look hopeful. It was clear Johnny thought he was making a terrible mistake by coming back. "If there is some way I can help…"

"You already have," Trask said, seeing how uncomfortable all this was making his friend. "I don't like putting you on the spot like this. I appreciate everything you've done. But I have it now." He stepped to his old friend, took his hand and pulled him into a quick hug. "I'm going to keep you out of this from this point on."

Johnny couldn't hide his relief. "Gordon's killer could still be around. If you start digging into the past…" He didn't have to finish. For a moment, he looked guilty for not wanting to be involved. Trask knew how much his friend had to lose.

"Listen, if you need anything, call me on the burner," Johnny said. "Don't worry about getting me into trouble." His old friend smiled. "You certainly tried to get me into trouble when we were kids."

"And succeeded." After he'd left town on the run, Trask had contacted his friend, needing to know what was going on with the murder investigation. He'd felt bad afterward, realizing he'd put Johnny in a tough position. It had been Johnny's suggestion to use burner phones to stay in contact.

Now he realized just how worried his old friend was. But was it friendship? Or did Johnny know more than he'd told him? He hated the feeling that his old friend was hiding something.

"Thanks for the food, for everything."

"Just be careful. I don't want a bunch of trigger-happy deputies coming after you."

Trask nodded. "Me, either." He watched Johnny disappear over the horizon before turning back to the fire. The flames had died down, making the night seem darker. Clouds scudded past the moon, leaving a break in the sky to reveal the stars. The light painted the forest around him in silver.

He moved to his bedroll, thinking of Lillie. What if Johnny was right and Lillie was ready to move on with someone like Wainwright? Was he a fool for coming back here to clear his name? What if he couldn't prove he didn't do it?

Trask let out a long breath as he lay down. The embers in the fire flared in the breeze. He could still feel the heat. A narrow ribbon of smoke rose, wavering before it disappeared into the dark overhead.

He tried not to worry about Johnny and the feeling he had that all was not as it seemed. He closed his eyes, picturing Lillie earlier holding a gun on him. He smiled to himself. That was the woman he remembered. The woman he loved. The woman he didn't want to live without any longer—no matter how much danger it put him in to come back here.

CHAPTER FIVE

LILLIE TOOK THE bottle of beer her brother handed her and put her feet up. It felt good to finally sit down after the bar closed for the night. They'd been busy all afternoon and evening, the time flying by. She'd hardly had time to think about Trask and speculate on where he might be. Or when he might show up again. A lie. He was *all* she'd thought about.

It had made for a tense day, fearing that he might foolishly show up at the bar any minute. He hadn't. She figured he'd probably left again. If he'd been arrested, she would have heard by now.

"Does it ever bother you?" Darby asked as he joined her in their nightly ritual after the place closed. He took a drink of his cola and glanced out the window.

Lillie didn't have to ask what he was referring to. She followed his gaze to the far pasture of the Cahill Ranch and the eight-by-eight metal fence around the missile silo.

"We don't even know if there is a manned missile down there after the disarmament agreements," she said.

"That's just it, neither do the Russians or the Chinese or whoever else wants us all dead. So when they decide to destroy us, they will fire at all of the missile silos. It will be Armageddon."

There were 450 active sites in Montana, Wyoming and North Dakota—two hundred of them in Montana alone. All of them were scattered around the state in pastures behind a chain-link fence much like the Cahills'. Their grandfather had been honored to do his part when it came to the nation's security. He'd gladly given the military the land they wanted for the missile site.

Everything about the sites were top secret. And that was the problem. If there was a malfunction, not even the sheriff could get involved.

"Truthfully? I forget it's even out there," Lillie said, taking a drink of her beer. Today especially, since she had other things on her mind. She'd gone for a drive after leaving her father at his cabin. It had given her time to think about things. She'd felt better by the time she'd come back to work her shift at the bar.

Now hours later, she and her brother were relaxing together. It was her favorite time of the day normally. Sitting there, she kept thinking of Trask. Worse, she was keeping it from the brother she felt closest to. How could she pretend that nothing had changed?

Her brother sighed. "Dad thinks something is going on out there."

"It's those aliens. They just won't leave him alone," she joked.

"It's because he is such a fine human specimen at nearly seventy."

She suddenly felt like crying. "What if it's real?"

"The air force has admitted that trained military men witnessed what they believe was a flying saucer hovering over some of the missile silos in March of 1967. Hell, whatever it was, it shut down the missiles, sent them off-line. If we'd been attacked during the more than twelve hours the missiles were inoperable..."

Lillie sighed. "If that really was an alien spaceship from some other planet, then we have more to worry about than the foreign invaders and the rest of our country's enemies on this earth."

Darby nodded. "I think it's what Dad saw all those years ago. Maybe he really was abducted by aliens, as crazy as it sounds. He wouldn't be alone. Aren't there hundreds of people who make that claim elsewhere in the world?"

"Maybe not hundreds." She could tell that he wanted to believe it. Or more than likely wanted other people to believe their father and quit treating him like a nutcase. "Or maybe what happened to him is more like a flashback from when he was in the Vietnam War. Let's not forget what he's been through before any of this alien talk."

Darby nodded and took another drink. Their father was a war hero. He'd been shot down and captured, spending months in a prison camp before being rescued. "So you don't think there is anything going on at the missile silo?" Darby asked.

"Is that one of the reasons you want to leave here?" Lillie had to ask.

"You have to admit, it's unsettling to think that an enemy country could nuke us at any time."

Did he really live with that fear every day? Not everyone had a missile silo in his backyard. But a whole lot of people they knew around here did. "Then I think I should find a way to buy you out and you should leave."

He looked at her in surprise. "Are you serious?"

"Aren't you?"

Slowly, he shook his head. "I don't know what I want. I just feel...antsy."

That was a feeling she knew well. She'd always blamed it on Trask. She'd lied to herself that she hadn't been waiting for him all these years.

But after this morning, she wasn't sure what she wanted. For years she'd wanted Trask. She'd played the fantasy of his return in her head. He would come back and beg her to forgive him, tell her what a fool he'd been, sweep her off her feet and... That was where she would stop imagining his amazing return.

There could be no happy ending. Not with a warrant out for his arrest. Even if there hadn't been, he'd never wanted to stay in Gilt Edge and run a bar. And she didn't want to leave. He'd known that. Maybe it was another reason he'd left her waiting that night nine years ago. They'd been at a stalemate. Nothing had changed.

Nothing except for the fact that they weren't those lovesick twentysomethings anymore. And if Flint got word that Trask was back, it would be only a matter of time before he was behind bars. Would Trask put up a fight? Would it end in gunfire?

She shuddered at the thought.

"You okay?" her brother asked.

"Just a chill," she said and took another sip of her beer. Through the open window, she could hear the frogs in the creek and the breeze whispering in the pines outside. She loved the peace that fell over the land in this isolated spot after the bar closed.

But tonight they'd closed early because business had been slow. Even so, she had too much on her mind to feel much peace. She finished her beer and got to her feet. "I'm tired. I think I'm going to call it a night."

Darby was looking at her as if he was trying to read what was really bothering her. "I'm not going to force you into anything on this place. I promise. I'm just talking."

She nodded, since that was the least worry on her mind right now.

"The old man is probably as fine as he can be, so there is nothing to worry about with him, either."

Lillie met her brother's gaze and considered telling him what was *really* bothering her. What would he suggest she do if she told him that it hadn't been a bear but Trask she'd seen earlier? Neither of them would call Flint, she assured herself. And yet Darby was more straight-arrow than her and the others. Darby would want nothing to do with harboring a criminal. That much she knew. She told herself she wouldn't put the bar in jeopardy.

But was she already risking everything by not telling someone about Trask's visit?

FLINT HAD SPENT a long day dealing with one small crisis after another, waiting for Anvil to call and say he'd heard from his wife. Now it was late and he realized there was nothing at home to eat.

He was also second-guessing his decision on Jenna Holloway as he pulled into the grocery store lot before it closed for the night. Earlier he'd been hesitant to start treating the Holloway farm like a crime scene. He told himself he would give it twenty-four hours. It was that long before he could put out a missing person's report on an adult female. That would give Jenna time to have second thoughts and come home.

If she was still alive.

That was what haunted him. By then, Anvil would have had plenty of time to cover his tracks even more than he already had. Flint knew that appearances could be deceiving. Anvil was definitely distraught. It was probably because of their argument, his wife's infidelity and absence, his guilt for having slapped her. But it could also be because he'd killed her.

He decided as he pushed open the door to the grocery store that he'd put out a missing person's BOLO on her and her vehicle first thing in the morning. He was still hoping that by tomorrow morning they would have news of her.

Tired, he put a frozen dinner, some eggs and a quart of orange juice into his cart and looked up to see his ex-wife, Celeste. That was the problem with living in such a small town. Fortunately, they somehow avoided each other for months at a time. Just his luck that tonight wasn't one of those times. He was in no mood for her and the feelings she evoked.

"Flint?"

Her voice alone was enough to bring it all back. Bitter memories tainted the sweet ones from his youth. Celeste was still a stunner, her blond hair cut in a perfect bob that framed a perfectly made-up beautiful face. Diamonds glittered at her throat, her ears, and the big one weighed down her ring finger.

"Celeste." He noticed that her grocery cart was filled with party food for a crowd. His own was nearly empty, making both it and him seem pathetic.

Her gaze scanned the contents of his cart before returning to him. She confirmed what he already figured she thought of him. The food in his cart practically announced it to the world. Here he was, the poor jilted ex struggling to survive. He wanted to say, "I'm doing just fine. Better than fine. Yes, you hurt me. We hurt each other. But I'm happy enough right now. Except when I run into you."

Instead, he asked, "How's Wayne?" and could have mentally kicked himself for it. He really didn't give a damn how her husband was doing. There were at least two reasons to dislike Wayne Duma. A rancher, philanthropist, all-around good guy, Wayne wallowed in his family's wealth. Wayne had also been sleeping with Celeste when she was still married to Flint.

"Wayne's fine. Busy. I try to get him to slow down... We're having a few people over tomorrow night. As you know, I don't like waiting until the last minute to shop." She motioned to her cart, looking as uncomfortable as he felt.

He recalled those late nights she went out for groceries and had really been meeting her future husband. A bitter taste filled his mouth at the memory.

When her green eyes locked with his, he remembered the two of them together, bodies glistening with sweat. It was a memory he would have preferred to forget.

"How are you, Flint?"

"Couldn't be better." Even to his ears, it sounded angry.

"I heard you're seeing someone." She frowned as if the name hadn't been on the tip of her tongue. "Midge. No, Maggie. Maggie Johnson, no Thompson." She smiled as if pleased that she'd remembered.

Flint felt his stomach roil. He didn't want to talk about Maggie with Celeste, hated that she knew any of his business. But he especially hated that she knew he and Maggie were dating. Crazy as it sounded, he felt he needed to protect Maggie from Celeste, as if his ex might do something to hurt her. He doubted Celeste gave a minute's thought to either of them.

"I should get going before my dinner thaws." He'd lost his appetite and wished he hadn't stopped by the store. But he had no choice now but to head to the front, where the checker appeared anxious to close soon.

Celeste looked disappointed that he was going. He'd seen her interest spark when she'd mentioned Maggie. It made him angry. She'd dumped him for Wayne Duma. She had no right wanting to know anything about his life, anything about Maggie, especially since Maggie was the best thing that had happened to him in a very long time.

He felt her gaze on him as he'd tried not to hurry to the checkout. That Celeste wanted to know more about Maggie worried him for reasons he couldn't put his finger on. Just curiosity, he told himself.

But a part of him wondered if Celeste was regretting the choice she'd made. That thought made him laugh. Wayne had given Celeste everything she'd ever wanted. Everything Flint had sorely lacked. And when he was being honest with himself, it still hurt like hell.

"DARBY?" LILLIE HESITATED. She wanted to tell him the truth about Trask, but she realized she couldn't involve him. For all she knew, Trask was gone again.

End of story. The back door was propped open to let in the night breeze. It chilled her as she looked at her brother. "It's just been a long day, since it began so early and at the sheriff's office." She smiled to take the edge off her words. She really hadn't minded getting their father out.

"You want me to take a look out back in case that bear came back?" Darby asked, finishing his cola and getting to his feet.

"No. I'm sure it's long gone." The last thing she wanted was for Darby to go out and possibly run into Trask. She honestly didn't know what would happen. All of her brothers knew that Trask had broken her heart. At the very least Darby would want to kick the crap out of him. She'd often wanted to do the same thing herself.

"Be careful driving home. Deer will be on the road. Don't want to have to bail *you* out of jail in the morning for speeding or what Flint might see as reckless driving."

"After drinking one cola?"

"Convince Flint that's all it was," she joked. Darby had been sober for three years and attended the local Alcoholics Anonymous meetings faithfully.

"An alkie owning and running a bar? What is wrong with this picture?" Cyrus had wanted to know.

"I still love bars," Darby had said. "I just won't be drinking."

"There is something totally messed up in that," his brother Hawk had said. Cyrus and Hawk loved ranching. They didn't understand why Darby would choose standing behind a bar over chasing cattle from the back of a horse.

Darby had merely shrugged.

"You're sure about this?" Lillie had asked him later.

"Positive. Watching other people drink too much, talk too much, argue and fight too much because of booze makes me glad I made the choice I did. Anyway, these are my people. I have a pretty good handle on who should drive home and whose keys I should take and get them a ride."

She'd been skeptical, but Darby had stayed sober and seemed happy. Except when he talked about leaving.

"I'll lock up, sis. Sleep well."

She started toward the back of the building and the stairs that would take her up to her home over the bar.

"I love you," Darby said behind her.

She stopped to look back, but he had already turned out the lights. "I love you too," she said, not sure if he'd already left, since he didn't answer.

As she reached the stairs, she made a quick detour and stepped outside. A crescent moon hung in the midnight blue sky along with trillions of twinkling stars. Out here there were no streetlights to wash out the view. She loved being able to see the stars.

Tonight, the mountains were etched deep purple against the night sky. The white snowcapped tips gleamed silver. Nearer, silhouetted pine trees swayed in the breeze as if in a slow dance.

"You are such a romantic," Trask had once told her. "Are you sure you want to open a bar? You should be writing poetry."

She'd laughed. "How do you know I don't?"

His eyes had locked with hers. "You are such a mystery to me. I want to spend the rest of my life unlocking all your secrets."

Lillie shook off the memory as she searched the pines and the hillside beyond for any sign of him. She caught the sweet scent of spring grass and pine. She heard an owl hoot off in the distance. She felt her heart beat slow in disappointment. Maybe he really *was* gone again.

She told herself it was for the best.

Going back inside, she locked the door and headed up the stairs. She thought of Darby and what he'd said before he'd left. They weren't the kind of family that said they loved each other. It was a given.

So what was up with that? Was he having trouble staying sober? Would he tell her if he was? Also doubtful.

Or maybe, she thought, slowing as she reached her apartment door, maybe there was something else going on with him. She wished he would find someone to love. But her brother rarely dated. Cyrus and Hawk both said Darby was too particular. Like either of them dated much. Maybe they were all doomed to be alone.

She got ready for bed, worrying about her family, determined Trask wasn't going to occupy her thoughts anymore this day. Climbing into bed, she closed her eyes. For only a moment did she wonder where Trask was sleeping tonight or if he was on the road miles from there, which was more than likely the case.

Lillie woke to darkness an instant before a large warm hand clamped down over her mouth.

CHAPTER SIX

"DON'T SCREAM," a familiar deep, sexy male voice whispered in her ear.

She grabbed Trask's hand, flinging it away from her face as she sat up and turned on a light. "Have you lost your mind scaring me like that?" she demanded when she caught her breath. "How dare you come into my house like a prowler. Had I got to my gun, I would have shot you."

"Which is why I didn't give you a chance. Not that I really believe you would shoot me," he said with a tentative smile.

"I figured you left town again."

He shook his head. "Not until I take care of some old business."

"Old business? Like going to prison for Gordon Quinn's murder?"

"You know I didn't kill him."

"Do I, Trask? I thought I knew you, but I'm not so sure I ever did." She saw the hurt in his eyes and felt her own heart ache at the sight.

"I know you're angry. That night when I told you I'd come for you, I couldn't do it. I couldn't drag you into the mess I'd made of my life. I didn't want to leave you behind, but I knew it was the best thing for you. You'd just bought this place with your brother, you never wanted to leave Montana, let alone go on the run with me."

She said nothing, thinking of her heartbreak when she'd realized he'd taken off without her. She didn't want to think how long she'd waited in the dark for him. Or how long she'd waited over the years for him to come back. She'd been ready to give up everything to be with him. He'd left her behind without a word all these years.

"Nice, you had the decency to come by to tell me that instead of letting me wait for you."

"I knew that if I saw you, I would change my mind and ruin your life." He noticed her sleeping attire and shot her a grin filled with devilment. "I see you still sleep in one of my old T-shirts."

She'd been feeling nostalgic earlier and had seen it in the bottom of her drawer. Now she regretted putting it on, especially since the fabric was so laundry-worn-soft that you could almost see through it.

Lillie pulled the covers up to her neck. "Why are you hanging around here? Do you have a death wish? Flint is still looking for you."

"I had to come back. I realized that I would risk everything for you. You're all I thought about. Lillie, I never got over you."

"Well, I got over you." It was a lie and she figured he knew it, since he'd just found her alone in a queen-size bed wearing his old T-shirt.

"You loved me once. I'll do whatever it takes for you to love me again."

She shook her head. "Do you realize how dangerous this is, you being back here? You're wanted for questioning in a *murder*."

"I've had a lot of time to think about things over the past nine years. I understand now why your brother was so sure I'd killed Gordon. Someone set me up and I intend to find out who and clear my name."

"So you haven't gotten any smarter is what you're saying?"

He gave her a sad smile. "I don't have a choice. If I want you back, I have to clear my name. But first I had to see you. I had to tell you that I never stopped loving you."

She thought she'd known him, had known him since they were kids. But the man who'd left her waiting for him that night... She didn't know him. Wasn't sure she knew this man before her now. Did he really expect her to pick up where they'd left off? She had no idea where he'd been all these years or what he'd been doing, and said as much.

"I'll tell you everything once I'm a free man," he said as he rose from the bed and stepped over to her vanity, where he picked up the bottle of perfume he'd bought her for their first-year anniversary. The smell had become a part of her as familiar as her skin—

until Trask left. She hadn't used the scent for nine years. It reminded her too much of him.

Trask sprayed a little into the air, the scent rushing at her with all the memories of the two of them. She felt that old pull, stronger than gravity. When he looked at her, naked desire burned hot in his blue eyes. Clearly, the scent had the same effect on him.

"Just know that leaving you was the hardest thing I've ever done."

"Yet somehow you managed it." She wished he'd put down the perfume and leave.

"I don't expect you to believe me any more than your brother Flint does, but I didn't kill Gordon. Yes, I punched Gordon, believe me he had it coming. Then I went for a long drive up into the mountains. I knew hitting him was wrong. But I was more worried about you being disappointed in me. I needed that job for us."

"He was all right when you left him?" she asked, needing to hear him say it again.

"He got to his feet and threatened to have your brother lock me up on assault charges, so he was his normal self. That's why I decided to lay low for a while. I stayed up in the mountains, built a campfire, slept in my truck. It wasn't until the next morning that I came back into town. By then I'd decided to try to make amends. I knew I couldn't work for Gordon anymore, but I thought I could get on at the construction site, where Johnny was working. I'd been paying on an engagement ring for you—"

"I don't want to hear this." She'd thought he couldn't do anything more to hurt her. *An engagement ring?* She felt as if her heart would burst.

"It's true. I was going to ask you to marry me as soon as I got paid and picked up the ring."

She couldn't take any more of this. How did she even know he was telling the truth? Maybe he was just saying what he knew she desperately needed to hear. She met his gaze, saw pain in his blue eyes and felt another piece of her heart break.

"Then I heard that Gordon was dead, that he'd been killed with a pitchfork in his barn and that your brother was looking for me. I got scared. But I swear to you, Gordon was alive and well when I left his ranch."

Her voice cracked when she asked, "If all this is true, then why didn't you stay and prove you were innocent?"

He raked a hand through his dark hair, making her own fingers ache at the memory of its silken feel. "That was just it. I couldn't prove I didn't kill him. I had his blood on my shirt. I had no alibi. And let's face it, I'd been in enough trouble that I couldn't blame your brother for thinking I killed him. Not to mention, I'd threatened to kill him earlier in the day."

"So I guess you're right back where you were nine years ago."

"No, I was twenty-two, just a saddle tramp who courted trouble nine years ago. I had nothing. I had nothing to offer you. And all of a sudden I'm

wanted for murder? You were the only person who
believed in me. Your brother wanted me gone as it
was." He held her gaze, his eyes pleading for her to
understand. "Running was what I knew. Look at my
mother, my old man. Things get tough, bail."

"So you bailed. I ask again, what's changed?"

He put down the perfume bottle and stepped toward the bed. "I needed to grow up and I did. I spent
those years working hard, saving every dime and
investing that money. All I could think about was
coming back and making things right with the law,
but especially you." She started to interrupt, but he
stopped her. "I'll do whatever it takes to get you back
because all I've ever wanted is *you*."

These were words Lillie had dreamed of for years.
But she couldn't let herself trust them. He made it
sound so easy, as if he could just come back and
clear his name. The case had gone dead cold in nine
years. How could he possibly prove his innocence?
He'd run. He looked guilty. Maybe *was* guilty, she
thought, even though in her heart she didn't believe
it. Would never believe it.

"Lillie, tell me there's a chance for us once I'm
free of all this."

No fool would trust her heart to this cowboy. She
thought of the years she'd yearned for him, hoping
for just a word, anything. She hadn't even known if
he was still alive.

"I'm sorry, but it's too little, too late," she said
with a shake of her head. "Nine years ago I was in

love with you. Nine years ago I would have done anything to help you. But you left me waiting for you. You broke my heart." The admission came out on a ragged breath before she could stop it. She raised her chin in defiance and lied through her teeth. "I've moved on."

He cocked his head. "I don't think so. You're sleeping in a queen-size bed all by yourself wearing my old T-shirt. I know you've hardly dated since I left."

He'd been keeping tabs on her through someone here in town? She bristled, outraged. "You kept track of me, but you didn't bother to contact me?"

"I couldn't. I knew your brother would expect that." He sat down on the edge of the bed again. She moved to the far edge away from him. "I'm so sorry I hurt you, Lillie. I was a fool. But I never stopped loving you. No matter what happens now, I'm not leaving until I get back what I lost." He reached for her.

Lillie jumped up, dragging the quilt with her to put distance and clothing between them. She'd seen that look in Trask's eyes too many times. It had always sparked a burning desire in her that matched his own. She didn't know how much Trask had changed, but how he made her feel hadn't. It would have been so easy to fall back into that empty bed with this man, this man she'd ached for all these years. Just to feel his arms around her...

"You need to leave before I call Flint," she said,

her voice warbling with both fear and a yearning that made her sick with need.

"You won't do that, even if it is true and you don't love me anymore. I only came here because I couldn't let another day go by without telling you how I felt. I can understand that you've moved on." His look said he didn't understand it, couldn't accept it. "But know this, I am no longer running when things get tough. I'm sticking it out. I love you, Lillie. That will never change no matter what."

She said nothing. They stayed like that, eyeing each other across the empty bed, the crumpled sheets between them a reminder of what they'd once shared.

"I'm going to clear my name. Once I do, I'm coming for you. I'll spend the rest of my life making it up to you. Or fighting for you, if that's what it takes." With that, he stood, turned on his boot heel and headed for the door.

"Wait a minute."

Trask turned expectantly and almost took a step in her direction.

"How did you get in here?" she demanded.

He looked surprised. "Seriously? I was picking locks before I was ten." Sometimes she forgot the kind of family Trask had come from. His father had been a trick roper, traveling all over the country with a carnival. Trask's mother had taken off when he was a boy. He'd had a stepmother of sorts for a short while, just long enough for him to think his life was going to settle down, before she took off with her son, Emery, from another relationship.

Trask had been raising himself most of his life. But after the so-called stepmother had left, Trask, then fifteen, had started getting into trouble. Nothing big, just enough trouble that the local law knew him well and would come looking for him when something happened—like the murder of Trask's boss after there'd been an altercation that had been witnessed.

Lillie followed him at a safe distance to lock the door behind him. Not that it would do any good if he decided to come back. She'd have to get better locks if she hoped to keep him out. Too bad there wasn't a lock for her heart.

She felt a chill and realized she was still wearing his old worn T-shirt. She raced back up the stairs, shivering. She could still smell his male scent mixed with the night air and the cloying scent of her perfume. It made the ache deep within her hurt even worse.

Stripping off Trask's old T-shirt, she threw it in the hamper and dug in the bottom of her dresser for the brand-new flannel nightgown some aunt had given her for a college graduation present. Pulling it on, she stepped to the window, opened it and let the cold breeze cool the heat that had her cheeks flushed, her body damp with perspiration.

She heard the sound of a truck engine start in the distance. Would he head for town? She listened until the sound died off in the distance, relieved when the truck headed for the mountains. At least he was smart enough to hide out. But then what?

Her mind reeling, she closed the window and climbed into bed, even though she knew she wouldn't be able to go back to sleep tonight.

EARLY THE NEXT MORNING, Maggie Thompson picked up her scissors and cut one-hundredth of an inch off the hank of hair spread between her fingers, her mind on her date tonight with the sheriff instead of this morning's long list of difficult clients.

She felt a bubble of excitement rise in her at the thought of tonight. Her relationship with Flint—she could think of it as that now—was about to go to the next level. They'd taken it slow, since both of them were leery after their former bad experiences. But they seemed to click. It was time to see where this was going.

"Not too short," Mrs. Appleby warned. "You know Herbert complains if it's too short."

"Yes, Sandra. I'm just trimming off a tiniest bit just to shape it up." They'd had this conversation so many times that Maggie could have recited it from memory.

Sandra Appleby touched her thinning gray locks and considered her profile in the mirror. "Did you hear about Jenna Holloway?"

Beauty shops were a hotbed of gossip. Maggie didn't encourage it, but she also knew that her clients came here to relax and catch up on who was pregnant, who was getting a divorce, who had gone into the nursing home and who was seeing whom since their last visit.

Some clients thrived on being the first to know what was happening in town—and spreading it. It was the nature of a beauty shop in a small town. Maggie did her best to keep out of it. She didn't want to hear in town that she'd said something she hadn't. So she kept quiet as she finished the haircut.

"I heard she's missing," Sandra said. "How could she be missing?"

Maggie had no idea and said as much. Sandra was one of those who loved to be the first with the town news. It helped that she had a niece who worked as a dispatcher at the sheriff's office.

"I thought the sheriff would have told you," Sandra said, eyeing her in the mirror. "You two are still seeing each other, right?"

"I don't tell him about my clients and he doesn't tell me about his cases," she said.

"Well, I suppose that's for the best given some of your clients." Sandra chuckled at her joke. "Still, you can't help but wonder if Anvil did something to her."

In the second chair, Irma Tinsley piped up. "He kept her on a short leash, that's for sure. Maybe she just got tired of it."

"She was so sweet and shy," Daisy Caulfield said as she combed out Irma's short do. Maggie had hired Daisy after she'd come out of beauty school looking for a job. She was young and full of life and was darned good at her job.

"I did her hair not all that long ago," Daisy was saying thoughtfully. "I remember because she didn't have an appointment. Just walked in and said she wanted something different." Daisy's eyes widened in alarm as she met Maggie's in the mirror. "Maybe the haircut was the start of something."

Maggie laughed and brushed it off, though it was strange that Jenna of all people would just show up without an appointment. "We hope all our haircuts are the start of something for our clients."

"I'd like to start up something," Irma said with a laugh. A small dark-haired woman in her late fifties with a great sense of humor, Irma had been widowed now for five years.

"There is always Merrill Forster," Sandra said, tongue in cheek.

Irma laughed gaily. Merrill was the over-fifty bachelor who apparently read the obits regularly because he turned up at each new widow's door like clockwork.

"I already gave Merrill a whirl," Irma said, making Sandra gasp.

"She's joking," Maggie assured her client.

Sandra looked disappointed. "I've heard stories about Merrill. I was hoping you could verify them."

Everyone laughed but quickly stifled it as the sheriff pushed open the door. Flint stood for a moment just inside the door. He looked afraid to come into this female domain.

"I was just leaving," Irma said as Daisy finished with her. "You can have my chair. Looks like you could use a trim."

Maggie smiled at him. "I believe he prefers Tim's Barbershop down the street."

"That's where Herbert goes," Sandra said. "You think they don't gossip like old women down there? Ha!"

"I'm almost finished," Maggie said, running a brush through Sandra's thinning hair. "What do you think?"

Sandra studied herself in the mirror. "It makes me look younger, wouldn't you say?"

"I would," Maggie agreed.

"Definitely," Daisy agreed and thanked Irma for the tip she gave her.

Flint held the door open for Irma and waited as Sandra settled up and left, as well. "Can you sneak away for lunch?" he asked Maggie.

"Sorry, not today. I have a highlight coming in." She glanced at the clock on the wall. "Actually, Angie should be here." Angie North was running late. That surprised Maggie. Angie was always early. She loved to come in and visit with whoever was getting their hair done before her appointment.

Maggie always got the impression that Angie had too much time on her hands. Either that or she was just glad to escape the house for a while. Not that her husband, Bob, didn't call at least once while she was in the chair to see when she'd be home.

"I'm going to run over to the drugstore for a milk shake," Daisy announced. "Can I get you something?"

Both Maggie and the sheriff declined.

"Smart girl," Flint said.

"She can take a hint." She smiled at the man she'd been dating for several months now. It still seemed too good to be true. Sometimes she had to pinch herself. It also scared her. Flint Cahill could break her heart without even trying.

He stepped to her, looked toward the street as if to make sure no one was watching and gave her a quick kiss. "I can't wait to see you tonight."

She nodded, making him smile. Flint seemed as excited as she was. Neither of them had actually come out and said that they would make love tonight. But somehow, they both seemed to be on the same page and knew that they would.

Flint cleared his voice and went back to sheriff mode. "I also wanted to ask about Jenna Holloway."

"We heard that she's missing," Maggie said. Flint seemed surprised for a moment. Like her, he probably forgot sometimes how news traveled in this small town.

"Did she have her hair done here?"

"Daisy was just talking earlier about the last time Jenna was in."

"Anything unusual happen?"

"Kind of. She was a walk-in. So that was odd.

She always made an appointment way in advance. Also, when she sat down in the chair, she said she wanted a new do, which might mean absolutely nothing. Except that she'd had the same hairstyle as long as I've known her. I don't think it was an impulsive decision. I think it had been coming for some time."

Flint nodded. "Jenna was one of the least impulsive people I've ever known. Isn't that what you got from her?"

Maggie chuckled. "I'd put her in the top five for sure." She could tell that he was worried. "If I hear anything…"

He smiled. "Thanks." He had a great smile that made his gray eyes crinkle. She was almost sorry he was so handsome. Wasn't there a country song about why a man should marry an ugly woman? She thought it might go both ways.

Daisy returned with her milk shake and Flint left after saying, "See you tonight." His stopping by, even on sheriff's department business, made her day. *See you tonight.* She smiled as she began to clean up around her workstation. Angie still hadn't shown up.

When she'd finished, she glanced at the clock on the wall. "Maybe I better call Angie. It isn't like her to forget a hair appointment," she said, picking up the phone.

"Mine's late too," Daisy said. "Maybe there's a traffic jam." They both chuckled at that, since they didn't even have one stoplight in town and most people felt stop signs were just suggestions. Gilt Edge was a small town with small-town problems. Traffic wasn't one of them. Daisy sucked on her straw. "Oh, this shake is to die for."

Maggie dialed the number. It rang four times before voice mail picked up. "Just wanted to remind you about your hair appointment, Angie. You're probably on your way." And yet, as she hung up, she had a bad feeling that something must have happened.

DARBY TOOK ONE look at Lillie the next morning when she came down to the kitchen at the back of the bar and let out an oath. "Rough night?"

He had no idea. "I had trouble getting to sleep."

"Probably worried about that bear you thought you saw."

Something about the way he said it put her on alert. "Probably. I'm just glad I have the day off. I think I need it."

"I looked around out back this morning when I got here," he said, his gaze intent on her face. "I didn't see any tracks. At least no bear tracks."

"That's good to hear. I'm sure I imagined it," she said, trying to laugh it off. "It was probably just the stress of Dad being arrested and all that."

"Lillie, if there's more bothering you—" Darby handed his sister a cup of coffee. "Seriously, if you aren't feeling well—"

She cut him off with a shake of her head as she took the coffee. "Thanks. I'm fine."

"Flint called earlier," her brother said.

Her pulse thundered in her ears. She tried to keep her face blank. Her first thought was that Flint had caught Trask. Which meant he was either behind bars or possibly dead.

"What did Flint want?" She hated that her voice broke.

"Said he wanted to get together soon and talk about Dad. It felt more like he was checking up on one of us than Dad, though." She saw worry in Darby's expression and knew at once which of them might cause a person to worry.

Lillie wasn't sure if she should be relieved or not. At least Flint hadn't been calling about Trask. "Did you tell him we're all fine and we don't need him checking up on us?"

"No, I saved my breath, since we both know it wouldn't do any good." He frowned and studied her openly. "You did have a rough night, huh? You should try to get a nap today. Otherwise, I pity Wainwright."

She stared at him, uncomprehending. "Wainwright?"

"Your big date with him tonight. Don't tell me you forgot."

"That's *tonight*?" She let out a curse and slapped her palm against her forehead. Just when she thought things couldn't get any more complicated.

"You can always renege on the bet."

The one thing a Cahill never did was renege on anything. Even a stupid bet. "You know I can't do that. Maybe he had enough to drink that he won't remember."

"I wouldn't count on that," Darby said. "He likes you and has for some time, but I think you already know that."

Junior Wainwright had asked her out several times over the past few years. Then he'd caught her at a weak moment a week ago when he'd suggested they let fate decide if she should go out with him. He was in the bar drinking with friends and everyone was having a good time.

"One date, dinner, maybe dancing, definitely champagne," Junior had said. "Your luck against mine." He had rattled the leather container with the dice in it that was kept behind the bar to roll for drinks or money for the jukebox.

"And if I win?" Lillie had asked.

"I promise to leave you alone."

She'd laughed. "You're on!"

He'd looked a little crestfallen as they shook hands on it.

She'd always had good luck when it came to the dice. She'd rolled and damn fickle fate, she now had a date with Wainwright. The timing couldn't be worse.

CHAPTER SEVEN

FLINT WAS SMILING to himself as he left the beauty shop. Seeing Maggie always brightened his day. She made him feel good. Nothing like he felt around Celeste.

Running into Celeste last night hadn't just ruined his sleep. It had given him vivid, disturbing nightmares. In the only one he remembered before he'd awakened, he was in the woods with a shovel in his hands. When he looked down, he realized that he'd dug a grave. He hurriedly started to fill in the grave, when suddenly the earth under his last shovelful of dirt moved. A hand poked out, then a head.

He shuddered even now at how real it had been. But he remembered the overwhelming sense of relief and then horror when he realized it wasn't Celeste in the grave. It was Jenna Holloway. The right side of her head had been caved in and her right eye dangled from the socket.

But as he'd stared down at her, her face began to change... Suddenly, it *was* Celeste. Her face had contorted into a smile, that one green eye on him as she said through dirt-crusted lips, "You did this.

You aren't any better than the people you put behind bars."

Any dream of Celeste was a nightmare, but this one had rattled him more than he wanted to admit. His ex-wife had always made him feel he wasn't good enough for her. That her beauty demanded someone more…important. Apparently, it had demanded a man like Wayne Duma.

He tried to put all thoughts of Celeste out of his mind as he pictured Maggie and felt himself smile again. Maggie, tall and pretty with her long, curly natural hair the color of burnished mahogany. Maggie with her sweet disposition. She always had a kind word for everyone, a ready smile. And her laugh? It was like sunshine after a rain shower. If anything, Maggie seemed unaware of how attractive she was. So completely different from Celeste.

Still, remnants of the nightmare seemed to follow him like a dark cloud as he walked down to the library. He didn't believe in omens, but that dream…

Clearing his head, he told himself he had to find out what had happened to Jenna Holloway. He was worried about Anvil and what he might have done. This morning, with Anvil still not hearing from her, Flint had put out a statewide alert on her car, along with a description of Jenna. Without her having a credit card that could be traced, it would be more difficult to track her down. Hopefully, she would call home.

If she was alive, he needed her found. Otherwise,

he would have to begin treating the Holloway farm like a crime scene. Right now, he still held out hope that Jenna would turn up alive and well.

With her still missing, Flint decided to follow up on his computer theory. The cool library with its wonderful smell of books was exactly what he needed this morning, Flint thought as he stepped inside. Deirdre "Drey" Hunter greeted him from behind the main desk as he entered. They'd gone to school together, often in the same classes, though they never dated. She'd dated his brother Hawk. He still wondered why they'd broken up.

Drey's long dark hair was pulled into a ponytail. She wore a white tank top over jeans with a navy blazer. She was still as pretty and slim as she'd been in high school.

He wondered if the reason she'd never married was because she hadn't gotten over his brother. They'd dated for over two years. Had she been more serious than Hawk had been? Hawk refused to talk about it. Strange that neither of them had tied the knot with anyone else.

"How are you, Flint? I don't think I've ever seen you in here before," she said.

"It isn't that I don't read," he said, quickly feeling as if he was being called on the carpet. "I like my own books." He shrugged, feeling embarrassed.

Drey laughed. "And I thought you were just avoiding me. A joke," she added quickly, no doubt feeling like he did and that they'd gotten off on the wrong foot. "Can I help you find something?"

"I'm here on sheriff's department business," Flint said, finding safe footing behind his star. "I need to ask about one of your possible patrons. Jenna Holloway. Have you seen her in here? Possibly on one of the computers?" He motioned to the three computers in the corner with the free-Wi-Fi sign over them.

Drey shook her head. "Sorry, but I've *never* seen Jenna in here ever. I can check, but I don't believe she even has a library card with us."

It had been a thought.

"Did you try the internet café uptown? They have computers. Maybe she used theirs."

He nodded. "I'll do that." He glanced around the library at all the books. "I do love books," he said, his gaze coming back to her. "I don't have much time to read and on top of that I'm a slow reader. My books would always be late. I'd owe you money all the time if I borrowed books from the library."

"I'm sure we could work something out," she said. "You could fix my parking tickets. A joke," she added, making them both laugh.

He thanked her and left, realizing how much he liked Drey. Too bad it hadn't worked out between her and Hawk. She would have been a good addition to their family.

At the internet café, he got the same answer. Jenna Holloway hadn't used their computers.

So that meant that if she'd met "someone" it must have been the old-fashioned way.

He glanced toward the grocery store, the only one in town. From what Anvil had told him, there were only a few places in town that his wife probably went: the grocery store, the gas station, the beauty shop—but only for special occasions—and the dress shop.

Anywhere along the way she could have run into a man who, seeing a vulnerable woman, had taken advantage of her. He couldn't imagine that the love had been mutual. Was it possible a man as vulnerable as Jenna might actually have fallen for the farmer's wife? Anything was possible, he'd learned in law enforcement.

What bothered him was that Jenna hadn't turned up yet. It had been almost thirty-six hours. And yet she hadn't called. And no one had seen her. That didn't bode well.

Flint hadn't gone but a few blocks from the café when his cell phone rang.

"Sheriff Cahill." He listened to the dispatcher for a moment, then said, "Patch him through." It was Bob North calling. Hadn't Maggie just said that Bob's wife, Angie, had a hair appointment and was running late?

"I can't find Angie," a distraught Bob cried without preamble.

"What do you mean *find* her?"

"She isn't in the house. She isn't at her hair appointment. It's like she disappeared out of thin air."

Or was abducted by aliens, Flint thought, keeping the family joke to himself.

"I'll be right there."

HER BROTHER, LILLIE REALIZED, was still studying her. "Where are you off to so early, anyway?" Darby asked. They'd shared the same womb together and had always been close. He probably knew her better than anyone—except Trask.

She realized she had her truck keys in her hand. "I've got an errand I have to run. You need anything from town?"

"We have a food delivery this morning, so I'm good. If you aren't going to try to get out of your date with Wainwright, then you'd better be thinking about what you're going to wear. Do you even own a dress?" he joked. "As I recall, he said he was picking you up at six. Dinner, possibly dancing and champagne."

"I own several dresses, for your information." Not that she wanted to wear any of them for a date with Wainwright. "I don't know why he wants to go out with me anyway."

"Because you're beautiful, Lillie, inside and out."

She loved her brother for saying so, but as she glanced in the mirror behind the bar, she would definitely have argued that. Her gray eyes were huge and there were dark spots under them, her skin pale. Her dark hair was pulled up in a ponytail, loose hair escaping to fall in dark wisps against her skin. She'd pulled on a pale green Stagecoach Saloon T-shirt and jeans that hugged her slim curves. She looked young and vulnerable and…scared. Trask was back and she was terrified what would happen next.

"Really, if you aren't feeling up to it, call Wainwright," Darby said.

"No, I lost the bet. But Junior is going to regret this. I will be the worst date he's ever had. He'll never ask me out again."

"That's the attitude," he said sarcastically. "Come on, is he really so bad? He's crazy about you. Anyone can see that. I thought one day…" He shook his head. "You're sure nothing else is bothering you other than this date?"

"Nothing that this coffee won't cure." She took another gulp.

"I didn't mean to yell at you yesterday about Dad."

She'd forgotten, given what else she'd had on her mind. "What if he really can't live alone?"

Darby rubbed a hand over his face. "Then you might as well put a gun to his head. Nothing could be worse than keeping him from what he loves. I think he's fine."

"Are you just saying that because you don't want to deal with it any more than I do?"

He smiled. "I've never thought of Dad living long enough to have to make decisions for him."

Lillie moved behind the bar to see what was on the menu for today. They would be opening soon. She wondered where their cook, Billie Dee, was this morning. She didn't want to have to fill in for her. In her state of mind, she would burn everything.

"Maybe I'll stop by the old man's place and see how he's doing tomorrow," her brother said.

"Good idea. If I go, he'll swear I'm checking up on him." They would be opening soon, which meant that their alternate bartender should be arriving any minute, as well.

When they'd first hired Kendall Raines, Lillie had thought for sure that Darby would end up falling for her. Kendall was cute, with blond hair and big blue eyes. She was also sweet, stacked and funny. She was the whole package. But Darby, while joking with Kendall and seeming to like her, had never made the first move.

At one of their after-hours talks, Lillie had asked him why he wasn't interested in the young woman. "She's perfect."

"Perfect for someone. Just not me."

"I will never understand men."

"Apparently not," Darby had told her, and that had been the end of it.

Kendall breezed through the door all smiles wearing a tan Stagecoach Saloon T-shirt, jeans, boots and some kind of nice-smelling perfume. She was fifteen minutes early for her shift. On top of everything, she had turned out to be the perfect employee and patrons of all ages loved her. Lillie could tell that they weren't as happy on the nights that she worked instead of Kendall.

"What is that you're wearing?" she asked the young woman. "I love that scent."

"Here," Kendall said, digging a small spray bottle out of her purse. "You can wear it on your date tonight."

Did everyone know about her date? Lillie almost told her to forget it, but the scent felt so fresh and actually made her feel better.

"There's only a little left," Kendall said. "It's all yours."

"Thank you." She spritzed some on and breathed in deeply. Last night's lack of sleep after her "visitor" seemed to fade a little along with the other perfume scent that reminded her so much of Trask.

She fell silent for a moment as she heard a vehicle approaching. Her heart did that crazy lurch in her chest. Would Trask have the all-out gall to just walk into the bar in broad daylight?

But as the vehicle neared, she recognized the bad tailpipe and sighed in relief. She wasn't going to have to cook. Billie Dee had arrived.

Kendall went in the back to put her things away and get ready for her shift.

The back door banged and a moment later a short, heavyset middle-aged women with bright red dyed hair came through the door whistling the tune "Dixie's Land." She grinned broadly when she saw Lillie.

"I don't really wish I was in Dixie," she said in her Texan accent. "My car started and it's not snowing."

She stopped in the middle of the room and held out her arms as she did a little soft-shoe and then took a bow. "The day can't get any better than this."

Lillie hoped Billie Dee was wrong about that as the cook laughed and headed for the kitchen. "I'm making myself an omelet. Ya'll want to join me?"

"Why not?" Darby said.

Kendall declined, saying she'd already eaten.

"Not me, either, I have to go." Lillie had done her best to pretend that everything would be fine, but there was no way that seeing the only man she'd ever loved after all this time hadn't turned her life upside down—no matter how it ended.

She couldn't just sit around waiting, wondering when she would see him again. If it could be in another nine years. Or any minute.

CHAPTER EIGHT

FLINT DROVE THE ten miles out to the North Ranch. The main house sat back against the mountainside overlooking the valley. As he parked and got out, he told himself that Jenna Holloway's disappearance and possibly Angie North's weren't connected. Both women lived out of town, but that was where the similarities ended. Angie was a small, thin nervous woman who lived in a nice, new house, married to a well-to-do rancher. Her hobby, other than getting her hair done once a week, seemed to be shopping. Flint had seen her in town numerous times coming out of the dress shop or the grocery store or the drugstore, loaded down with packages.

He rang the doorbell and waited. When Bob North came to the door, he had his cell phone in his other hand. Flint had a second to hope that Angie was on the other end of the line before Bob motioned him inside.

"Well, if you see her, please tell her to call me at once…Yes, that's right. I have the sheriff here… Okay, I'll let you know." He disconnected and turned toward Flint.

"I take it none of her friends have seen her?"

"No, and she didn't show up for her hair appointment and I can't reach her on her cell phone."

"You saw her leave this morning?"

Bob ran a hand through his already rumpled hair. "No, I was in the stables checking one of the horses. But heard her leave."

"And she was alone?" Flint asked.

"Of course. Why would you even ask that?"

"Why don't we sit down." He followed Bob into the kitchen.

"Coffee?"

Flint nodded, thinking it would give Bob a chance to calm down some. He watched the man fill two cups with trembling hands. He took the cup he was offered and sat down at the kitchen table. Bob remained standing, appearing too nervous to sit.

"So when was the last time you saw her?"

"At breakfast."

"How did she seem?"

Bob shrugged as if he hadn't noticed, but then changed his mind. "Distracted. I thought it was because of her hair appointment. She likes to go in early. She seemed a little put out when I asked her to fix me some eggs and bacon this morning."

"Bob, I'm trying to understand why you're so upset. You saw your wife several hours ago. What makes you think she's missing?"

"I always call her to make sure she got into town without any trouble. I usually check with her to see when she will be finished with her hair appointment. She always answers her phone. But when I called this morning, it went to voice mail."

"Okay. Maybe her phone isn't working."

"Oh, it's working." Bob reached over on the counter and picked up a cell phone. "It's right here. You see? She didn't even take her phone."

Flint stifled an impatient sigh. "She forgot her phone, which explains why she isn't answering your calls."

"She *never* forgets her phone. I always remind her to take it because she knows I am going to call her and it worries me if she doesn't answer."

"Apparently, she forgot it this time."

"Fine, let's say that is the case. Then why hasn't she shown up for her hair appointment?"

Bob had him there. "You said she was distracted, which could explain her forgetting the phone and even forgetting her hair appointment."

"No. You don't understand. This isn't like her." His words echoed Anvil's.

"I can't put out a missing person's alert on her until she's been gone for twenty-four hours. At this point we have no reason to believe she's in trouble."

"I *know* she's in trouble."

Flint felt a stab of worry. "Based on what? You need to tell me if there is something more going on here."

LILLIE'S HEAD THROBBED as she drove away from the Stagecoach Saloon. She'd awakened with a killer headache, which she blamed on Trask. She was furious with him, but just as much with herself. She'd let him drag her back into his life, this man who'd hurt her more than she would ever admit.

She felt the push-pull of Trask's presence. She'd wanted to rush into his arms. She'd also wanted to shoot him. He'd left her. She could never forgive him for that. He'd told her he would take her with him and then hadn't. What made it worse was that this was the last place she ever wanted to leave. She had only agreed to go with him because she'd felt she couldn't live without him.

But she *had* lived without him. It had hurt, still did, but she'd survived. She'd even thrived without him. If anything, she was stronger because of it.

Which was why she couldn't let him back into her life. How could she ever trust him again?

At the same time, she couldn't let him go to prison for a murder he hadn't committed.

That was the thought that kept coming back to her.

That and the change she'd seen in Trask. The years had filled out his slim body. Hard work had built a taut physique. He was stronger in other ways, as well. But the biggest change was his quiet confidence.

Trask had always been cocky as a boy. He'd hidden a lot of pain behind that charming grin of his. Somehow, he seemed to have dealt with the pain of those years growing up with his sketchy background. The Trask who'd visited her last night had become his own man. A man who'd come back to do exactly what he said he was going to do—clear his name if not win her back.

But how after all this time?

She felt torn between the ache she always felt for Trask and the need to keep her heart safe. She couldn't trust her heart to him again. She wouldn't.

While she wasn't looking forward to her so-called date with Wainwright tonight, she realized it was the best thing that could have happened. Trask hadn't believed that she'd moved on. He'd obviously known how little she'd dated since he'd left. But this date would convince him that it was true. She should have moved on years ago. It made her angry that she hadn't. That she couldn't.

She drove to the sheriff's office, debating what she was about to do. As much as she loved her brother Flint, they'd never understood each other. He thought he was so reasonable, so levelheaded, so sure that he was right. He'd never been in love like she had with Trask.

Sure, he'd loved Celeste. Loved the idea of her, anyway. But he would never have agreed to take off with her and leave everything he knew behind. His hadn't been that kind of love, so he couldn't understand what she was going through now, let alone nine years ago.

As she pushed through the door, she caught Deputy Harper Cole flirting with the dispatcher, a woman a good ten years his junior—not that age would slow the deputy down any more than a rut in the road.

The door closed behind her, making Harp turn. "Hey, Lillie," he said and smiled broadly as he started toward her. His black eye from Ely's punch was open, but the skin around it was varying shades of yellow and gray.

"Is my brother in?" she asked, looking past him to the dispatcher.

"He's out on a call," Harp said, drawing her attention back to him.

"I'll wait in his office, then," Lillie said and started past him.

"Maybe I should wait with you," the deputy said behind her.

"I don't think so." She stepped into her brother's office and closed the door in Harp's face.

IT WAS CLEAR to Flint that his little sister hadn't heard him enter his office. She'd been too busy going through his files.

"It isn't in there," he said behind her, making her jump as he closed his office door.

She spun around. He could see indecision on her face as she struggled with whether to lie or tell him the truth.

It took her a moment to make up her mind. He waited, expecting the lie.

"I want to know everything about Gordon Quinn's

murder," she said, planting her hands on both hips. "You owe me that."

He laughed, surprised she'd gone with the truth. Or at least part of it. "I *owe* you that?"

"Yes, you know how I feel…felt about Trask Beaumont. I need to understand what happened and why you thought…still think he's guilty."

"After all this time? Nine years? *Now* you need to know?"

"Yes." She raised her chin, her look defiant, and yet he could see how vulnerable she really was.

"Mind if I ask what's changed," he said as he walked around his desk and lowered himself into his chair.

"I think I can handle the truth now."

He wasn't so sure about that. "Have a seat and I'll tell you what I can, since the case is still open. But it's common knowledge that he lost his temper. We have witnesses that overheard his fight with Gordon, heard him threaten to kill the man and then hit him and knock him down."

"But you don't have witnesses that saw him kill Gordon."

"No."

She seemed to breathe. "So you really don't have anything."

"I didn't say that."

Her face set in determination, she said, "I want to look at the file."

"You know I can't let you do that." He noticed

her purse on his desk, the handle of a small crowbar sticking out of it. "Really, Lillie?" he asked, pulling out the crowbar. "Were you planning to use this on *me* if I just happened to be in my office?"

"Fortunately, you weren't," she said, shooting him an impatient look that said she was joking. "I saw that your SUV wasn't outside, so I assumed you were on a call. You're not the only member of the family with detective skills."

"So you brought a crowbar to break into my files."

"I doubted you would open them for me. Anyway, growing up, you always told me to think for myself. I did."

"Cute. Sit down," he said as he put the crowbar back into her purse.

With obvious reluctance, she pulled up a chair. "I really don't need a lecture. I need specifics. Just because Trask punched his boss after an argument in the stables, doesn't mean he killed him."

"He threatened to come back and kill him. I have reason to believe he came back later, caught him in the stables and did just that. He was seen hurrying out just before Gordon's body was found." He saw that this was news to her.

Flint had figured that nine years ago Trask had told Lillie his side of the story before he'd left town. He'd always been curious what Trask had admitted to her. Obviously, he hadn't told her everything.

"He didn't mention that he'd gone back that night, huh?" he said.

"It still doesn't prove he killed anyone. That's all the evidence you have against him? Circumstantial at best?"

He rolled his eyes. "You watch too many crime shows on TV."

"Who is this eyewitness?"

"You know I can't tell you that," Flint said. "I shouldn't have told you as much as I have." But if he could help her get over Trask, he'd bend a few rules.

She waved that away. "Did you look at any other suspects at all?"

"Of course I did." Sometimes his little sister annoyed the hell out of him. "I did my *job*. I looked at Gordon's wife, Caroline. Her alibi checked out."

Lillie mugged a face. "Did you consider that she might have paid someone to kill him while she was allegedly elsewhere?" Lillie had heard that Caroline was in Billings shopping. "Everyone knew she and Gordon weren't getting along."

Flint nodded. That was the joy of living in a small town. Secrets were hard kept. "If she paid someone to kill Gordon, there is no record of her doing so."

"Did she have a large insurance policy on him?"

He groaned. "No. She barely got enough to pay off her husband's debts. Are you happy now?" She didn't look happy. She looked as if she might cry. He didn't want that. "I also looked at his partners in the construction company."

"J.T. Burrows and Skip Fairchild? There was a rumor going around that Skip was sleeping with Gordon's wife," Lillie said. "Gordon was barely in his grave before Caroline and Skip were seen together."

Flint nodded and continued, "I looked at everyone associated with him, including his children, Patrick and Brittany. They were eleven and sixteen at the time. They too had alibis."

She set her jaw stubbornly. "Trask didn't do it. Did you ever even consider that?"

"Yes. Lillie, just between you and me, I looked for anything that might clear him. I knew how you felt about him. My feelings aside, I didn't want him convicted of murder, for your sake—if not for his."

She sat back in the chair with a look on her face that broke his heart.

"I'm so sorry."

She nodded as if too close to tears to speak.

Was she looking for closure or was there another reason for this now? The only other reason he could think of was that Trask had contacted her.

"Lillie, if you hear from Trask—" he held up his hand before she could deny it "—tell him to give himself up. I will do what I can for him. He was young. With his family background—"

She was on her feet. "I have to go."

He could see her jaw set and knew her well enough to know there would be no getting through to her. If Trask had been in contact, then Lillie would do her best to help him even though the man had broken his sister's heart.

Flint swore under his breath as she stormed out.

For all these years there had been no word on him, even though there was a BOLO out on him. He'd thought about and analyzed Gordon Quinn's murder for years. He'd lived with it hanging over his head, wondering if Trask was dead or if he'd turn up some day and he'd have to arrest him. The thought had made him sick to his stomach, because if that day ever came, he feared he would lose his sister.

LILLIE LEFT HER brother's office telling herself that Trask wasn't a killer and there had to be some way to prove it. She'd convinced herself that once she helped him clear his name it would release the spell he had on her. Then Trask would be free and she would get on with her life, as well.

All the evidence made him look like a killer, though. There'd been an eyewitness who could put Trask at the stables at the time of the murder.

How was that possible? There had to be another answer. Someone else had gotten away with murder. And if Trask was right, they were willing to let him take the fall for it. Maybe planned it that way after hearing about his argument with Gordon.

Yet, she had to ask herself, how far would she go to help him prove his innocence?

It was the answer to that question that had her determined to talk to Skip Fairchild. She remembered a rumor that had been going around nine years ago that Gordon was liquidating his assets. Did that mean he had wanted out of the construction company? There was only one way to find out.

She tried Skip's house first. When he wasn't home, she swung by the construction site.

Skip Fairchild looked up as she walked into his office without knocking. He blinked as if surprised to see her. Lillie hadn't spoken more than two words to the man over the years. He seldom came out to the Stagecoach Saloon, and when he did, he would sit alone at the end of the bar, order two gin and tonics, drink them and leave.

He always looked…sad, like a man with a heavy weight on his shoulders.

"Ms. Cahill," he said, getting to his feet.

"I need to talk to you about Gordon Quinn's murder," she said as she closed the door behind her and took a seat at his desk.

He stared at her for a moment before lowering himself back into his desk chair.

"Is it true that Gordon was pulling out of the construction company?"

Skip leaned back, clearly taken aback by her abruptness. "What? Where did you hear that?"

When she didn't answer, he said, "He might have been talking about leaving…"

"Who inherited his part of the company on his death?"

Skip shifted in his chair. "That really isn't any of your business."

"Is there some reason you don't want to tell me?"

Skip opened his mouth and closed it again as he leaned back in his chair. She could tell that he hadn't expected her to be so direct or to know as much as she did. But she didn't have time to beat around the bush. She could feel the clock ticking. Once Flint heard Trask was back in town...

"We all know who killed Gordon. I can understand why you might want to throw suspicion on someone else other than your boyfriend, but—"

"Trask didn't kill Gordon." She was on her feet. "I'm going to prove it."

Skip looked as if he didn't want her to leave his office until he dissuaded her. He picked up the phone on his desk and said into the receiver, "You'd better step in here."

A few moments later, J.T. Burrows opened the office door behind Lillie. He was a big man, dressed impeccably in a dark suit and tie. That alone made him stand out in Montana, where only lawyers and morticians wore suits and ties.

"What's going on?" J.T. asked, glancing at Lillie in confusion before turning his gaze on Skip.

"I've been asking about Gordon's murder," Lillie said. "My questions seem to have upset your partner."

"She heard that Gordon might have been leaving the company."

J.T. shot Skip a what-the-hell look. "That was only a rumor—"

"I don't think so," Lillie interrupted. "If I can prove that Gordon was leaving the partnership—"

"Why would you want to do that?" J.T. demanded.

"It gives you both a motive to want your partner out of the picture before he pulled the plug on the company he'd started. Trask didn't kill Gordon. So maybe one of you—or both of you—did."

The men exchanged a look. "That's ridiculous," J.T. said. "It sounds to me like you're just stirring up more trouble than you can handle." Even though he hadn't outright threatened her, she heard something in his voice that made a chill creep up her neck.

She'd come in here hoping to get a reaction to her bluff. But she hadn't expected one quite like this. Suddenly, she wanted out of this small cramped office, but J.T. was blocking the door.

"If the two of you have nothing to hide…" She moved toward the door to leave. J.T. didn't budge. Her hand snaked into her pocket and closed on her phone. She pulled it out, ready to hit 9-1-1. "Maybe we should get the sheriff over here to see what he thinks."

"We have nothing to hide," J.T. said and stepped back. "You're wasting your time."

She didn't think so as she left, her heart pounding.

CHAPTER NINE

FLINT TRIED NOT to worry about his sister. He had two missing women he had to find. In a place with so little crime, this was a rarity. He wasn't as worried about Angie. He thought she'd turn up soon. He drove through town, which didn't take long, looking for Angie's little red convertible. If she was parked along the main drag, he figured she would be easy to find.

But there was no sign of her car or her. Pulling into the parking lot, he got out and went into the post office. There were only a couple of places in town where everyone turned up at some point or another: the post office and the grocery store.

He asked the postal clerk, an older woman who'd been behind the counter for as long as he could remember, if she'd seen either woman and got the same answer before walking over to the local grocery.

Flint had just entered when his cell phone rang. He saw that it was Maggie and stepped back out onto the sidewalk. "Hi," he said and found himself smiling.

"Angie North just walked in. She had a flat tire, forgot her cell phone, tried to fix it herself. She said a man from Wolf Point stopped and helped her. She's a little worse for wear, but she's fine. I just wanted you to know."

He let out a relieved sigh. "Did she call her husband?"

"First thing. Got a lecture and now she's in my chair and about to get her hair done, so all is well."

Flint laughed. "You're like a stylist and a psychiatrist all rolled into one."

"Yep, that's me," she said and laughed.

He loved the sound. He also loved that Maggie never took herself too seriously. He lowered his voice. "I can't wait to see you later."

"Me too."

As he disconnected, smiling from ear to ear, he turned to find Celeste standing behind him. One look at her face and he knew that she'd heard most of the conversation, especially the last part.

"That's how it is with you and Maggie?" she said, her eyes shiny with tears.

He didn't know what to say, so he said nothing.

She gave him a brave smile. "I'm happy for you. Really." A tear caught at the corner of her eye. She reached up and wiped at it. "Allergies. Always get them this time of year. Have a wonderful night." And with that she was off down the street, leaving him wondering what that had been about, since she'd been the one to leave him. Maybe she really was having regrets? He realized that he didn't know how he felt about that.

LILLIE HADN'T GONE far when she had to pull over, she
was shaking so hard. J.T. and Skip had something to
hide, there was no doubt in her mind. But murder?
She thought either of them was up to it. Maybe J.T.
more than Skip.

After her run-in with them, she felt shaken and
even more afraid. She had to see Trask. Last night,
he hadn't given her any idea when she would see
him again. Nor had he mentioned a way they might
communicate now that he was back.

When she was talking to Flint earlier, she'd remembered something. In high school, she and Trask
used to leave messages in the hollow of an old tree
on the ranch. Ely hadn't been around much. But Flint
had made his feelings about Trask clear from the beginning. So they'd sneaked around.

She'd always thought that Flint hadn't been fair
to Trask, who'd never had much, had worked since
he was a boy, and as tough as things had been he'd
managed to survive on his wits. Something Lillie
had always felt her family didn't give him enough
credit for.

Back when she wasn't supposed to be seeing
him, they'd leave messages in the hollow when they
needed to reach each other. If she knew this Trask
who'd returned, then there would be a message waiting for her this morning.

She couldn't trust Trask with her heart, but she
also couldn't desert him when he needed her help,

she thought as her pickup rumbled down the dirt road toward Cahill Ranch.

The ranch was small by Montana standards. But it sprawled across the rolling foothills east of town to the edge of the national forest in the Judith Mountains. Two creeks meandered through the spring-green grass. In the distance, she could make out the brown and white of Herefords dotting the hillsides. Closer to the house, a huge red barn loomed up. Next to the road, a half-dozen horses took off, their manes blowing back as they ran with the wind.

Lillie pulled into the ranch where she'd grown up. It was only a few miles up the road from the stage-coach stop. As she parked, she was relieved to see that both Hawk's and Cyrus's pickups were gone. Out doing chores? Or maybe off somewhere for supplies or a new bull?

She knew they weren't still out on all-night dates, since neither courted. Talk about a family with intimacy issues, she thought. And wasn't it ironic that the one person in the family everyone thought was crazy had stayed married for more than thirty years before losing his wife.

Getting out of her pickup, she was glad both of her brothers were gone. She didn't want anyone to know what she was up to. If they saw her checking the tree, they would know that Trask must be back. She was in no mood to argue about it.

The day was warming up as she walked behind

the main house to where the creek widened into a clear, green pool. The smell of the creek and the cottonwoods around it brought back memories of hours spent back there as a young child with her brothers and their friends.

She'd had an idyllic childhood. Growing up there meant being outside most of the time. All that wide-open space had been their playground and they'd never grown bored with it.

Lillie found the tree easily even though it had been almost a decade since she'd checked the hole for a note. She'd come the morning after Trask had left her waiting for him. She'd been so sure he would have left her a message. He wouldn't have left without telling her why he hadn't come for her.

The memory of that disappointment made her hesitate. He'd let her down nine years ago. Was she strong enough to go through it again? What if she helped him find out the truth and the truth was that Trask really was guilty?

Her heart in her throat, she reached into the hole in the tree. Her fingers found dead leaves. Nothing else. She dragged them out, surprised at her disappointment. Apparently, either Trask hadn't remembered the tree or he hadn't left her a note.

As she brought out the last of the dried leaves, her fingers brushed against paper. She felt light-headed with joy as her hand closed on what was clearly a note—one that had been hidden under the dry leaves but not for nine years.

She pulled it out, cupping it in her palm and simply breathing her relief. Trask wasn't a stranger. She knew him. Knew that he was innocent.

Taking a breath, she slowly opened the paper. At Trask's neat printing, her heart did a little leap. She couldn't help but remember the beautiful love letters he used to write her.

She took a breath and read what he'd written. Then read it again.

What had she expected?

I'm sorry about last night. If you need to talk, leave me a note here. Or I will be at our meeting spot this afternoon until dark. Otherwise, I'll know you don't want to be bothered and I'll leave you alone. For now.

She balled up the note in her hand. She wouldn't leave a note. She hadn't brought anything to write with anyway, since she'd left her purse heavy with the crowbar in the pickup. Also, she didn't know what she would have written.

Not just that, she didn't like the idea of Trask sneaking onto the ranch. All he had to do was get caught by one of her brothers.

As she started to step away, her cell phone rang. The name Junior Wainwright came up. She groaned and checked her watch. She had time to meet Trask before her deadline. Of the three dresses she'd told Darby that she owned, none of them were appropriate for tonight. She so seldom wore a dress that the ones in her closet were ones she'd bought to wear for Trask.

She let the call go to voice mail and then listened to the message.

"Just wanted to check and make sure we were still on for tonight. Six?"

She texted back. See you at six.

With a sigh, she headed for her pickup. She didn't know what she wanted to say to Trask right now anyway. She'd go shopping for her date, since, if she knew Wainwright, which she did, he'd be dressed up. So jeans were out.

It took her a while at the only clothing store in town to find a dress for the date. Her heart wasn't in it. She kept thinking about Trask's note.

Finally, she found a dress that was anything but sexy, bought it and headed for her pickup. The sun was setting. It wouldn't be long before it was dark. She sat behind the wheel of her pickup for a moment before she slipped the key into the ignition.

She'd known where she was going, since she'd found the note in the tree. She'd fought it, spending hours looking for a dress. But as she drove out of town, she knew she had to see Trask. At least one more time.

CUSSING HIS LUCK at running into Celeste yet again, Flint pushed her out of his thoughts and entered the grocery store. Angie North had turned up. He was hoping Jenna Holloway would too and soon.

He knew the two checkers working by name. It was that small of a town. Betsy was a heavyset woman with a perpetual smile.

"Hey, Sheriff," she said. He'd realized he was out of milk at home, so he grabbed a quart. "This it for you?"

He nodded and tossed down a couple of dollars. "You haven't seen Jenna Holloway around, have you?"

Betsy frowned and looked over at the other cashier, who was leaning over the wall that divided them as if not to miss anything.

Lyla was a nice woman, tall and thin with a bunch of kids. Townies remarked she had teeth like a horse, but only in the best way because she had an easy smile. "I haven't seen her for a week or so, I'd say."

"Have you ever seen Jenna in here with anyone?"

"Like who?" Betsy asked, lifting a brow.

"A man who might have been paying attention to her or her to him?" Flint knew this would get the rumor mill going for sure, but he couldn't see any way around it. These women saw people come through their lines every day. They were the heart of the town, since the one thing that everyone needed was food.

"A man?" Lyla scoffed at that and turned back to take the customer who'd walked up.

Betsy lowered her voice. "I saw her once talking to our former butcher, George Fisher, if that helps, but other than that..."

Last he'd heard, George was still in town managing a motel on the outskirts. The kind of motel Jenna Holloway might have gone to after the fight with her husband.

After taking his milk home to the refrigerator, Flint stopped by the motel even though George was a long shot for Jenna's boyfriend. But the fact that he was now apparently managing the motel could at least answer one question. Jenna would have had a place to stay.

George was a big beefy man with heavy shoulders and arms. Flint guessed his age at somewhere around fifty. His face was flushed red and he was sweating profusely as if it was hot back in the apartment directly behind the registration desk. Flint tried to see what Jenna Holloway might have seen in the man. Maybe it was enough that he was the opposite of Anvil physically. George certainly didn't look any more fun, though. Nor did his prospects seem like much of an improvement over what Jenna had.

"A word?" Flint asked, and without hesitation George waved him behind the counter and into the small cramped apartment.

"I was about to have lunch," George said. On the apartment-sized stove a large hamburger patty wallowed in a pan filled with hot grease.

"Have you seen Jenna Holloway in the past few days?"

"Who?" The man looked genuinely confused.

"Jenna Holloway." He gave him a quick, more flattering description than was actually true of Jenna.

"Doesn't really ring a bell."

"She shopped at the grocery when you worked there."

"If you could tell me what she had me cut for her, I might remember her."

Flint had no idea. He thought of the run-down farm. "Something...inexpensive and probably never more than two of each cut."

"Farmer's wife, right? Wait. Two pork chops, cut paper thin. Said her husband didn't eat pork. She always acted guilty for buying them for herself." He shrugged. "I might have given her a deal on them. Felt sorry for her. Is that what this is about?"

"Is that why you aren't at the grocery anymore? Too many deals?" Flint asked.

George looked angry for a minute but then checked his expression. "I got sick of cutting meat. This gig is a lot better."

Flint doubted that but didn't argue. "Was that the only time you and Jenna talked?"

"Talked? You call that talking? She'd ask for two very thin pork chops, I'd cut under her watchful eye and tell her to have a nice day. You call that talking, okay." He frowned. "What are you getting at, anyway?

"You'd remember if Jenna checked into the motel in the last couple of days," Flint said.

"You think she checked in here?"

"Did she? I can get a warrant to check the register if I have to."

"No, she didn't check in here. A warrant? What's going on?"

"She's missing."

"Missing?" he repeated. "And you thought she'd come here?"

"She might have been seeing another man."

George let out a bellow of a laugh. "Me and the pork chop? Not a chance in hell. I'm insulted." He looked insulted.

"If you see her, would you give me a call?" Flint turned to leave.

"I'm not going to see her. I don't even know why you would ask me about her. It's that busybody Betsy at the grocery. She was always starting rumors based on what people had in their baskets. A bottle of wine? A nice couple of steaks? A carton of the good ice cream and she had them having some illicit affair. But me and Pork Chop? Seriously, I'm pissed."

FLINT CALLED THE only other two motels in town, asked if they knew who Jenna Holloway was and if she'd checked in. He had to describe the woman, since apparently few people knew her. She hadn't stayed at either motel.

He then went by the gas station where she bought gas. The only person working was a teenager, pimply and too busy playing video games on his cell phone to be having an affair with an older woman. His boss, who Flint found working under a car in the garage, didn't know who Jenna was.

That left the town's only clothing store. The woman behind the counter said to her knowledge that she'd never seen Jenna Holloway in the store. She suggested that if Jenna had bought a dress recently maybe she'd gone to the not-so-big big-box store just outside of town.

"Sure, I've seen her," the girl at the cash register told him at the small big-box store. "She usually just wanders around looking at stuff, then leaves without buying anything."

"Have you ever seen her buy makeup?" he asked.

"Makeup?" the girl scoffed. "I've never seen so much as lip gloss on her."

He had a thought "You've never seen her looking at makeup?"

That stopped the girl. "It was strange. She would pick up stuff like mascara and read the container, then put it back. I didn't pay much attention because she always left without spending a cent."

According to her husband, Jenna had been wearing makeup. She had to get it somewhere and this would be the most likely place. Would she be too embarrassed to buy it, thinking people would talk? "How often does makeup get shoplifted?"

The girl's eyes widened in alarm. "You think she stole it?"

"No, I'm just asking. Would you have known?"

The girl shook her head. "Makeup items are our biggest losses because they are so easy to stick in a pocket or a purse. I wouldn't have noticed if she'd taken anything nor would any alarms have gone off at the door if she had. Do you think she's been stealing stuff this whole time?"

He didn't know. "I'm just asking questions. I don't know that she stole anything ever from the store." But he had a gut feeling that it was exactly what the prim-and-proper Jenna Holloway had done.

The beginning of a life of crime? Or at the very least, a life of lies?

When Anvil called, Flint thought for sure it was to say that Jenna had returned, that they'd patched up their differences and all was well again out on the farm.

"I found something I think you need to see," the farmer said, sounding upset.

Flint's first thought was evidence. "Don't touch anything. I'm on my way."

TRASK LOOKED AT his watch, then at the ribbon of dirt road that stretched across the valley. No sign of a vehicle. Lillie had probably forgotten about the spot where they used to leave notes for each other. Even if she went to the tree and found it, that didn't mean she was going to come.

She'd been pretty clear about how she felt. He'd broken her heart and she wasn't going to let him do it again. Mentally he kicked himself. He should have stayed all those years ago and faced the music. But he feared he would have spent the past nine years in prison if he had. The evidence against him was damning.

Or maybe he'd just been too young and had seen only one way out—run. He should never have asked Lillie to go with him. At first she'd said she couldn't leave, but he'd known that she would. She would do it just for him. He still regretted asking her. At least he'd come to his senses before he'd picked her up. She had a good life here. She and her brother had made a go of the stagecoach stop. He remembered how excited Lillie had been about turning it into a bar and café and preserving the building.

He was thankful that he hadn't taken her away from her family for a life on the run. He'd seen her waiting outside the stagecoach stop that night in the moonlight. It had taken all of his strength to keep going.

It had killed him to do that to her. No wonder she couldn't forgive him. She'd been ready to leave everything behind to go with him. How long had she waited in the cold morning air for him to come for her?

He couldn't bear to think about it.

With a sigh, he told himself Lillie wasn't going to show now. Had he really expected her to? It was probably for the best anyway until he cleared his name.

Out of the corner of his eye he saw dust boiling up in the distance. His heart raced. Lillie?

It wasn't until she was a few hundred yards away that he recognized her pickup. He told himself that she might have called her brother and that it could be the sheriff now racing down the road toward him.

But in his heart, he knew it was her.

The pickup came to a dust-boiling stop yards from him. Sun glinted off the windshield, hiding her face behind the wheel.

The driver's-side door opened and he waited where he stood.

Lillie stepped out and came around the front of the truck. She stopped, hands on her hips. He smiled at her, thinking he'd never seen anything more beautiful in his life as this woman with her dander up.

"I'm going to help you clear your name. But that's it."

Trask couldn't help being touched. He shook his head. "No, darlin', you're not. I have to do this myself. I can't have you involved. I only contacted you because, like I said, I couldn't let another day go by without telling you how I feel."

"Let me finish," she said, those beautiful gray eyes of hers catching fire in the waning sunlight. How he'd missed this fiery female. Whatever she did, she did it with a passion. He was glad she hadn't changed. "I'm going to help you whether you like it or not, but it doesn't change anything between us. I have to move on."

LILLIE WAITED FOR Trask to say something.

He took off his Western straw hat and raked his fingers through his thick hair. His blue eyes never left her face. "Why *are* you helping me, since you say you don't love me anymore and that you've moved on?" Trask finally asked. "It isn't because once I clear my name you're hoping I will leave, is it?"

Lillie had told herself that Trask couldn't get to her anymore. But that blamed grin threw her off balance. She was reminded of the first time they'd made love. The memory sent an arrow of desire straight to her core. She'd believed they were made for each other. She'd also believed nothing could tear them apart.

"Don't do that," she said.

"Don't do what?"

"Look at me like that."

"Like I want you more than my next breath?"

She turned away.

"Lillie," he said, touching her arm and gently turning her back to him. "None of this matters without you. Nothing does. Even if I go to prison—"

"You're not going to prison."

"You know that morning I was supposed to pick you up?"

She waved a hand through the air in an attempt to shut him up.

"I couldn't take you away from here, away from your family. I couldn't take you on the run with me."

She glared at him. The last thing she wanted to be reminded of again was that morning when she'd waited for him for hours only to have her brother Darby find her bawling her eyes out after Trask stood her up.

"I don't want to talk about it."

He raised both hands. "If you have any doubts about me..."

She let out a bitter laugh. "*Doubts?* You can't be serious. I think I've lost my mind. I know I have." She turned her back on him, had to. She didn't want him to know how badly he'd hurt her. Didn't want him to see how much she'd loved him, would always love him. He was her first. Her only. But loving Trask was one thing, trusting him again with her heart was another. Trask was her Achilles' heel. He could destroy her if she let herself fall for him again.

"We're just old friends. I'm helping an old friend," she said, turning back to him. "That's all I have to offer you."

He settled his hat back on his head. She could feel the heat of his gaze and braced herself. "Okay, you've moved on," he said after a moment. "Just know this. I am not leaving. I'm sticking it out. I love you, Lillie. That will never change no matter what. Trust me."

"Trust you?" She let out a croak of a laugh. "Why would I do that?"

"Because you *know* me."

"Do I? Maybe you don't remember, but I do. The weeks before Gordon was murdered? I didn't recognize the man you were back then. I loved you still, but I was almost afraid of how angry and upset you were *before* Gordon's murder."

"It wasn't something I could talk about."

"So you left me in the dark and you were surprised when I hesitated leaving with you all those years ago? That was before you convinced me to go and then left me without a word. You want me to trust you *now*, when you still aren't telling me the truth?" She started to turn away from him, but he grabbed her arm and turned her back to him, this time not letting go.

"I was protecting Johnny."

She stared at him in surprise. Johnny had been his best friend since they were kids. "*Protecting* him?"

He nodded. "There was a problem between us. I didn't want to tell you. I thought I could fix things…" He shook his head. "Like I said before, I was young and foolish. But I never wanted to scare you with my dark mood. I just didn't know how to handle the situation."

She pulled free of his grasp and crossed her arms over her chest. "But you're going to tell me now." She saw him hesitate and was about to turn to leave when he finally spoke.

"I saw Johnny loading material from one of the jobs into his pickup. The moment he saw me, I knew he was stealing it."

"Stealing from the construction company where he worked?" She thought of earlier when she'd confronted Skip and J.T.

Trask nodded. "He said it had been ordered incorrectly and that he was returning it."

"But you didn't believe him."

He shook his head. "Then one day he stopped by the Quinn ranch, where I was working in the stables," Trask continued. "I saw him take one of Caroline Quinn's silver-and-turquoise bracelets that I thought she must have dropped after her ride that morning."

Lillie was having a hard time believing this. *"Johnny?"* Unlike Trask, Johnny had grown up with two parents, a nice home, an easy life. An overbearing, demanding father, but still… "He tried to steal it?"

"That's what's so crazy. He said he'd found it on the floor and was putting it back. But I distinctly saw him take it out of his pocket when he realized I'd seen him."

"That is crazy," Lillie agreed. "He didn't need the money, so why would he take it?"

Trask shook his head. "I knew he was keeping something from me."

"Did you ever find out what?"

"Johnny told me that he didn't find Caroline's bracelet on the floor of the stables. He found it in the office trailer at the construction company. Caroline had left it on one of her visits to the office."

"So she really was having an affair with Skip Fairchild," Lillie said.

Trask nodded. "Johnny had seen the bracelet and picked it up, afraid if Gordon stopped by the office, he would recognize it and realize what was going on."

"But why steal the construction materials?"

"He said his father had instructed him to pick them up and return them."

"So he wasn't stealing them."

Trask sighed. "I didn't believe him. I wasn't even sure I believed the story about Caroline's jewelry. Something was going on between the partners, but Johnny wouldn't tell me what. Then Gordon was murdered with everyone believing I killed him and that was that."

"There was a rumor going around that Gordon was pulling out of the partnership. I talked to Skip and J.T. earlier. They didn't confirm it, but my asking certainly upset them."

"Lillie, I don't want you—"

"I told you. I'm going to help you, whether you like it or not." Lillie sighed. "Johnny is now one of the partners with Skip and his father. If there is something going on there…"

"I know. That's why I'm still worried about him. But you know how he is when it comes to his father. He is determined to make the man proud, no matter what. I'm worried Johnny's in over his head—and was nine years ago, as well."

It was so like Trask to be worried about his friend instead of himself. She thought of the times she'd run into Johnny since Trask left town. She'd always liked Johnny and wasn't angry at him for telling Trask what she'd been up to after he'd left. But Johnny and his friendship with Trask reminded her of the past and right now she couldn't deal with that.

"Johnny is upset that I've come back. I don't think he's comfortable with the possibility of anyone discovering we've been in contact all these years."

"Johnny has to know that you want to clear your name. That you couldn't have killed Gordon. I would think he would applaud what you're trying to do."

Trask shrugged, but she could see the hurt. Trask made friends for life. He and Johnny went way back.

"We should talk about the murder," she said, determined to stay on track. Still she hesitated before she said, "You were seen leaving the stables just minutes before Gordon was found dead. You didn't tell me you went back that night."

"Because I didn't. Who said they saw me?"

She shook her head. "Flint wouldn't tell me. But whoever it is, that person is his eyewitness who puts you at the murder scene." They stared at each other for a long moment.

"The killer must have heard my earlier argument with Gordon. I was the perfect patsy, wasn't I?"

"The eyewitness saw the real killer leave but mistakenly thought it was you," Lillie said. "Or the eyewitness is actually the killer."

"Lillie, you are brilliant. All we have to do is find the eyewitness," Trask said and grabbed her, pulling her into his arms and swinging her around. He swept her off her feet, literally. In his arms, all those old feelings rushed at her like a locomotive. She felt a drowning wave of desire, but even stronger was that old bond between them.

He set her down carefully as if feeling some of the same emotions. A heavy silence fell between them. "We were so young when we fell in love, weren't we?" Trask said softly into the golden late afternoon around them.

Her throat tightened at the memory.

"We were so innocent. Remember?" She felt the heat of his gaze at even the mention of their initial lovemaking. It had been the first time for both of them. Heat and passion. It had always been that way between them back when Lillie had still believed in soul mates and true love everlasting.

Heart pounding, she found her voice. "That was a long time ago." She turned toward her pickup. "I have to go. I have a date."

CHAPTER TEN

JUNIOR WAINWRIGHT WAS TALL, handsome and wealthy, something he was more than a little aware of. But when she wasn't being critical, Lillie had to admit there was something also shy about him—at least when it came to her.

"You look…amazing," Junior said as she opened the door. He almost blushed. Word around the county was that he was a ladies' man and yet she'd never seen him with a woman at the bar. Nor had she ever heard of him being serious about anyone.

She felt guilty when she thought of how she hadn't wanted to go on this date. She could see how much it meant to Junior. As crazy as it seemed, she felt as if she were cheating on Trask. She mentally smacked herself. She and Trask weren't together. Might never be together again, but she couldn't go there right now.

"Thank you," she said. "You look nice yourself."

Junior smiled. He had a nice smile, the kind made by an orthodontist. She well remembered his crooked teeth from grade school.

"I thought we would go to the steak house. Not a

lot of options in town. If I'd been thinking, we would have left earlier and gone to Billings."

At least she could be thankful that he hadn't been thinking earlier. "The steak house is just fine."

They descended the stairs from her apartment over the bar and walked to his car parked out back in the pines. She didn't look around. If Trask was out there, good. Let him see that she'd moved on. It was for the best, she kept telling herself.

At the front of the bar, there were a half-dozen pickups. She could hear the thump of the bass coming from the jukebox inside and the sound of voices. While there were more trucks per capita in this county than cars, Junior had driven a luxury sedan.

"Are you trying to impress me?" she joked.

"How am I doing?" he asked as he opened the passenger side for her.

She didn't tell him that she would have been happy with an old pickup and burger at the In-N-Out. Too bad the drive-in theater was closed. She would have loved a date like that.

Or maybe she was just remembering her first date with Trask, splitting a large cola, a bucket of popcorn and a box of Hot Tamales. She couldn't recall being more happy.

They talked little on the drive to the steak house. Junior asked how she'd been. Fine. He'd been the same. Had she seen the new subdivision outside of town? She hadn't. Well, it was his development. His and Pyramid Peak Construction Company. They'd teamed up together, he said. "Johnny Burrows is involved. He's as excited about it as I am."

She ground her teeth at the thought of the men involved in the construction company. Not to mention she hated to see pasture turned into rows of identical houses and realized she sounded like her father. She didn't like change any more than Ely did. Also, she liked old things, not cookie-cutter houses in long, boring rows. But she tried to be polite, since it was clear that Junior was very proud of the project.

"That's right, Johnny is one of the partners along with his father and Skip Fairchild," she said, thinking about what Trask had told her.

"They're an ambitious bunch over there," Junior said, smiling. "Johnny works harder than the other two, I can tell you that. But he's young and eager."

She had to chuckle. "Like you."

He almost blushed. "I'm arrogant enough as it is." He smiled as if he'd heard that she thought he was arrogant.

Lillie felt bad that she'd thought it about him.

The steak house was dimly lit and only half-full. Junior had made a reservation, so they were led right into the back to a quiet, secluded booth. She could tell it was what he'd asked for. She almost felt sorry for him. Where did he think this bet date was going?

He ordered champagne, overruling her argument that he was overdoing it. The waiter poured them both a glass, then left. "Remember, I promised dinner, maybe dancing, and definitely champagne." He raised his glass and waited for her to do the same. She complied, regretting not reneging on this date.

"How many times have I asked you out?" he said when she finally lifted her glass.

Did he really expect her to remember?

"This is something I've wanted to do for a very long time. I know I had to practically trick you to get you here." He waved his free hand through the air, not wanting her to answer that. "But I'm serious about liking you. A lot."

She couldn't think of what to say and was thankful when he touched the rim of his glass to hers and took a drink.

The bubbles made her want to sneeze. She drank half the glass and put it down. Feeling as if she was compelled to say something, she searched for an answer to his words. What came out surprised them both.

"You put a frog down my blouse in sixth grade."

He seemed startled at first but then laughed. "That's what you have to say to my confession? You're not any better at this than I am."

That made her smile because it was true.

"I know you're still in love with Trask," he said and stopped her from arguing the point. "But he's gone. I'm here and I'd like to see you on a real date unless this night goes so far south that you never want to see me again."

All the arrogance she usually saw in him had been dropped. He was just a man doing his best with a woman he liked.

"That seems fair" was all she could think to say. Because Trask wasn't here in the restaurant, but he *was* back. He was teetering on the edge of every breath she took.

WHEN FLINT REACHED the farm, Anvil was sitting on the porch swing, his face in his hands.

He looked up as Flint got out of his patrol SUV and walked toward him. The man's expression made Flint think the worst. Anvil had aged years in the hours that Jenna had been missing.

"What's going on?" Flint asked, dreading what Anvil had supposedly found.

Without a word, the farmer led him into the house, through the kitchen and down a hallway to what was apparently Jenna's sewing room. When Anvil opened the closet, Flint braced himself, not knowing what to expect—evidence or something worse.

Instead, he found himself looking at trinkets, all still wrapped in plastic, still marked with price tags. There must have been a hundred different items crammed in the back of the closet, including unopened perfume, nail polish, tiny ceramic dolls, candle holders and candles. None of the packages appeared to have been opened or used.

Flint looked to Anvil. "What is this?"

The man shook his head.

"Could they be presents she was stocking up?"

"Presents for who?" Anvil demanded.

Flint had no answer. He thought about what the

clerk had told him at the big-box store and had a bad feeling Jenna's life of crime had been going on for some time.

But what, if anything, did that have to do with her disappearance or her confession that there was someone else in her life?

He wondered if the confession had been as bogus as her "shopping."

"I don't know what to tell you, Anvil." He didn't see any reason to share his theory with the man. He figured Anvil had come to his own conclusions, since he hadn't given her money for these things. It was clear that Jenna had a life that her husband had known nothing about.

"Anvil, I put out a missing person's report on Jenna," he said. "It's gone statewide, so if she's out there somewhere…"

Anvil nodded.

It had been a long day. He asked Anvil to hang on to the stolen items for now and drove back to town. Glancing at his watch, Flint realized he had to hurry if he was going to make his dinner date with Maggie. Just the thought of spending the evening with her made him smile.

Tonight, he hoped they would make love. They'd taken it slow for long enough. He was sure Maggie was as ready as he was. It had been four years since his divorce from Celeste. Maggie had a more recent breakup with a man she'd lived with for a while. But he could tell they were both ready now to take the next step. He smiled, realizing something he hadn't felt in a very long time. He was happy.

Maggie sounded as happy as he felt when he called her to tell her he was running a little late and had to stop by his office before he went home to change.

"Take your time. Don't worry, I'll be waiting."

Flint pulled into the parking lot at the sheriff's office building and hurried inside. Once behind his desk, he connected his cell phone to his desktop to retrieve photos he'd taken out by the missile silo. Still smiling, thinking about his call with Maggie, he scanned through the photos.

He stared at the images on the screen. Just as he'd thought. He recognized the prints from a tanker spill some years ago. Whoever had made the huge footprints out by the missile silo had been wearing a hazmat suit.

Flint glanced at his watch, hating how late he was running. Still, he had to make the call before he could leave. Picking up his desk phone, he dialed the local air force commander, a man named Bruce Smith. They weren't exactly friends, but they'd caught a few trout at the local stream together on more than one occasion.

"What can I do for you, Flint?" Bruce asked, no doubt thinking this was a personal call.

"I know there were men out at the missile site on my family's ranch the other night. They were wearing hazmat suits. They left tracks in the dirt."

Silence on the other end of the line.

"If there is a problem out there, I'd like to at least have a heads-up," Flint continued.

"Sheriff, I shouldn't have to tell you how this works."

"That military trumps local law enforcement every time," the sheriff said. Bruce was right. He knew exactly how this worked. It was hands off anything military. "That missile silo on our ranch is the closest one to town. I know there have been problems before out there. If there is a problem and you don't let me know so I can get residents on that side of town evacuated—"

"You know I can't do that. Anything at the sites is classified."

"I'm familiar with other missile sites where civilians have died because the military was trying to keep the problem *classified.*"

Bruce cleared his voice. "Sheriff—"

"I just want you to know. I'm going to be watching that site, and if I see any more hazmat suits, I'm going to start evacuating residents and you can explain to the press what's going on."

He heard a smile in Bruce's voice when he spoke. "See you on the stream, Flint." With a *click*, the commander was gone.

TRASK FELT THE darkness slowly envelop the mountainside. He breathed in the cold sweet scent of the spring evening, surprised how good it felt. He couldn't imagine ever leaving there, but prison still hung over his head.

It was why he had to find out the truth. He was finally ready. He hadn't wanted to stay away so long, but he knew he couldn't come back until he'd made his fortune. It wasn't the money. He'd had to prove himself. Nine years ago, he'd been exactly what Gordon had called him, a saddle tramp with an attitude.

The years of hard work had been a discipline that he'd needed. Before that he hadn't been able to control his temper. Now, though, he thought before he spoke in anger. Now he could walk away from a fight. He'd become the man he wanted to be. A man who was ready to deal with the past—and win back the woman he loved.

Except the woman he loved was now on a date.

He tried not to think about it. After today and what she'd told him, he had more hope that he could find the real killer. He couldn't help being touched that Lillie wanted to help him. That had to be a good sign, no matter what she said about it being strictly friends.

Trask tried to concentrate on how to find Gordon Quinn's killer. He'd had years to think about it. When he'd heard that Gordon had been murdered, he'd told himself that he just needed to get out of town until the real killer was caught. He'd thought it was just a matter of time.

But that hadn't happened. As far as Sheriff Flint Cahill was concerned, Trask was still responsible for Gordon's death and there was no statute of limitation on murder.

Well, now he was back. He needed to track down everyone who hated Gordon enough to kill him. He suspected that list was long. He'd put Caroline, Gordon's wife, at the top of that list, then Gordon's partners in the construction company, where Johnny still worked.

Unfortunately, he couldn't depend on Johnny's help. He was on his own. Except for Lillie.

But now she was on a date.

He threw another log on the campfire to chase away the dark beyond it. At the sound of a twig breaking, he picked up the rifle lying next to his bedroll.

All his instincts told him it wasn't Johnny.

ELY CAHILL LIT the lantern as darkness blanketed his cabin. He hadn't wanted electricity, could get water from the creek behind his house and liked his outhouse just fine. He needed to live simply and couldn't explain why, not even to himself.

The lantern light made the small cabin glow warmly. Earlier, he'd walked the perimeter of his yard making sure he was alone.

Now inside his cabin, Ely pulled the leather-bound notebook from its hiding place along with the pen.

Sitting down, he opened the worn leather to a clean page. He'd started writing down what he knew about the missile silo and the aliens years ago, looking for a pattern. Now putting down what he'd seen wasn't just a form of therapy. He planned to make sure this notebook got into Flint's hands. Once Flint read it, he'd finally see what Ely had known for years.

The military would try to gloss it over like they always did, but with what he had in this notebook, maybe, just maybe, it would save his family.

He set about writing in his small, tight script about what had happened the night he'd come out of the mountains and what he'd seen. Then he sketched what he'd seen and signed and dated it. Toward the end, his hand shook some. He was still scared.

After he finished, he glanced through the notebook, checking the dates of other sightings. A chill raced through him as he saw something he hadn't noticed before. The visits were getting closer together. Not just that. It appeared that while he'd been tracking what was going on at the missile silos, someone had been tracking *him*. The sightings had all been when he came out of the mountains. That couldn't be a coincidence.

They knew when he came out of the mountains. He dropped the notebook, his heart pounding. They must have implanted some kind of tracking device under his skin. For a moment, he almost headed down to the main ranch to tell his sons. Fortunately, he came to his senses first.

Flint thought he was losing his mind. Ely had heard him pushing Lillie on doing something about him. It would be a cold day in hell before he went into some kind of old folks' home.

He had to believe that once Flint saw the accounts in the notebook, it would change his mind about his old man. But by then, Ely feared he would be dead. If they were tracking him, then they must know he was a danger to them.

Putting his notebook back in its hiding place, he told himself that enough people thought he was crazy that he had to keep this to himself as long as possible. He couldn't let the military get hold of the notebook. Or worse, the aliens.

He sat for a long time considering what he now knew. Maybe he could use the tracking device inside him to his benefit. Wherever he went, they would be watching.

He still didn't know who they were—just that they were out there and they must be worried about what he was going to do next.

FLINT AND MAGGIE had just gotten to his house after dinner when his cell rang. As a small-town sheriff, he didn't have the luxury of ignoring the call. He checked to see if it was his office. To his surprise, he saw that the call was from his ex-wife, Celeste. He let it ring again but then worried that something had to be wrong for her to call. He said to Maggie, "I need to take this," and stepped away.

In the next room, he answered it on the fourth ring. "Celeste?"

"I was getting ready to hang up."

He heard fear in her voice. "What's wrong?"

"You're going to think I'm crazy. Wayne is away on business and there's someone outside my house."

"You should have called 9-1-1."

"Isn't that only for emergencies?"

He glanced back into the other room. Maggie was looking through his books pretending not to listen.

"Is the man still out there?"

"Yes. Next to the shed. He seems to just be standing there, watching the house."

"I'll send a deputy over. Stay inside and keep your doors locked."

"Do you have to send a deputy? I thought since you are only a few blocks away…"

He cursed under his breath.

"I'm sorry. You're probably busy. Maggie is probably there. I shouldn't have called you."

Flint told himself he wouldn't be able to relax and enjoy his night until he knew Celeste was all right. Like she said, she was only a few blocks away.

"I'll be right over." He disconnected and looked back at Maggie.

"Celeste."

He nodded as he walked back into the living room. "She says there's someone outside her house."

"I heard. You should go. Maybe you could drop me off on the way."

He stepped to her, taking her shoulders in his hands. "This is not the way I wanted this night to end."

"Me neither. But you're the sheriff and Celeste is…Celeste."

"Wait here or come with me. This shouldn't take but a minute—"

"It's late and I have a color appointment first thing in the morning."

He kissed her. "Let me make it up to you tomorrow night."

She smiled, but he could tell she was upset. "We'll see."

He dropped Maggie off with a quick kiss and drove over to Celeste's. She lived in a huge, old three-story house on the outskirts of town that took up two city blocks. As he parked and got out, he saw that all the lights in the entire house seemed to be on.

Maybe she really was frightened. Or maybe she had just wanted to interrupt his date. He hated that uncharitable thought. Since their divorce, he'd done his best to put all the hurt and anger behind him. Celeste could be manipulative, but she wouldn't do something like that.

Still, like today on the street, he swore it was as if she couldn't stand him moving on, which made him wonder where her head was—let alone her heart. She'd been the one who wanted out of their marriage. He hadn't known it at the time, but she'd been seeing Wayne Duma behind his back. He'd been so oblivious that he hadn't even suspected there was another man.

In his more uncharitable moments, he damned

well knew what she saw in Wayne: money, security, a husband with an upstanding role in the community. He thought of that old Elvis song about a house without love. Was that the problem? Was she sorry now?

He unsnapped his holster even though he doubted he was going to have to use his gun. But that was the thing about being the law. You never knew when you were going to need your weapon. Better to be prepared than caught off guard.

Unfortunately, he was already angry at himself for giving in to Celeste and coming over here. A man in that state of mind could make a mistake and get himself killed.

TRASK TENSED AS another twig snapped, closer by. He stared at the crest of the hill, waiting for whatever it was to show itself. As something dark emerged, he lifted his rifle.

"Don't shoot!" came a once familiar male voice. "I come in peace."

Trask swore under his breath. His former not-legally stepbrother, Emery Perkins, was the last person he'd expected to see on this mountain. His mind raced. How could Emery have known he was back in Montana, let alone that he'd be hiding out up there?

Because, he realized with a curse, he and Emery had camped up there one time years before. But that still didn't explain how his stepbrother knew he was back. Maybe Lillie had changed more than Trask thought.

"No need for that," Emery said as he stopped a few yards away. His dark, close-set eyes looked from Trask to the rifle and back again. "Would you shoot your own brother?"

"You're not my brother."

"Stepbrother by almost marriage," he said with a laugh.

"*Almost* only means something in horseshoes and shit throwing."

"Just cuz my old lady and your old man didn't officially tie the knot. We're still brothers. Hell, we were a family for a while."

"A very short while." At first he'd been glad to have a brother. Until he got to know Emery.

"By the wayside, heard from our mom lately?" He laughed at his joke, exposing a few black spaces where teeth should have been. After Trask's so-called stepmother had left with Emery, he'd never heard from her again.

"How did you find me?" Trask asked.

"Well, that's a funny story." He took a toothpick out of his shirt pocket and stuck it into the corner of his mouth. "Ya put down that rifle and I'll share it with ya."

Trask hesitated, but only for a moment before he set the rifle aside, keeping it close enough that he could go for it if he had to.

Emery moved closer to the fire. "Remember Vernon?"

"Vaguely." Vernon had been some kid Emery's mother said was a cousin. But they all suspected the teen had been her lover. Vernon only showed up when Trask's father was on the road with the carnival.

"Well, he seen ya over in North Dakota and he happened to mention it."

"So you came looking for me." Trask felt a wave of relief. It hadn't been Lillie. He also understood why his so-called stepbrother hadn't gone to the sheriff with the information.

Emery's face lit up like he'd just won the lottery. He probably thought he had. "When they said you'd quit yer job for that oil company in North Dakota after nine years, I just had this sneakin' suspicion that you'd come back here. I always wondered how ya could leave behind a babe like Lillie Cahill."

He winced at the word *babe* but let it go. He figured Emery had just begun to piss him off. He might as well wait until he was good and mad. "So you found me."

"Yep, remember ya and me come up here one time when we was boys. It was your special place. Nice view. Should be able to see anyone headin' up the mountain." His grin widened, exposing more dark holes. "'Course, I knew that, so I come over from the ravine to the east."

He could see how proud Emery was of surprising him. Trask fought the urge to push Emery for the point of his visit, not that he didn't already suspect what was coming.

"Kind of a long walk up the mountain to talk old times," Trask said after a few moments of watching Emery chew on his toothpick.

"Sure was. Made me downright thirsty. Ya wouldn't have any beer, would ya?"

"Afraid not. There's water in the creek, though."

Emery glanced back in that direction and for a moment Trask feared the man hadn't come alone. That would definitely complicate things and make Trask a whole lot less congenial.

"Here's the thing," Emery said, finally getting to it. "I didn't go to the sheriff after Vernon told me about seein' ya. I know about the ten-thousand-dollar reward for your capture—"

"Actually, Caroline Quinn is offering ten thousand dollars for the arrest and conviction of the killer or killers of her husband, Gordon. It's not a reward for me."

Emery smiled at that. "Now yer just messin' with me. Everyone knows ya killed that man, and with good reason, from what I heard. Heard he almost beat a horse to death with a club."

"It was a piece of wood, not a club. I did pull him off the horse, I did threaten to kill him if I ever saw him treat a horse like that again, and when he said he'd do whatever he wanted with his animals, I hit him. But I didn't kill him."

His stepbrother eyed him with a tilt of his head.

"Reckon it's yer word agin the sheriff's, but we're gettin' off topic here. We're kin. I couldn't turn ya in to the law for no reward."

Only because it would take patience to wait through a trial to get his money, Trask thought. And that was if Trask was actually convicted.

"But I think I deserve somethin', don't ya?"

"What for?" Trask asked, playing along when he really wanted to knock Emery into the next county for this blackmail attempt.

"For *not* goin' to the sheriff. For lettin' ya know that Vernon seen ya. For my trouble." He grinned. "It was a long hike up here. That has to be worth somethin'."

"You're right," Trask said, taking a step toward Emery. "Sneaking up here to blackmail me deserves something, all right."

Emery took a step back. He was as tall as Trask but skinny. Not that he wasn't mean as a rattlesnake and wiry strong even as a kid. Also, Trask knew from experience that Emery never fought fair.

"Now hold on here," the man said, raising his hands and taking another step back. "We're just negotiatin' right now."

"No, we're not. I won't be blackmailed. Go to the sheriff, but you won't be collecting any reward, since I didn't do it, and even if I couldn't prove it, my conviction would take years. You'd be old and gray before you got that money, and then the IRS would take half of it."

"Now that's just sad." His eyes shifted again to the ravine he'd come up through.

Trask swore under his breath as he pulled the pistol from the back of his jeans and pointed it at Emery's head. "Who'd you drag up here with you?" he demanded.

"What? That's crazy talk. I come alone."

"I don't think so. Call them out, right now." He leveled the gun at the spot between Emery's eyes. "I could shoot you, bury you up here, and no one would be the wiser. Just give me another reason."

For the first time, Emery looked worried. "I always thought ya had killin' in ya. But I swear I come alone."

"Call the person out. *Now!*"

"Vernon! Ya might as well come on out."

There was the sound of rock cascading down into the gully and several grunts and groans before Vernon's head popped up over the rise followed by a large, heaving body.

Vernon had always been big as a teenager. He'd gone to seed since then. He hoisted his bulk over the crest of the ravine and stumbled toward them. He was breathing hard by the time he reached the campfire.

"Hey. Trask. Don't. Want. No. Trouble." He bent over as he tried to catch his breath.

He realized the man must have still been climbing up the mountain all the time they'd been "negotiatin'." Vernon was lucky he hadn't had a heart attack, since he was obviously in poor shape.

Trask stared at them, realizing his troubles had just doubled. "Now, let me make something clear to the two of you. I won't be blackmailed. I'm not giving you money. So, Vernon, I want you to catch your breath, then relieve Emery of his weapons. You'll find a gun on him, I'm pretty sure. And definitely a switchblade if I know him as well as I used to. Otherwise, I can just shoot the two of you now and do myself a favor."

"He's bluffin'," Emery said, but Vernon apparently wasn't so sure, since Trask was holding a gun on them. Emery probably wasn't, either, because he let his friend take his gun and knife.

"Toss them both into the fire," Trask ordered. "Good job. Now, what do you have on *you*?"

"Nothin'. You can search me if you don't believe me."

"I just might do that. But right now I want you to sit down on the ground. Both of you sit down."

"Come on, Trask. We can talk this out," Emery said but sat down in the dirt.

"Now take off your boots. Both of you."

"You can't leave us up here without our boots," Emery said, looking scared. "Them rocks and sticks'll tear our feet up bad."

"Your boots, Emery. I'll leave your boots on the trail partway down the mountain. But if I have to ask you to take them off again, I won't be leaving yours at all."

Vernon had already gotten his off. He sat poking his fingers into the holes in his socks and staring at the ground, looking scared, as if he thought Trask was still going to shoot him.

Emery took off his boots in angry jerking motions and tossed them at Trask's feet. "You're going to pay for this."

He picked up Vernon's boots with his free hand. "Now, here's what's going to happen. I'm going to toss a few things into my pack and leave the two of you here. Your boots will be on the trail down the mountain. It's dark, so I suggest you stay here for the night by the fire and go down in the morning in daylight. You don't know the way down as well as I do—and I have a flashlight."

Emery looked furious. Vernon was still playing with his socks. This hadn't been his idea. He'd merely let Emery bully him into it.

"When you get down the mountain, I'm sure you'll go to the sheriff. Give him my regards. It was just a matter of time before he found out I was back in town anyway." He was bluffing and he figured at least Emery knew it. But it was also true. "If I ever see the two of you again, I'm not going to be so nice."

He set down the gun long enough to tie their bootlaces together, all the time almost daring Emery to try something. He wanted badly to punch him and had to remind himself that he'd changed. Unfortunately, Emery hadn't.

Hooking the bootlaces over his shoulder, he

slipped the pistol into a pocket of his pack, picked up his pack and his rifle.

"I'm going to find you again, only next time you'll be the one in the dirt," Emery blustered.

"There are a lot of places to hide in these mountains. I wouldn't count on finding me, but you're sure welcome to try."

Emery looked as if he could chew nails. "My mother never liked you," he said, spitting out the chewed-up toothpick.

Trask laughed. "If you're trying to hurt me—"

"Oh, I'm going to do more than hurt you the next time we meet," Emery threatened.

"I'd think twice about that, *bro*. We've already had this reunion. I don't care to have another one. Stay out of my way or do it at your own risk."

With that, he started down the mountain. Pretty much as he'd anticipated, Emery jumped right up, grabbed a rock and hurled it at him. The rock clipped his shoulder just enough to register mild pain, but mostly irritation.

He kept walking. He wouldn't be leaving Emery's boots on the trail partway down the mountain.

CHAPTER ELEVEN

JUNIOR WAINWRIGHT KEPT the conversation light, talking about growing up in this valley surrounded by mountains ranges. Summers were spent floating on the spring creek, going up to Crystal Lake camping, riding horses, building forts out of hay bales and catching frogs in the small creeks.

"You were such a tomboy," he said not unkindly.

"What makes you think I've changed?"

"You haven't and that's one of the things I like about you. I hated, though, that you could always outrun me when we were growing up. That's why I'm surprised I got that frog down your shirt. I thought maybe you let me because you liked me."

"I love the way boys—and men—think," she said with a laugh and realized she was enjoying herself.

She'd dated some since Trask left only to prove to everyone that she wasn't going to die of a broken heart. The dates had been disastrous and had lasted all of one evening.

They ordered and ate in a companionable silence. She was seeing another side of Junior, a side she'd

not let herself see—because she'd given her heart to
Trask and he'd run off with it.

"Dessert?" he asked hopefully after they'd finished their meals.

"Why not?" Thinking about Trask and the past
had almost dragged her back into her bad mood. The
steak house's famous chokecherry cheesecake would
take care of that. The area held a chokecherry festival each year to celebrate the abundance of the berries. Fat juicy dark berries were stripped from bushes
and the tart juice extracted to make jelly and syrup.
It was an acquired taste. Most Montanans preferred
the sweeter huckleberry.

The cheesecake was delicious. Junior entertained
her with stories about his college days at the University of Montana, where he'd gone on a football
scholarship. She'd attended Montana State University in Bozeman, a rival university.

"Wasn't there someone special you met in college?" she asked, curious. "After all, you were the
star quarterback. You must have had women falling
all over you like rain."

He laughed. "I had to get good grades and play
well, so I didn't date much. I met plenty of girls."
He shrugged. "If you must know, I found myself
comparing them to you and they usually fell short."

She shook her head, flattered, embarrassed and
a little uncomfortable.

"It's true."

A silence fell between them.

"Sorry, I should have kept that to myself. Now you think I've been mooning over you since the frog incident."

She licked the last bite of cheesecake from her fork. "Using me as your standard should have set the bar low enough that you could have found someone by now."

"I like the original," he said, grinning at her. It wasn't a bad grin, but it was no Trask high beam.

"Did you say dancing?" she said to chase away any more of those thoughts.

They went to a bar at the edge of town that had a good country band and danced a half-dozen country swing songs before a slow one came on.

"Let's sit this one out," she said. "I could use a drink."

He nodded, but she could tell he was disappointed. She was too. She'd been having fun, but the idea of dancing to a slow song with anyone but Trask...

"Trask may be gone, but he's not forgotten, is he?" Junior said gently. "Even if he's a murderer?"

She met his gaze. "He didn't kill Gordon Quinn."

"How do you know that?"

"I know."

He nodded. "Then who did?"

She'd thought about nothing else for nine years. "One of his business partners."

Junior seemed to consider this. "Why?"

"Money, probably." She saw a change in his expression. "What?"

"Just something I heard back then." He tried to wave it off.

"Tell me."

She could tell he was sorry he'd brought up Trask. "That Gordon was leaving the partnership and going out on his own."

"I heard that too. How would that have affected the company?"

"Nine years ago during the recession?" Junior said. "Since Gordon had the controlling interest in the company, I would imagine it would have bankrupted Skip and J.T."

Lillie sat back and tried to catch her breath. No wonder they had gotten so upset earlier. "Good motives for murder, wouldn't you say?"

Junior sighed. "This is not what I thought we would be talking about on our first date."

"I'm sorry." This wasn't fair to Junior. But with Trask back in town… "No more talk of murder." But she couldn't help thinking about what he'd told her. If true…

The bar was dark and smelled of stale beer, much like most bars at this time of the night. There were only a few people on the dance floor, moving slowly to the song. Junior came back with the beers and sat down next to her in the booth, where he could see the dancing couples. She moved over to let him in and felt his thigh brush against hers.

Desire raced along her nerve endings. But not for

Junior. She took a swig of the beer to steady herself. She'd had only the one glass of champagne earlier. The date had been going well enough that she felt she needed to keep a clear head. Would she have felt that way if she hadn't known that Trask was back in town?

Would she be feeling this wave of desire right now for Junior if she didn't know Trask was out there somewhere right now? Or maybe even closer, she thought with a start as she saw a cowboy at the back corner of the bar deep in the shadows.

She swore under her breath and took another drink of her beer. When she looked up, the cowboy was gone, making her wonder if it really had been Trask. How could he have known she was here unless... Unless he'd followed the two of them from the restaurant?

Lillie couldn't believe he would be so reckless. What if someone had recognized him?

"Are you all right?" Junior asked when she reached for her beer bottle and overturned it. Beer went everywhere. He jumped up to grab a rag from the bar to clean it up.

The cowboy she'd seen returned. Not Trask. The man didn't even resemble him. What had she been thinking?

"I'm sorry. I think I've had enough for tonight," she said when Junior came back to the table and cleaned up the spilled beer. His gaze met hers and she nodded. "I need to go home."

THE SHERIFF MOVED toward the shed behind the Duma house and the dark shadows next to it. The moon peeked out from behind the clouds. If there was someone standing there watching the house and saw him approach, they would run and he could be able to see them.

He was almost to the shed when he caught the flash of light. He pulled his gun only to realize it was the moonlight glinting off a ladder propped against the shed. With a curse, he holstered his gun and headed for the house.

Celeste met him at the back door. "Did you see him?"

"It was a ladder leaning against the side of the shed."

"Oh, I told you I was just being silly. I feel like such a fool."

No, he was the one who felt like a fool as he saw what his ex was wearing.

"Come in. The least I can do is offer you a drink, since I ruined your night."

"It's not ruined and no, I don't need a drink." He started to turn away.

"Please don't be angry with me. I got scared and all I could think about was calling you."

He turned back to her. "Maybe Wayne should

think about getting you a security system, Celeste. The next time you get scared, call 9-1-1."

"You *are* angry."

"I don't have time for this."

"Of course, Maggie is probably waiting for you."

"What is going on with you, Celeste?" he demanded, definitely angry.

She made that pouty little-girl look that he'd once thought was precious. "I don't know what you mean."

"Today on the street you were practically in tears."

"I told you, it's my allergies."

"You never used to have allergies."

"You never used to talk to me like this."

"Whatever is going on with you, don't make it my problem. You understand? Good night." He turned and walked away, but he could sense her still standing in the doorway.

The familiar scent of her perfume seemed to chase after him. He'd recognized the negligee she was wearing. It was an expensive one he'd bought her for their first anniversary. He didn't think it was a coincidence she just happened to be wearing it tonight. Nor that Celeste had known he'd had a date with Maggie tonight and looked out and seen something that scared her.

As he left, he drove past Maggie's. Her porch light was out. Only one light burned deep within the house behind drawn curtains.

He didn't stop but drove on home, wishing with

all his heart that Celeste was out of his system. How could he move on with Maggie until she was?

"DID I DO something wrong?" Junior Wainwright asked Lillie on the drive out of town.

"No, in fact that was the nicest night I've had in a long time." It was true. Tonight could have gone so differently if it wasn't for Trask's return. She'd enjoyed herself. She actually liked Junior, could have seen it going somewhere—if not for Trask. But he was back and until he was gone again... "I'm not ready for this."

"After nine years, you're still not ready?"

Her throat closed and she fought tears. Damn Trask. If he hadn't come back... If she'd gone on this date believing he was out of her life. If she hadn't given him her heart and not gotten it back.

"Is it me? Or is this about Trask?"

"It's not you." It would always be Trask turning her life upside down if she let him. Junior pulled into the back of the bar near the entrance to her apartment upstairs.

It was quiet back there. Whatever had the bar hopping earlier had slowed down. There were only a few pickups out front. She couldn't hear the boom of music. When she'd bought the place, she'd made sure the floor separating her house and the bar were super insulated so the bar downstairs didn't bother her on the nights she wasn't working.

Junior shut off the car and looked over at her. She

listened to the tick of the engine as it cooled. "I'd ask you if we could do this some other time—"

Impulsively, she leaned over and kissed him.

He was as startled as she was by the kiss. It was a short, sweet impulsive kiss.

"Thank you for a lovely evening," she said and, opening her door, climbed out before she heard his door open. He was out of the car when she came around.

"At least let me see you to your door," he said.

She thought of Trask. If he was out there in the dark watching, she hoped he wasn't fool enough to do something more stupid than he already had by coming back here. "That's not necessary, but I appreciate the thought. I really did have a nice time."

Lillie went straight to her door, opened it and slipped inside. She was breathing hard as she locked it and, leaning against the door, realized that she was crying. Damn Trask.

With relief, she heard Junior drive off. She'd been afraid Trask might go after him. It would be a foolish thing to do, but probably no more foolish than threatening to kill your boss in front of witnesses and then skipping town when someone did kill the man. He'd already proved to this town that he was a hothead.

She remembered how angry her brother Flint had been. "Your boyfriend is looking at more than assault. He's looking at murder. How can you be in love with a man like that?"

Lillie still didn't know the answer to that one.

Love knew no reason. But right now, as she went upstairs, she found herself waiting for Trask to show up and hating herself for loving him.

It was much later that she heard the footfalls on the stairs and braced herself.

To her surprise, it wasn't Trask. Darby knocked at her door. Trask would have come right in.

"How was your date?" he asked and noticed that she'd been crying. "If Wainwright tried something with you—"

She reminded him that this wasn't high school. "Anyway, he was a perfect gentleman. I actually had a good time most of the date."

"So what are the tears about?"

She looked at him with what she knew was her hangdog face until he swore and said "Trask" under his breath like a curse of its own. "Are you ever going to get over him?"

"I don't know. I thought with time…"

"Nine years weren't enough?" he demanded.

"Apparently not. You don't have to tell me how stupid I am."

He softened his words as he came over and sat down next to her. "You're not stupid."

"Pathetic?"

"Yeah, definitely that." He put an arm around her.

She leaned into her twin, leaving fresh tears on his shirt. "I don't know what I would do without you."

"You're never going to have to find out."

"I hope not."

"See you tomorrow," he said as he got up and headed for the door. "Get some sleep. Things always look better in the morning."

"You sound like Mom," she said to his retreating back as he closed the door and was gone.

She couldn't help but wonder if his life was as complicated as her own. As close as she was with her brother, she didn't know that much about his life away from their bar.

For hours after she'd gone to bed, she lay there listening for the sound of Trask's boot heels coming up her stairs. She thought she caught a whiff of his male scent mixed with the night air. She thought she felt the whisper of his touch. She thought she felt his breath against her cheek.

She finally fell into an exhausted restless sleep in which she was searching for something in her dreams, something that left a horrible ache inside her.

Lillie was awakened at first by what she thought was a dream. She shot up, wild-eyed in the middle of her bed, feeling like a dangerous animal hunkered in the room with her.

CHAPTER TWELVE

LILLIE TRIED TO talk herself out of it. Only a crazy woman would do what she was about to do because of some…intuition. The realization had come to her in that gray area between deep sleep and wide-awake. As she'd sat up blinking, she couldn't throw off the feeling that had awakened her.

Before she'd fallen asleep, she'd been thinking about Trask, wondering what he was doing tonight. No wonder it had come to her. When she'd awakened, she'd known what Trask would be doing tonight—and what she needed to do.

She quickly changed her clothing and, taking her keys, binoculars and flashlight, headed for her pickup. She'd seen how worried he was about Johnny. He'd said he thought something was going on at the construction company—the one Gordon Quinn had been involved in.

It all made a strange kind of sense when she thought about it. If Trask hoped to clear his name, he had to find out what was going on with Gordon nine years ago. Trask would have waited until tonight—Friday night when he was sure everyone was gone from the construction lot for the weekend.

She shivered. She had tried to convince herself that she didn't know this Trask who'd come back. But she *knew* him. She knew how he thought. Which meant when she'd thought about it, she knew exactly where he would go tonight.

The office of Pyramid Peak Construction was located outside of Gilt Edge at the bottom of a hill. The complex took up several acres. Large construction equipment stood silent in rows to one side of the property. Near a creek on the other side was a small nondescript rectangle building that served as the office just as it had before Gordon's death. Inside the office was where Johnny had found the bracelet belonging to Gordon's wife after Caroline's tryst with his partner Skip Fairchild.

The single large outdoor light inside the construction company's property illuminated the tall chain-link metal gate barring the entrance. She could see that the gate was padlocked as she assumed it would be on weekends when no one was around.

Trask wouldn't have any problem picking the lock, but he would be seen by anyone driving past. Not that the road out there got much traffic. But there were two ways into the construction site and he would know that. So she assumed he would come in through the back way that ran from the mountains along the creek.

She parked on the side of the hill where she had

a good view of the office. Her truck was partially hidden by the pines as she killed her engine to wait. Darkness settled in around her. Her eyes ached after a few minutes of watching the office through the binoculars.

The night was chilly. It didn't take long for the pickup cab to grow cold. She should have grabbed a coat, but she'd been in too much of a hurry. Had she lost her mind coming out here in the middle of the night? She told herself she would be in her warm bed asleep right now if it wasn't for Trask.

But she couldn't leave yet. The feeling when she'd awakened so abruptly had been too strong. Trask would show up. As time passed, all she could think about was Trask's handsome face grinning down at her and how empty her bed was going to feel if and when she ever got back to it. She hated the old feelings he evoked in her.

She'd never thought of herself as a fool. But only a fool would be out there in the middle of the night because of intuition and some crazy idea about a psychic connection between them. Where was that connection over the past nine years? She wanted to know.

It made her angry with herself. Even angrier with Trask that worrying about him had her freezing, sitting in her pickup and waiting for him. He'd left a cannon-ball-sized hole in her heart. And now he thought he could just walk back into her life with a grin and another worthless promise? Maybe her brother was right about him.

So where was he staying when he wasn't breaking into her house? Up in the mountains, camped out, probably.

She couldn't bear the thought of the only man she'd loved being out in the cold when she was snug in her bed. The thought made her shake her head angrily. She wasn't warm and snug in her bed. She was sitting in a cold pickup staring down at an empty construction company office.

Still, she had to wait just a little longer. Trask was a wanted man on the run. She knew Flint wouldn't hurt him if he caught him. But what would one of her brother's trigger-happy deputies do if they stumbled across him? A deputy like Harper. The thought sent a shudder through her. Harp would definitely use force to bring Trask in.

Nothing moved below her. She sighed. She'd been so sure this was where Trask was headed.

Cold and cussing herself, she was reaching for the ignition key to leave when she saw something move on the hillside below her.

A dark figure came out from behind one of the large heavy equipment rigs and moved toward the office building. In an almost primal way, she recognized the way the man moved and felt again those old emotions that made her heart ache.

Trask.

She'd been right, but it gave her little satisfaction.

Now that she was there, she realized she had no idea what she planned to do. This kind of behavior wasn't like her. She always thought things out. Except for that one time when she'd agreed to run away with Trask, an alleged felon on the run.

This was ridiculous. Did she really think she could protect him somehow? She saw that Trask had disappeared into the office, having no doubt picked the lock.

She should go home, go back to bed… As if she would get a minute's sleep knowing where he was and what he was doing. Still…

A set of headlights topped the rise on the back road into the construction site and then went out. She watched with growing terror as a vehicle with its headlights off pulled into the back of the construction lot. A friend of Trask's? Not likely.

He'd told her that Johnny wanted nothing to do with any of this. She doubted Trask had trusted anyone else with the news that he was back in town.

Through the binoculars, she saw a man exit his vehicle. Something about the way he moved seemed familiar. The man headed toward the office. He was almost there when he pulled an object from his coat pocket. It glinted in the starlight for a moment before the man dissolved into the shadows.

The man had a gun.

OPENING THE OFFICE door was a piece of cake. Trask slipped inside and took a moment to lock the door and close the blinds before he pulled out a small flashlight and looked around.

When Gordon was alive, there'd been two small offices. Skip Fairchild had the larger one to the back, no doubt where Johnny had found Caroline's bracelet. The outer area had been a general office for the other partners, since neither J.T. Burrows nor Gordon Quinn spent much time there. Skip had seen to the day-to-day running of the place.

It hadn't changed since Trask had come by there years ago to see Johnny. Even the old file cabinets looked the same. Trask quickly went through the desk drawers but found nothing of interest in either desk. He feared he was looking for a needle in a haystack. He had no idea what might be going on there, just a feeling he couldn't shake that Johnny was in trouble and that it might have something to do with Gordon's murder nine years ago.

Trask moved to the filing cabinet. Nothing of interest in the first four. He reached for the bottom one. Locked.

His interest peaked. He hadn't found any keys in the desk drawer. Nor was there a small file drawer key on the board on the wall where keys were kept for the construction rigs parked outside.

Why would there be a locked drawer? Fairchild wasn't stupid enough to leave money at the office. But what about paperwork he didn't want anyone to see? Or was it possible that the old file drawer had been locked since Gordon was part of the company and no one had cared what was in it?

Trask quickly picked the simple lock and pulled open the drawer. To his surprise, there were only three thin file folders.

He took them over to the desk and sat down. Shining the flashlight on the folders, he saw that the first was marked Project A. He opened the folder. On top was a letter from the bank. The date jumped out at him. March 3 nine years ago. He quickly scanned the letter. The president of the bank, Robert Wainwright, had approved a business loan request for Gordon Quinn. Not the construction company, but Gordon alone.

Trask opened the second file folder, noticing that it was marked Project B. Inside was another letter approving the loan. He started to open the third folder when he heard a sound outside. He quickly scooped up the folders, stepped to the filing cabinet and quietly closed and locked it like he'd found it—sans the file folders—before extinguishing his flashlight. Heavy footfalls sounded on the steps outside. The door handle jiggled.

Glancing around the office, he realized he was trapped. There was only a small window at the back, certainly too small for him to escape through. Nor was there anywhere to hide except for the bathroom, since there was no back door in such a small office. Climbing under one of the desks was also not an option.

He stepped toward the bathroom. It had only a sink and a toilet and an even smaller window. He would instantly be discovered in there.

The door handle jiggled with more force. Trask noticed a small narrow door in the corner of the bathroom. Opening it, he found the hot water heater, some old mops and brooms, and a sliver of a space that he might be able to wedge himself into.

At the sound of breaking glass, he knew he had no choice. He had barely squeezed himself into the broom closet and closed the door as much as he could when he heard the front door bang open.

Heavy footfalls thudded across the floor. Trask held his breath as he heard desk drawers being ransacked, then metal file drawers. It sounded as if the contents were being dumped on the floor.

Clearly, the man was looking for something in particular. The file folders he was holding? Trask heard him try the bottom file drawer. A loud curse came from the office. The walls were so thin that Trask thought he could smell the burglar's sweat.

The man began to beat the file cabinet, apparently unable to get the drawer open. Silence fell over the office and for a moment Trask thought that maybe the burglar had left. Or worse, that he was coming into the bathroom. Maybe looking for something to pry the drawer open with in the broom closet?

He tensed, prepared to take the man by surprise.

But then he heard grunting and groaning as the man must have found something in the desk to use.

There was a loud pop, a curse, and then the mangled file cabinet door was jerked open. Another loud curse filled the office followed by what sounded like a metal file drawer being kicked.

Trask hugged the three folders to his chest, his adrenaline racing as he heard more swearing before the man began to destroy the office. Would he be content with just the office area? Or would he feel the need to wreck the whole place, bathroom included?

The noise stopped so abruptly that Trask held his breath, all his senses zeroed in on the next room.

Heavy footsteps started toward the front door but stopped to kick something out of the way. Then the footfalls turned and headed toward the bathroom.

Trask readied himself as much as he could for what he feared was coming. The floor groaned under the man's weight. A moment later the bathroom light flipped on.

Through the crack between the broom closet door and the wall, Trask blinked at the sudden light. The man's face came into view as he stepped toward the broom closet door. Shock ricocheted through him as he recognized him.

As the man reached for the broom closet door handle, the sound of a car horn filled the air outside, almost blocking out the roar of an engine clearly headed in their direction. Trask heard a loud crash, metal meeting metal. It took him a moment to realize that someone had just crashed through the front gate.

The burglar turned quickly and hurried out, the

front steps into the office groaning under the man's running weight. Trask realized he was still holding his breath as the night fell silent again. What the hell, he thought as he eased open the broom closet door and looked out.

The front door of the office stood open. Past it, a familiar pickup sat running, the front dented from where the driver had just rammed through the closed metal gate of the complex. If he hadn't already been crazy in love with Lillie, he would have fallen for her right then and there.

CHAPTER THIRTEEN

LILLIE GRIPPED THE steering wheel of her pickup as the passenger-side door swung open.

"I have never been so glad to see you," Trask said as he climbed in.

"Have you lost your mind?" she cried, still too shaken to even look at him. As she had crashed through the gate, barreling toward the construction company office, the man with the gun had come running out to disappear behind the construction equipment.

She'd thrown on her brakes, coming to a dust-boiling stop in front of the office, petrified that she was too late. She'd heard the man's vehicle motor, the sound growing fainter as he left, while she sat praying that Trask was alive and would come out that office door.

For too many breathless moments, no one else had emerged from the office. She'd imagined the worst. Trask dead, lying in a pool of his warm blood, shot to death. The thought of him dead…

"I can see that you're upset," Trask said.

"Upset?" She swung to look at him, glaring,

angrier with him than she'd been years ago as she fought tears of relief.

"I get it. I scared you. Drive me up to my truck and I'll follow you to your place. The construction company security firm checks in soon, so we have to get moving."

How did he know that? He'd been staking out the place. He'd been taking all kinds of chances before tonight.

Remembering how terrified she'd been, she wanted to yell at him, to pummel him, to…to beg him to hold her. She fought the conflicting emotions as she shifted the pickup into gear with hands that shook.

"Good thing you have a guard bumper on this thing," he said with a grin and a shake of his head. "I can't tell you how surprised I was to see you. Or how glad." His grin broadened. "You *do* care."

She swallowed the lump in her throat and fought tears of relief and fury. Trask was fine. He wasn't lying inside the office shot to death. Her heart rate could drop back to normal anytime now. But she still wanted to punch him.

"My truck's right up here," he said, pointing to a dark spot in the back behind the equipment.

"You could have been killed. That man had a gun. I thought if I didn't do something…" Her voice broke. A big, fat, hot, salty tear rolled down her cheek. She tasted it on her lips.

"You did great, Lillie." He touched her arm. She jerked it away. "I'm sorry I scared you. The last thing

I expected was someone else to break in tonight. This will do right here." He started to open his door to get out but then turned in his seat. "Just follow this road out. I'll make sure you get back to your place without any trouble. If you want to talk then…" He motioned to what he was carrying. She hadn't even noticed until then that he had file folders tucked under his arm.

She was so angry with him. She wanted to tell him that she never wanted to lay eyes on him again. But she couldn't get the lie past her lips. All she could do was grip the wheel and stare straight ahead as she waited for him to get out of her truck.

"It's going to be all right, Lillie. I swear to you." She really had her doubts, but she said nothing as he climbed out. "Drive straight home. I'll be right behind you." And he was gone, disappearing into the darkness.

She followed the road away from Pyramid Peak Construction Company's yard. One of her headlights was out, but other than that, her pickup ran fine. Glancing in her rearview mirror, she spotted headlights behind her. Trask. She gripped the steering wheel. She'd lost him nine years ago, not knowing if he was alive or dead. Tonight she'd almost lost him for good.

Another large hot tear broke free and rolled down her cheek, followed by another and another as the road ahead blurred.

HER BROTHER WAS waiting for her when Lillie came down from her apartment the next morning. "What happened to the front of your pickup?" he demanded. "Are you all right?"

With everything that had gone on yesterday, her pickup had been the last thing on her mind. "I hit something," she said.

"I can tell *that*. What?"

Lillie looked at her twin. If she told him about crashing through the gate at the construction office last night, she'd have to tell him about Trask. Neither would go over big with her brother and right now she didn't have time for the lecture. Not to mention him demanding Trask turn himself in to Flint before they both got killed.

She didn't want to lie, but all of this had gotten even more complicated. It was bad enough she had to keep a wanted felon secret, she couldn't put that on her brother. Last night, as terrifying as it had been, had proved they were onto something. They were close to finding the killer. She could feel it.

If they stopped now… "You know how bad the deer have been on the road out here," she said, evading an outright lie.

Darby frowned. "So you hit a deer. But when I left you last night, I thought you were headed for bed. You went back out?"

"I couldn't sleep and went for a drive." This too was true.

He nodded. "It happens. Don't worry, I can get my buddy down at the body shop to fix it for you.

Lillie felt a stab of guilt. Darby was so sweet and

trusting. "Thank you." She felt close to tears. She felt as if she hadn't gotten any sleep last night. Trask had followed her back to the stagecoach stop, but she'd refused to let him in.

"I can't do this right now," she'd said. It had been so easy to tell herself she could keep her heart safe from Trask while helping clear his name. But last night had proved what a lie it was. She loved him. The thought of living without him...

"Lillie—" Trask had tried to hold her. She'd stepped away, knowing that if he touched her she would be lost. Once in his arms, she didn't think she would be strong enough to ever step away again. She couldn't let herself go back to that place of despair where Trask had left her nine years ago.

And she had to face it. Trask was teetering on a tight wire. Arrest and prison? Proving his innocence and staying here? Or leaving again? She didn't like the odds for any outcome that involved the two of them finding their way back to each other.

"I can't do *this*." She had motioned in the space between them.

"You're exhausted," Trask had said. "Get some sleep. We can talk tomorrow." He'd thrust something into her hand. "I got this for you."

She'd looked down at the cheap cell phone in her hand.

"It has only one number on it. Mine," Trask had been saying. "Call me and we can talk."

As he stepped away, she remembered the files and

the man with the gun. But she'd been too exhausted and emotionally wrung out to ask about either.

The realization of how much she loved him had left her too shaken. She'd never stopped needing him. Would always yearn for him. She'd stood cupping the cell phone in her hand as he'd disappeared into the trees behind her house. She'd heard him leave but hadn't move.

The nine years had seemed like an eternity impossible to cross. Then last night... It had shaken her to her core.

This morning she hadn't felt any better. When he'd first come back, she'd told herself that it was over, that she didn't know this man, that she couldn't trust him, that after all those years there was no going back. She'd been hurt too badly.

After last night she could no longer lie to herself. She'd waited all these years, knowing in her heart that he would return. And now he had. She couldn't go on pretending that he wasn't the only man she'd ever loved—would ever love with this kind of intensity. It scared her so badly that her stomach roiled.

The past was still a painful reminder of how badly Trask had hurt her, how badly he could hurt her again. Last night as she stood outside in the cold after Trask had left, she'd kept reliving the day Flint had come to her with the news. She'd been shocked. Trask had told her he'd gotten into a fight with his boss. Flint had said that Trask had killed Gordon.

"I need to talk to Trask," Flint had said. "Where is he?"

She hadn't known, since he hadn't shown up last night. Her suitcase still sat by the door, where she'd left it when she'd realized Trask wasn't coming for her.

Flint had followed her gaze to it and let out a curse. "Tell me you weren't going with him."

She hadn't been able to do that. That was what hurt the most. She *would* have gone with him. She would have left her family, left everything she loved, to be with him all those years ago. And last night she'd realized those feelings hadn't changed—and weren't going to.

"Where are you off to?" Darby asked now, still studying her.

"I have an errand. I'll be back before my shift. Don't worry." But as she climbed behind the wheel, she could tell that her brother was more than worried. He was *suspicious*.

As she shifted her pickup into gear, she knew it was time to take control of her life again. There was only one way to do that.

A quarter mile down the road, she pulled out the cell phone Trask had given her and called his number. "Where do you want to meet?"

"How was your date?" Maggie's coworker Daisy asked the next morning as she came into the beauty shop and put down her things.

Maggie thought of her dinner with Flint. Everything had been so perfect. They'd talked. Flint had seemed relaxed. He'd seemed happy. She'd thought for sure that they would finally make love.

"The date was nice—while it lasted," she said, hating how awful she felt this morning. Maybe she should have waited for him at his house while he went over to Celeste's last night. Or gone with him. But the truth was, Celeste calling had destroyed any chance of them making love last night. She feared Celeste would keep them from having a relationship at all.

Daisy groaned. "What happened?"

"*Celeste*. She called. Thought there was someone hiding in her backyard."

"Seriously? Why didn't she call 9-1-1?"

"Flint asked her the same thing, but in the end, he went over there. He's still involved with her," Maggie said. "That's the problem."

"The problem is that she doesn't want to let him go," the hairdresser said. "But when you say he's still involved with her, you don't mean…"

"No, it's not physical, but it is definitely emotional. She's got some hold on him that I don't understand. She left him for Wayne Duma! Why would Flint still have feelings for this woman?"

Daisy shook her head. "Men, I've never been able to understand them."

Maggie laughed, since her coworker was only twenty-two. "I want to blame her, but it's not all her fault. If he runs over there every time she bends her little finger… I saw his expression when he checked his phone and saw that she was calling."

Daisy looked pained. "He's a fool if he loses you."

She smiled a thanks at her friend. When she'd opened the shop, she'd been so happy to have Daisy join her. Daisy was young and fresh and full of ideas. Maggie felt old around Daisy sometimes even though there was only a ten-year age difference.

"What makes me mad at myself," Maggie continued, "is that I knew he was still hung up on his ex. That's why I didn't go out with him the first couple of times he asked. I wanted to wait, give him time to get over Celeste. But it's been four years! I thought that by now…" She shook her head, hating how much it hurt. She'd had a crush on Flint for years, but there had always been Celeste—even after Celeste had married Wayne Duma, there was still Celeste.

Her early-morning color client came in the door. Maggie smiled and tried to forget her disappointment of last night. If only Celeste was a client. She fantasized about what she would do to her if she ever had Flint's ex in her chair.

FLINT HAD SLEPT little last night after everything that had happened. He'd thought about calling Maggie and apologizing again, but he'd showered and gone to work instead, telling himself he would make it up to her tonight.

He'd gotten busy with sheriff's department business, which included another visit out to the Holloway farm. Anvil had called to say he'd done what the sheriff had asked and gone through Jenna's things to see what was missing.

"Can you tell me what clothes she took?" Flint said as he walked down the hall to the bedroom Anvil had shared with her.

The closet door was open. From what Flint could see, not much was taken.

"There was a yellow dress that I always complimented her on when she wore it. It's gone. Some high heels that her sister gave her. I never saw her wear them. She liked low-heeled shoes. She's tall, you know."

He did know. "What else?"

Anvil looked at the floor. "Some…underwear that was a joke gift from some girls she went to high school with."

"Sexy lingerie?"

He nodded without meeting the sheriff's eyes. "I told her to throw them away."

"How do you know she didn't?"

"I saw it still in the drawer recently."

Flint caught the slip. "Why were you looking in her underwear drawer even before she left?"

Anvil didn't answer for a few moments. "The makeup. I thought if she was wearing the makeup that maybe she was also wearing those awful underthings. They were in the drawer with even more that I'd never seen before." He sounded embarrassed.

"Maybe she just wanted to look more attractive to you."

Anvil looked panicked. "Why, after all these years, why would she want to do that? I mean, she was still attractive to me. I didn't need...any of that other stuff."

But maybe *she* had.

"Anvil, there's going to be some forensics people coming out here. They need to do some tests."

"Tests?" he asked as they returned to the kitchen.

"They need to be sure that nothing happened to Jenna out here."

Realization made the man slump into a chair. "You still think I harmed her."

"I don't know what to think, but I have to do everything to make sure you didn't."

Anvil looked at the floor. "There's something else. She had more money than I thought," he said as if his life couldn't get any worse. "I found out that she'd set up a charge account at the grocery store and has been paying a little out of her grocery budget and hiding the bill from me for months."

"How much money do you think she had?"

"A couple hundred dollars socked away, from what I can tell," he said.

"Any idea what she might have been planning to do with the money?" Flint asked, pretty sure he knew if Anvil didn't. Jenna had been planning her escape. Alone, though, or with another man?

"I know you think I'm naive, but I think she just

wanted to get away for a while to think. Or she could have been saving up for something. Maybe something she wanted that she didn't want to ask me for the money."

The man was clutching at straws. It was a hard thing to watch. It also made it hard to believe that Anvil had killed his wife, hidden her body somewhere and dumped her car in a gully.

But it wasn't unheard of. Often after a traumatic event such as cold-blooded murder, a person could step outside reality, come up with a wishful story that became more real the more they told it.

"Our anniversary is coming up," Anvil was saying. "We never gave each other presents on birthdays or anniversaries. Jenna always said it was a waste of money, since we had everything we needed. But I suppose it could have been something like that."

Apparently, Jenna hadn't had everything she needed if there was another man. Anvil seemed to realize the irony of what he'd said and fell silent as he looked at the floor and fought tears.

It wasn't until later after he'd left the Holloway farm that Flint's stomach growled, reminding him that he hadn't eaten. He swung into the Country Cabin Café in the heart of town. It was late morning before the lunch rush. He took a booth and the waitress, an elderly woman named Ethel, came over to take his order.

Ethel was his favorite at the café. She always had a smile, usually a joke to tell him and a sympathetic ear for those late nights when he would stop in starving and exhausted from a long day. Those were the nights soon after his divorce when he hadn't been able to face an empty apartment.

Ethel was like a mother to him. Nothing like the mother he'd had. Mary had been quiet, shy, easygoing, a patient women who'd put up with Ely all those years.

Ethel was loud and fun and often inappropriate. She was just what he needed.

"The special sucks. If I were you, I'd go for the pulled pork. Cook made it for tomorrow, but I can sneak you some on a nice grilled bun with a side of fries. How's that sound?"

"Like heaven."

"I'll be right back." True to her word she returned a few minutes later after having an argument in the back with the cook. Clearly, she'd won because she came out giving him a thumbs-up.

"So what's new?" she demanded as she slid into the booth opposite him.

He figured she already knew, since no one had her ear to the ground like Ethel.

"Jenna Holloway is missing."

She raised one finely arched brow. "You don't say." Clearly, she'd already known.

He knew at once that he should have come there first instead of all the investigating he'd been doing around town. "What?"

"Just that it explains a lot. I saw her last week

coming out of the post office. She had a bundle of letters. When she saw me, it startled her and she lost her grip on them. Several caught the wind. I chased them down for her, since she had her hands full."

He laughed, knowing full well why Ethel had chased after them. "And you just happened to notice who they were from."

Ethel chuckled and nodded. "Shocked even *me*. Who thought Jenna Holloway of all people?" She shook her head, enjoying making him wait. "I handed them back and pretended I hadn't seen a thing. Strange, to say the least, but I'm not one to judge."

"Spill it," he said.

The bell dinged in the back, signaling that his meal was ready.

"Be right back."

He shook his head in irritation and amusement as she sashayed off, returning with his food.

She took her seat again. "Eat," she ordered. "I'll talk. You don't have to put me under a naked lightbulb. But if you ever just want to get naked…"

He took a bite. He really was starved and he knew she wouldn't talk until he did.

"Prison pen pals."

He almost choked on his sandwich. "What?"

"Swear it's true. Had their numbers on the envelopes. I had a no-good husband who did time. I recognized that envelope right away. Definitely from two different prisoners."

"What prison?"

"Deer Lodge, at least the two I saw were from the state prison, but there were others I didn't get a gander at."

Flint couldn't believe this. He'd spent the past few days looking at every man on the street wondering if he was the one Jenna had fallen for. Now this.

"I suppose it's possible she went up to the prison to visit one or all of them," Flint said and took a bite of his pulled pork sandwich, swallowing before he asked, "How many letters were there?"

"A good half dozen."

Unbelievable. Was one of them the man she'd fallen for? The one she feared Anvil would kill if he knew the man's name?

"You don't happen to remember the name on the envelopes, do you?"

She gave him a disbelieving look. "One was a T. White. The other was Lester Branch." She beamed and reached over to steal one of his fries.

"You could have come to me the moment you heard Jenna was missing," Flint chastised.

"I could have, but I thought she would have turned up by now. It isn't like I thought one of her pen pals had broken out of prison and done her in. Her pen pals are all locked up."

"Maybe," he said between bites. "Or maybe one of them got out."

She raised a brow again. "And Jenna was waiting at the gate for him? Never thought it of her, but more power to her. Why not have some excitement in her life? She sure wasn't going to get it from Anvil."

Flint thought of the makeup, the missing sexy underwear and money she'd been able to collect by charging her groceries. He groaned inwardly as he finished his meal and pushed the dirty plate away. He couldn't imagine how Anvil was going to take this news. Unless he'd already found the letters...

"I hope I'm wrong about this," the sheriff said to Ethel. "Otherwise, I have no idea where Jenna Holloway could be right now or if she's even still alive."

CHAPTER FOURTEEN

LILLIE DROVE UP to the cabin in the mountains. Since Trask's return, she'd been caught in a whirlwind of emotions. She'd been angry at herself—and Trask. She'd felt betrayed and gun-shy, hurt by his leaving and leaving her behind… She'd thought she could use those feelings to keep her emotional distance from him.

But after last night, she no longer believed that. She loved Trask. She knew it wasn't that simple, especially given the circumstances. He was still wanted for questioning in Gordon's murder. But she was tired of fighting something that felt as if branded to her DNA.

She didn't need anyone to tell her what a risk she was taking. But the heart wanted what the heart wanted. She had to have faith that between the two of them they would figure this out. She had to believe that it would end the way it was supposed to, with them being together.

Lillie wouldn't let herself think beyond that point as she parked and walked the last couple of hundred yards up the mountain because the road didn't go all the way to the cabin.

The log cabin was small and rustic-looking, built years ago by some miner who'd come to these mountains in search of gold.

Trask came out of the cabin and down the front steps. He looked worried. She hadn't told him anything on the phone except that she had to see him.

She climbed up the last of the mountain to stop in front of him. The sun shone on his dark hair curling at the nape of his neck beneath his Western straw hat. His face was lit with the rays, making his features more pronounced. She'd thought he could never be more handsome than he was standing there.

"Are you all right? I was worried about you." He touched her arm.

She flinched and he drew back. His touch had sent electricity rippling through her. Desire warmed her to her center. All those old feelings coursed through her blood, through her nerve endings, making her tingle.

"Lillie, damn it, I'm so sorry I scared you last night. I never wanted to hurt you, not ever. Every dream I have involves you. Those nine years were hell, but I couldn't come back yet."

The scent of the creek and the pines carried by the wind transported her back to when she and Trask were lovers. Being this close to him…

"I don't even know where you were all those years or what you did to survive," she said, realizing she needed to know everything before she told him what she'd decided.

"I told you, I worked."

"Worked at what?"

Trask pulled off his straw cowboy hat and raked his fingers through this hair. "I got a job in the North Dakota oil field. I worked every shift I could. I got paid under the table, told my boss that my ex was trying to take me to the cleaners. I saved every dime with only one thought, coming back and proving myself to you."

Her heart dropped like a stone when he'd said he hadn't gone any farther than North Dakota. He'd been so close those nine years that it made her hurt with regret.

"I was tired of being the local screwup. I wanted to earn your respect—and your brothers'. If you don't believe me, I can give you the name of my employer."

She shook her head. She hadn't come there to argue with him.

He sighed. "So you're serious about Wainwright."

The question came out of left field and caught her flat-footed. "He's a nice guy."

"You mean he's everything I'm not."

It was the sadness of Trask's smile that needled her conscience. But she had wanted him to believe she'd moved on. *Only to protect yourself.* She'd thought that falling for Trask all over again was the worst thing she could do. *Really? The worst thing?* She could think of a lot worse things.

But right now all she was thinking about was kissing him, feeling his arms around her, tasting that mouth that she'd dreamed about for almost a decade. Her heart soared at the mere sight of him. Desire burned like a campfire inside her. She thought she would die if she couldn't have this man.

"Come inside," Trask said. "I brought in water from the spring." He thought she needed a drink from the longing in her eyes?

She followed him into the one-room cabin. He'd cleaned it up. His pack was against one wall, his bedroll tied to it.

He handed her a folding metal cup. She took it, the springwater ice-cold, and took a sip. "You didn't have to come all this way to tell me you never want to see me again. You could have done that on the phone."

She handed him back the cup. His brow was furrowed with worry, his blue eyes sad with regret. "That's not why I came up here."

"If it's about last night…"

"I was there last night because I know you. I know how you think. I know how you feel about things. You were more worried about Johnny than you were yourself." She stepped toward him. "I know you, Trask Beaumont, like I've never known anyone. I've fought that feeling because you hurt me."

"Lillie, I'm so sorry—"

She put a finger to his lips, lips she'd kissed a hundred times and hoped to kiss a million times more.

"I was afraid of those old feelings. I was afraid you would hurt me again."

"Never, I'll—"

She silenced him again. "I was afraid that I didn't know you anymore. But I know you, Trask Beaumont, on some primal level. I have no idea what will happen tomorrow, let alone today, but I've never stopped loving you. I don't think I'm physically capable of doing so."

His brows unfurrowed. His blue eyes lit from within. "What exactly are you saying?"

She grabbed the front of his shirt and pulled him toward her until they were mere inches apart. "I surrender." She kissed him, letting go of his shirt to cup his handsome face in her hands and kiss those amazing lips. It had been so long and yet like only yesterday. The feel of his lips, the taste of him, the smell of him. He wrapped his arms around her and dragged her to him. Her softer body fit into the hard lines of his, a lost puzzle piece now found. He deepened the kiss, tracing the tip of his tongue along her lips and then opening them to delve deep into her.

It was a complete take-no-prisoners surrender. She was Trask's. She always had been.

TRASK UNFURLED THE BEDROLL, lowered Lillie to it and lay down beside her. He'd been so sure she was coming up there to tell him she really had moved on—moved on with Junior Wainwright.

When she'd said she loved him, when she'd kissed

him… He still couldn't believe this wasn't a dream, since it had been one he'd had since he left.

She was beautiful. The afternoon light coming from the cabin window cast her in gold. "Lillie, are you sure about this?" he whispered as he trailed kisses from her mouth down her slim throat. She moaned softly and drew him closer.

He pulled back a little to stare into her gray gaze. Sometimes he forgot just how beautiful her eyes were. Especially when filled with desire. "I can't tell how many times I thought of you, I thought of us together again, I dreamed of this." He kissed her softly on her full mouth and felt a fire run through his veins. This woman was everything to him.

He drew back to pull her T-shirt over her head. The light caught on her shoulders, her flat stomach, the swell of her breasts above the white lace bra. He could see her nipples, hard and dark, pressing against the thin fabric. The blaze that her kisses had started began to roar inside him. He'd never wanted Lillie more than at that moment.

She reached behind her, unsnapped her bra and freed her beautiful breasts, making his breath come faster, his pulse a thunder in his ears as he bent to pull one taut nipple into his mouth.

LILLIE MOANED, ARCHING her back against his mouth as he sucked at her breast. Desire spiraled through her. He cupped the other breast and sucked the hard tip of her nipple into his mouth. Her palms were on his hard chest as he drew her on top of him.

She looked down into his blue eyes and lost herself in the need she saw there. He wanted her as much as she did him. The years faded away in that instant. It was as if they had never been apart. Would never be again.

Trask lay back to look at her as Lillie worked at his Western belt, then at the buttons on his jeans. Her fingers trembled in her need to have him inside her. He rolled with her until he was on top. Above her, she watched as he shed the rest of his clothing, then tugged her boots and jeans off, as well.

Their bodies glowed in the afternoon sun that slanted through the cabin window. She lay on the sleeping bag, looking into Trask's eyes. His gaze raked over her body slowly, intimately, as if memorizing every inch of her.

She reached for him, her hands grasping his strong biceps to draw him down to her. He kissed her, his body hovering over hers. As he drew his mouth away from hers, he trailed kisses down her neck to her breasts again, then across her stomach.

Lillie lay back as he continued down her body until she couldn't stand it any longer and arched against him until she cried out with a release that left her trembling.

Again she reached for him and this time he came to her, his body connecting with hers in the most primal of all contact. She clung to him as if on a wild horse ride, each galloping lunge taking her faster and faster, higher and higher until she cried out again. He followed quick behind her. Their bodies slick with perspiration, their breathing ragged, they collapsed in each other's arms, spent.

Trask glanced over at her. He was smiling, his eyes bright. Lillie curled against him, his arm around her. The surge of love she felt for him was so strong that she thought her heart might explode.

"Everything is going to be all right, you'll see," he whispered.

She nodded against his chest. "As long as we're together."

As LONG AS they were together. As long as Trask wasn't sent to prison for Gordon's murder. He'd never wanted more badly than at this moment to clear his name. He drew closer, just needing to hold her right now. Just needing to assure himself that this wasn't a dream. Lillie still loved him. They still had a chance for a future together.

That was enough for the moment. Trask chuckled, making her shoot him a look.

"What?"

"When your brothers find out I'm back in town, you know what's going to hit the fan."

"You're a fugitive, what do you expect?"

"They didn't like me even before that," he said.

"My father always liked you."

"I like your father too. How is he doing?"

"If you ask Flint, he's losing his mind. I had to get Dad out of jail the day I saw you. He was arrested for being drunk and disorderly. Dad's lucky it wasn't worse. He punched Harp."

Trask laughed. "Couldn't happen to a nicer guy."

Outside the dusty window, he could see that it was getting late. Lillie would have to go to work soon. They'd lost track of time making love.

"Can you stay a little longer?" he asked.

She nodded.

"Then I'd better get us some firewood for that old potbelly stove over there before it gets dark." It was still cold at night that high in the mountains.

As he started to rise, Lillie caught his hand. "Wait, I'm going with you to help." She scrambled to her feet.

He pulled her to him, loving the feel of her naked body against his. Carefully, he brushed a lock of her hair back from her face and looked down into those eyes again. He still couldn't believe his good luck all those years ago when she'd fallen in love with him. Trask Beaumont, the boy most likely to screw up his life.

"We better get that firewood," she said, drawing away to reach for her clothing. "I have to go to work soon."

"DID YOU KNOW that Jenna had pen pals?" Flint asked after Anvil Holloway was seated in the interrogation room. He'd already said the time and date and introduced Anvil into the video recorder running during this interview. Then he'd had the farmer tell what had happened that night before his wife disappeared. His story was the same.

So the sheriff decided it was time to tell Anvil about the prison pen pals.

"What?" The farmer looked only mildly surprised by the question. "You mean like kids in other countries?"

"No, like prisoners at Montana State Prison and possibly other prisons."

Anvil looked at him as if he thought he'd gone mad. "That's ridiculous. Where'd you get such a fool idea?"

"It's true. I contacted the warden. He's compiling a list of names of prisoners Jenna was writing regularly. He's looking for one who might have been released recently or is coming up for release. He's also checking to see if she has visited any of the prisoners."

Anvil shook his head as he sat rubbing his hands on the worn overalls that covered his thighs. He'd paled and begun to perspire.

Flint waited for him to speak.

"It just keeps getting worse, doesn't it? I thought it would be bad enough if she met someone in town or, worse, met someone online, some stranger, but this. Writing criminals? What could she have been thinking?"

"Anvil, your wife has told you there's someone

else, you find out that she's been lying to you, then you discover that she'd been stealing not only from local stores, but also from her grocery money, and now, writing men behind bars. Any spouse would be angry."

Anvil said nothing.

"Since all of this has come to light, is there something you want to tell me? If so, now is the time."

Anvil looked up, then directly into the video camera. "I didn't kill her."

"I have to tell you, it looks bad. You said you slapped her. Maybe you hit her too hard—"

"No, I told you her nose bled. The slap…it left a red mark on her cheek. That's all. But I felt terrible. I apologized. She was crying, backing toward the door, saying how sorry she was and that she'd never thought she'd fall in love."

"You mean in love with someone else."

He shook his head slowly. "No, in love. She told me that she respected me, cared about me, but that she never knew what love was until she'd met this other man."

Flint thought of the destroyed Sheetrock wall. "That must have hurt you deeply after all these years of marriage. You had to be angry."

Anvil shook his head. "I think I was in shock. I never expected…"

"Is that when she told you about the pen pals?"

He looked confused. "You were the one who told

me about them. Before that, I had no idea. I still have trouble believing it's true."

"Jenna must have said more about this man she'd fallen in love with."

"Just that he was kind and understanding and passionate. Passionate," Anvil repeated. His face was flushed now and Flint noticed that his hands were balled into fists.

"How did she know that?" he asked, but Anvil didn't answer.

"I thought I'd given her everything she needed, you know?" He frowned. "I took care of her. When I met her, she had no one. I made her my wife. I brought her out to the farm. I kept her fed and clothed and put a roof over her head. I didn't ask much in return. Just keep my house up and cook my meals. Was that too much to ask?" His voice had taken on a plaintiff whine.

"Then you found out that she'd betrayed you," Flint said.

"Betrayed me in so many ways. It's going to make me the laughingstock of the county when people find out about all this. Or maybe they already know and I'm the last one to hear about it." He looked down at his soiled boots. He must have come straight from the field when Flint called him. "Or maybe she will do worse to me," the farmer said slowly, lifting his head. "Maybe if you don't find her or she doesn't come back, she'll get me sent to prison for her murder."

"Doesn't that make you angry?" Flint said.

"Wouldn't you like to get your hands on her right now…?"

Anvil looked down at his hands balled into fists and slowly opened them to rub the fabric of his overalls again. "I just want her back. If that isn't what she wants, then I will let her go. I'm not a violent man, Sheriff. I'm a farmer. I grow things."

"What were your last words to her?" Flint asked.

The man seemed lost in memory of that night for a moment. When his focus cleared, he looked embarrassed. "I never wanted to admit this."

Flint held his breath.

"I fell to my knees. I grabbed her hips and buried myself in her stomach, crying and pleading with her not to leave me." When he looked up, Anvil Holloway was a man with nothing more to lose. He was irrevocably broken. "She shoved me away and said she never wanted to see me again. She was so cold, so distant. It was as if…" He seemed to strangle on the words. "As if she didn't care if I lived or died. As if she could just walk away without any thought to me at all after years together as husband and wife. I knew then that it was true. She'd never loved me. I was…just convenient at the time apparently. Realizing that, killed something inside me. She could have ripped out my heart and it couldn't have hurt more."

Flint said nothing. He thought of a jury hearing this and wondered if the farmer would spend any time in prison if this ever went to trial.

Anvil looked up, tears in his eyes. "I think I'd better have a lawyer now."

"Okay, Anvil," Flint said, giving it one last attempt. "But I can tell you right now that a jury will go easier on you if you tell us where we can find Jenna's body."

The farmer closed his eyes. "I'll speak with that lawyer now."

"I CAN'T KEEP lying to my brother," Lillie said as she and Trask walked through the trees away from the cabin, looking for wood for the stove.

"Flint?" he asked as he stopped to pick up a short dead branch.

Lillie shook her head. "Darby." She turned so she was looking directly at him. "He saw my truck and asked about it."

"What did you tell him?"

"I let him think I hit a deer, but he's no fool. He knew I was lying."

"So tell him," Trask said, meeting her gaze.

She shook her head. "He might go to Flint. Or insist I do."

He smiled. "It's just a matter of time before Flint finds out I'm back anyway."

"I think we should run away together. I have some money—"

He stopped to grab her arm and spin her around to face him. "Not happening, you hear me?"

"You being back, me asking a lot of questions,

I feel like we're too close to Gordon's killer. What if…" Tears filled her eyes. "I want to run away with you."

Trask slowly shook his head. "We're not going anywhere. I once asked you to leave behind everything you loved. That was wrong and thank God I didn't make you go with me. But that's never happening again. You've made a life here you love. I can't take you from it."

"They know we're looking for Gordon's killer and getting close. That man with the gun last night—"

"I saw his face right before you came careening through the front gate."

She felt a shudder. "Did he see *you*?"

"No, I don't think so, but I recognized him. Lillie, it was Johnny. Johnny Burrows."

She stared at him in shock. "Why would Johnny break into an office he has a key for?"

"Good question. I intend to ask him when I see him again."

"It makes no sense," Lillie said.

"It does if he wants his partners to think I broke into the office."

She couldn't believe this. "Not if he's your *friend*."

"I told you, my friend is in some kind of trouble."

"Something that has to do with Gordon's murder?"

Trask looked away. "I hope not, but my instincts tell me otherwise. I found some files in one of the locked metal cabinets. I'm not sure what or if they have anything to do with all of this."

She felt a chill crawl up her spine. For a while in his arms, she'd felt safe. They'd felt safe. But there was still a murderer out there and a murder charge hanging over Trask's head. Unless they left. Or stayed and proved who really killed Gordon...

"Each folder had a construction project that Gordon had proposed. Each one had apparently been approved by the bank."

"But the projects never happened because Gordon died."

"What's interesting is that these projects weren't through the construction company, but Gordon only," Trask said. "It looks like Gordon was planning on striking out on his own."

"Gordon was threatening to leave the company, which would have bankrupted it."

"Where did you hear that?"

She looked away. "Junior Wainwright mentioned it last night."

"On your...date. That must have been an interesting date if that was the topic of conversation."

She didn't take the bait, determined not to change the subject. "I doubt either Skip Fairchild or J.T. Burrows would have been happy about that. Add to that the fact that Fairchild was sleeping with Gordon's wife... Where are the file folders?"

"Hidden in my truck. I can show them to you when we leave." But he was studying her as if he had a lot more questions about her...date.

"You think Johnny was looking for the file folders?" she asked.

Trask shrugged as if it was another question he planned to ask when he saw Johnny. "If he'd learned about them, he might have been there to destroy them.

"We have enough wood," he said as he balanced his load of limbs. "We should head back."

TRASK COULDN'T TAKE his eyes off Lillie as they walked back toward the cabin. He felt more complete than he had in nine years. That she'd even suggested they run away had him worried, though. She was still scared and rightly so.

Gordon's killer was still out there.

Between the two of them, they'd stirred things up. If the killer was still in town, he would have heard.

Trask had to keep her safe. That meant finishing what he'd come home to do alone. She'd saved him last night. But he couldn't have her involved anymore.

Junior Wainwright. He tried not to think about her date with the man the night before. Whatever had happened, she'd come to him today, he told himself. Still, the old Trask wanted to pop Junior in the nose. Old habits died hard.

The sun had set. Soon Lillie would have to go back down the mountain, back to the Stagecoach Saloon, back to work with her twin brother. He hated that he'd put her in a position where she'd had to lie to Darby.

He moved across the rugged terrain as if he'd never left. He'd grown up camping in those mountains. He knew them like the back of his hand. What he hadn't expected was how much he'd missed them.

Next to him, Lillie was watching a hawk fly high above the cabin in the distance. He glanced from her to the hawk and froze.

"Wait." Trask stopped to listen. He'd heard a vehicle engine when they were looking for wood but had thought it had been on the road below the mountain, since he hadn't heard it since.

Now he heard nothing but the breeze in the pine boughs and the soft sigh it emitted. But there was something… He'd barely gotten the thought out when he heard the sound of glass breaking.

"Stay here!" he ordered Lillie. Dropping his load of wood, he ran toward the cabin through the pines when he heard more glass breaking. He'd gotten within fifty yards when the inside of the small old cabin exploded with flames, driving him back.

Someone had thrown Molotov cocktails into the windows. He stared at the cabin, completely in flames. No vandals would have climbed all the way up this mountainside to destroy an old cabin.

No, someone had thought he'd be inside. Inside with Lillie, since her pickup was parked down the mountain next to his.

Shock and fear rattled through him. If he hadn't

decided to get wood for the stove when he had... His heart in his throat, he turned at the sound of footfalls behind him. Lillie had dropped her wood. She stepped into his arms and he held her tight. What if she had stayed inside the cabin while he'd gone for wood?

"What happened?" she cried.

"Stay here." Grabbing up a large chunk of wood, he took off around the cabin, hoping to catch the arsonist.

But when he reached the other side, all he could make out was a dark figure disappearing into the pines far below the cabin site. The growl of a four-wheeler engine echoed through the pines as it sped away.

"You need to go," Trask said when he joined her again. The cabin was still ablaze, the old dried logs burning like kindling. "Someone is going to spot the fire and report it. Neither of us can be here when that happens." Mostly, he wanted her far away from him because being with him was now too dangerous. This changed everything.

CHAPTER FIFTEEN

THE LAST PERSON Maggie expected to see after last night was Flint. He pushed open the door looking sheepish. He still wore his uniform, but he was holding a bouquet of flowers.

She tried not to be touched by the gesture, but she couldn't help herself. It had been a very long time since any man had brought her flowers.

"I'd hoped to catch you before you left," he said, closing the door behind him.

"Well, you did." She smiled and heard it in her voice. Seeing him warmed her clear to her toes. She would love to have been coy, but her feelings for him were so transparent, even Flint, who often seemed confused about women's feelings, knew how she felt.

"These are for you," he said.

She took the flowers he offered and stuck her nose into one tiny white rose, breathing in its scent. "They're beautiful. If this is about last night—"

"No, it's about us," he said.

She could see that this wasn't easy for him. "Us?"

"I like being with you. I want to keep seeing you."

She waited for a *but*. When one didn't come, she said, "I feel the same way."

"Good." He burst into a smile. "I have a past, but it's just that, past. I haven't been interested in anyone in a really long time. I find myself smiling just thinking about seeing you."

Her heart did a couple of cartwheels in her chest. Her throat closed with emotion. She couldn't have spoken even if she tried. She stepped to him, kissing him lightly on the lips.

He pulled her to him and deepened the kiss. Her knees went weak. She leaned into him, telling herself that Celeste wasn't finished with him, but maybe, just maybe, Flint was finished with her.

"Tonight," Flint said when he drew back to look into her face. "Tonight, dinner at my house? No interruptions. What do you say?"

She smiled and nodded. "Sounds wonderful."

DARBY LOOKED UP as Lillie rushed into work half an hour late.

"Sorry I'm late. Had to run an errand," she said as she joined him in the kitchen. When she'd returned, she'd gone straight upstairs, showered and changed, not taking the time to wash her long hair.

"Yeah, you said that earlier." He nodded, studying her. "Your cheeks are flushed. You're never late for work. And I know how you feel about your pickup. You'd never crash into anything without being brokenhearted about it and you smell like a campfire.

Sis, I know something is going on. This have anything to do with Junior Wainwright?"

"No. Why would you ask that?"

"He's called, though, right?"

He had called three times and left messages about what a nice time he'd had and how he wouldn't mind doing it again. She had turned off her phone earlier when she went to meet Trask and left it and the cell phone he'd given her in her purse locked in the truck. Otherwise, it would be ashes right now.

"He called," she said as she pulled on one of the aprons and began to help with getting their daily special started. Tonight it was Billie Dee's Texas chili. At least Lillie could chop some of the vegetables for it. Anything to keep busy.

Darby watched her for a moment. "You know you can tell me anything."

She and Darby had always been close. Maybe it was the twin thing. Or maybe they just connected, unlike with their other siblings.

"I know," she said, her voice cracking with emotion. This was killing her.

Darby shook his head, clearly seeing that she was keeping something from him. "I just don't want to see you get your heart broken again." *In other words, I don't want you getting involved with another man like Trask.*

She didn't say anything, pretending that chopping the onions and peppers for the chili required all of her attention.

"Billie Dee can do that."

"I don't mind helping," she said without looking at her brother.

"You're worrying me," he said and went out to the bar. The regulars should be showing up any moment.

Lillie looked at the clock on the wall. She and Trask had parted company so quickly, she had no idea where he'd gone. As she'd driven away, she'd gotten the feeling that Trask had known who'd fire-bombed the cabin. Would he go looking for them? What if whoever had burned the cabin had seen the two of them leave and destroyed the structure knowing Trask would come looking for them? He could be walking into a trap.

"Lillie?"

She looked up, startled at the sound of Flint's voice, and almost cut herself with the knife.

"Sorry," he said quickly. "I don't think I've ever seen you being so...domestic. Or so lost in your thoughts. Dark thoughts, from the scowl on your face."

Fortunately, Billie Dee came in then with her usual good cheer and took over the chili and the conversation.

Lillie went out in the front with Flint, surprised to find Hawk and Cyrus sitting at the bar talking to Darby. "What's going on?" she asked, hating the tremor in her voice. All she could think was that Trask was about to be arrested, so Flint had called the rest of her family sans Ely to meet at the bar to console her.

"Can't we just stop by for one of your café's famous burgers?" Hawk asked, eyeing her.

"I've been craving one for days," Cyrus said. "Can we get Billie Dee to fry us up some?"

"I'm sure she'd be happy to once she gets her chili on," Darby said. "Have a beer while you wait."

Her brothers all siddled up to the bar and Darby served them while Lillie tried to get her pulse rate to drop back to normal.

If Flint was about to arrest Trask, he wouldn't have time for a burger and he sure wouldn't be having a beer.

"Day off?" she asked. He always looked like a sheriff, even in a plain shirt and jeans. His uniform wasn't much different—just a uniform shirt, jeans and boots. He always wore his side arm because he was the sheriff 24/7.

"Supposed to be," her brother said.

Darby slid a diet cola in front of her with lots of ice. "Relax," he whispered before turning back to the others to ask Hawk and Cyrus about the new bull, how the fencing was going and did they get as much rain down at the ranch as he did at his place.

She let her mind drift for a moment as she sipped her cola. This wasn't an intervention. It was just her brothers having a late lunch together.

The cell phone Trask had given her rang in her shoulder bag, where she'd dropped it at the end of the bar. She quickly stepped away, saying, "I need to take this." As she headed for the back door, she could feel Darby's gaze on her. Before she was out of earshot, she heard Flint ask Darby, "How did her date go with Wainwright?"

So *everyone* knew about it?

She didn't hear his answer as she hit Accept and asked, "Are you all right?" The fear in her voice surely a dead giveaway for a man who knew her so well.

"I'm fine. I was worried about you."

"I was late for work. Darby is suspicious, but I'm fine."

"I'm going to pay Johnny a visit after I hang up."

"Just be careful. Trask, do you know who burned down the cabin?"

"I have my suspicions. I can't get into it right now. You sound funny."

"My brothers are all here having a late lunch, so I should go."

"I love you," he said, softening his voice.

"I love you." She disconnected and went back inside. Billie Dee was singing and stirring a variety of ground chili powders into a big pot. As she walked past the kitchen, Billie Dee thanked her for helping with the prep work.

She put in her brothers' orders for burgers and tried to relax.

"So have you found Jenna Holloway yet?" Darby was asking when Lillie returned to the bar.

"Not yet," Flint said and, spotting Lillie, patted the stool next to him.

Lillie slid onto it and her brother reached over and

gave her a quick hug. This was what she loved about her family. They were all so different, often were at odds, and yet at these moments they could come together as a family as if nothing had happened.

"You think Anvil killed her?" Hawk asked.

Flint shrugged. "Not even sure she's dead yet. How was your date?" he asked, turning to Lillie.

She could feel all their gazes on her. "It was fine."

"Fine," Hawk repeated. *"That* great?"

"I had a nice time."

"Nice," Cyrus said and groaned. "If Junior tried anything with you—"

"He didn't," she said quickly before the whole bunch of them got up in arms.

Flint's cell phone made a sound alerting him that he had a text. He smiled as he read it.

"Big date with Maggie?" Cyrus asked.

"Don't make more of it than it is."

"And what is it?" Hawk asked.

"Two people enjoying each other's company. We're taking it slow."

"You don't have to downplay it for us," Lillie said. "It would be all right if you fell in love again."

Flint looked embarrassed. "I'm not having this discussion with you."

"You're giving yourself away, bro," Hawk said and laughed. "It's written all over your face."

"So tell the woman," Darby chimed in, sounding more serious than the others. "Don't leave her hanging."

Flint's cell phone went off again with another text. He checked it. "I'm going to have to take a rain check on that burger. Jenna Holloway's car's been found."

"So tell the woman? Don't leave her hanging?" Hawk asked Darby as Flint left. "You giving romantic advice is bad enough, but what's that about?"

"Just saying." Darby turned away to wipe down the back bar.

"Just saying what? Is someone leaving you hanging?" Cyrus asked, grinning at Hawk. The two of them loved to give their younger brother a hard time. "Sounds like you're making this personal."

Darby tossed down a bar rag and started for the kitchen.

"Leave him alone," Lillie said, making both Hawk and Cyrus turn to look at her.

"Come on, we were just teasing him," Cyrus said. "So what's the big deal?"

"Why are the two of you like this?" she demanded. "Because your lives are so boring and devoid of women that you have to pick on Flint and Darby?"

Both brothers looked surprised at her outrage.

"What's going on, little sis?" Cyrus asked, actually looking chastised. "You sure Wainwright didn't try something with you?"

"Honestly," she said with a sigh. "Get a life. Both of you. And leave Darby alone."

Cyrus held up his hands as he slid off the bar stool to go to the restroom. "Guess we can't tease either of you."

She shook her head, knowing the reason for her thin skin was that it was only a matter of time before they heard Trask was back. Then all hell was going to break out—and all of it in her direction.

"You're awfully sensitive," Hawk said, studying her. "You sure everything is all right?"

"It's fine." She'd had enough and headed for the kitchen.

"You don't have to defend me," Darby said when she joined him where he was helping Billie Dee with the burger plates. "I can take care of myself."

"I know you can. Sometimes they just annoy me."

He laughed. "They do need to get lives. We should set them up on blind dates."

"Like anyone around here would go out with them. They're like two old crotchety bachelors living out there on the ranch." She chuckled at the picture she'd painted of her brothers.

"I'm surprised that neither of them has asked out Kendall," Darby said.

She shot him a look as did Billie Dee. "They think *you* like her," they said in unison.

He raised a brow in surprise. "Where would they get that idea?"

WEEKS COULD GO by without Maggie running into Celeste. That was why she was shocked to see her now.

Flint's ex had her hair done across town at the Serenity Spa and Salon. The place wasn't as fancy as the name sounded. Maggie knew the owner, who

once confided in her at a beauty supply conference
that Celeste was the worst gossip in town and a pain
in the ass in her chair.

Since Maggie shopped for groceries after work
and Celeste had all day to shop because she didn't
work, they hardly crossed paths. Just her luck that
a moment ago Celeste had come in the door of the
local clothing shop.

Maggie had gone between clients to get a new
dress. She was standing in front of the mirror outside the dressing room considering the robin's-egg-
blue dress when she'd heard the bell over the front
door of the shop ding and had turned at the sound.

She knew her face must have fallen when she saw
Celeste. She tried so hard to be pleasant and not let
the woman see how much she disliked her.

"What a beautiful dress!" Celeste cried and made
a beeline for her.

Maggie groaned under her breath as she turned
back to the mirror.

"Special occasion?"

"Not really." The lie caught in her throat.

Flint's ex took hold of the price tag hanging from
the sleeve and let out a surprised, "Wow. If you're
going to drop that much, it must be a really big date."

It was none of the woman's business, but Maggie
was in too good of a mood to argue with Celeste.

"I'm glad Flint asked you out again. I'd hoped I
didn't mess things up for the two of you last night.
Flint said I didn't," she added before Maggie could

deny it as well, even though it wasn't true and she figured Celeste probably knew it. "I'm just happy he's found someone."

Clearly, Celeste didn't have as much trouble lying apparently.

Maggie could think of nothing to say, since somehow the words felt like a backhanded compliment.

"Flint is going to love that dress on you," Celeste said, staring at her in the mirror. "I have one just like it. In a smaller size, of course. Not that you probably want to hear that," she added with a laugh.

The clerk came over then to ask Mrs. Duma if she could be of help. Maggie winced at the solicitation in the clerk's voice. She hadn't been like that with her. But then she was no Mrs. Duma, was she?

After Celeste and the clerk disappeared deeper in the store, Maggie considered herself in the mirror. She'd loved the dress only minutes before Celeste had appeared. She thought she did look good in it. Did she give a hoot that Celeste said she had a dress just like it?

She stepped into the dressing room and took off the dress and hung it back on its hanger. As she put on her clothes to go back to work, she kept looking at the dress. Was she going to let Celeste ruin this for her?

Rebellion welled inside her as she took the dress and headed for the checkout counter.

"Oh, so you're going to buy the dress," Celeste said, sounding both surprised and maybe disappointed.

"As you said, it looks good on me and I think you're right about Flint liking it."

Now it was Celeste who seemed at a loss for words. Maggie didn't give her a chance anyway as she paid for the dress and left the store, her step a little lighter. Screw Celeste. She couldn't wait for Flint to see the dress on her.

TRASK DIDN'T HAVE any trouble finding Johnny Burrows's house. His friend answered the door at the split-level in a newer subdivision of Gilt Edge with a look of shock followed quickly by concern.

"What are you doing here?"

"We need to talk," Trask said, pushing his way in. "Are you alone?"

Johnny nodded. "But my fiancée will be back soon and my father called earlier. He's going to come by. What's going on?"

"I stopped by the construction site last night."

His friend's eyes widened in alarm. "Why would you do that?"

"You might recall that I'm back in town to find out who killed Gordon."

"What does the site have to do with Gordon's death?"

"I wish I knew, but I think it's somehow connected."

Johnny waved that away. "That's crazy."

"As crazy as me thinking you're in some kind of trouble?"

"I appreciate your concern, but you shouldn't be here. If anyone saw you—"

"I wasn't the only one at the construction site last night," Trask continued as if his friend hadn't spoken. "Someone broke in and tore the place apart as if looking for something." He saw that now he had Johnny's full attention. "I thought the person might have been looking for these." He pulled out the three file folders and dropped them on the end table next to him.

Johnny stared at them but didn't move. "What's in them?"

"Why don't you tell me."

His friend looked at his watch. "I really can't do this right now. My father—"

"If you're in trouble—"

"You're the one in trouble. Trask, you shouldn't have come back. It's too dangerous." He still hadn't moved to pick up the file folders.

"You already know what's in the folders, don't you, Johnny? Aren't you even curious to know who broke in and tore up the office looking for them?"

Johnny looked away, but not before Trask saw fear. "Is what's in those folders the reason Gordon was murdered?" His friend started to protest that he couldn't possibly know. "Whatever you're hiding—"

"It isn't about Gordon's murder. I swear."

"All those years we've been friends, I really thought I knew you," Trask said. "Could I have been that wrong about you?"

Johnny met his gaze. "I'll tell you everything. But not now. Meet me tonight. At the creek where we used to go all the time when we ditched school." When Trask got Johnny in trouble. "Give me an hour. But I swear. It has nothing to do with Gordon's death."

Trask looked at his friend and hoped with all his heart that it was true.

Johnny swore at the sound of a vehicle pulling up in the driveway. "That's my old man now. You know how he is. He'd drop a dime on you in a heartbeat. Go out the back way and, Trask? For your own good, don't come back here. If the wrong person saw you here…"

Trask went through the house, exiting out the back door, but not before he'd heard Johnny arguing with his father just like old times.

CHAPTER SIXTEEN

JENNA'S CAR WAS found in a gully only a few miles from the Holloway farm. Her purse and the bag she'd packed weren't inside. Nor was there any sign of an injury or a struggle. What was odd was the lack of footprints near the driver's-side door. If Jenna had been in the car when it went off the road and still alive, she would have gotten out of the car. There would have been tracks where she'd climbed out of the ravine.

Suspecting that the vehicle had been pushed off into the gully, Flint checked to see what gear the car had been left in. Neutral. Jenna Holloway hadn't been in the car when it left the road. There was a good chance that she hadn't gotten into the car and left her home at all.

"What are you saying?" Anvil demanded when he told him Jenna's car had been found and that he should come down to the sheriff's department.

"Are you sure you don't want your lawyer present for this?" Flint asked when the farmer showed up alone.

Anvil shook his head adamantly. "Given what he charges me an hour, no. Just tell me."

"The car was found in a tree-filled gully. It probably wouldn't have been found for months except for some boys hunting rabbits. They stumbled across it."

"You say her purse wasn't inside?"

"No, and no, I don't think the boys took it. I know them. They're good kids. Jenna wasn't in the car when it went off the road. It appears that someone wanted to hide the car."

"You think she got out of it and got into someone else's car, then tried to hide hers? Why would she do that?" Anvil asked, sounding near tears.

"Jenna might have dumped the car herself and gotten a ride somewhere. But as you said, why?"

Anvil shook his head as if it was all beyond him.

"Maybe she's terrified of you and doesn't want to be found." It was one theory, but not the one Flint believed anymore.

"I'm telling you, she's run off with that other man," Anvil said with a groan.

"Or she's dead and has been since the night you argued with her."

The words seemed to hit Anvil like a fist. "I don't understand how you can still think I killed her."

Had the man never seen a cop show? Kill your wife, get rid of her car, do everything possible to make it look as if she'd left—including packing a few things in a bag and making sure it looks as if she took her purse.

"You have to admit, it looks suspicious, Anvil. You washed the clothes you were wearing, you cleaned up the kitchen, you even mopped the kitchen floor."

The farmer looked confused. "I told you I got blood on it. Would you have had me leave it?"

"Whose blood?'

"Jenna's. The nose bleed. I've already told you all this…" Anvil buried his face in his hands. "She's not dead. She can't be."

"There is still a chance she's alive and just not ready to come back."

He hated giving the farmer too much hope because Anvil grasped on to it like a log in a flood.

"Even if she did take off with this other man, she'll eventually come home," Anvil said. "She'll want the rest of her things. Or maybe she'll tire of him." His voice broke.

"You would take her back?"

Anvil's tear-filled gaze held his. "You don't throw twenty-four years away like it was nothing. I behaved badly, I'll admit it. I should never have struck her. I swear on my life I never will again."

"Then let's hope we hear from her soon."

"You need to find the man she was seeing," Anvil pleaded. "He knows where she is."

"Anvil, we don't even know for sure that there was a man. She could have just told you that."

"I thought you said she could have met him online."

"I can't find any evidence that she has used any of the computers available to the public in town."

"Then it's someone she met in town or one of those prisoners she wrote to."

"As far as the prison has been able to determine, none of the men she wrote to have gotten out of prison."

"But they might have had a friend on the outside who she was in contact with."

Flint studied the man. Anvil seemed determined that they find this other man. To take the focus off himself? Or because he really believed Jenna had taken off with this other man?

LILLIE WAS BEHIND the bar working when she saw the two men come in. She recognized Emery right away, but while he looked familiar, she couldn't place the larger man with him.

She felt a start at seeing Emery. It had been years since that family had lived around there.

Emery pulled up a stool at the end of the bar and sat down. The large man sat next to him.

Lillie had a bad feeling about Emery turning up now, with Trask only back in town a few days. Her heart was pounding as she walked down the bar.

"What can I get you?" she said, tossing two bar napkins down in front of them. The two smelled like a campfire. Or a cabin fire.

"Remember me?" Emery asked with a bad grin. He appeared to be missing quite a few teeth. When he'd come in, she'd noticed that he was wearing flip-flops and limping.

She pretended not to recognize him. "Sorry?"

"Emery. Emery Perkins. Your boyfriend's former stepbrother."

"I didn't think your parents were ever married."

"A technicality. Trask is still my bro whether he likes it or not. And this is an old family friend, Vernon. Ya might remember him."

She shook her head. "It's been a long time. So what can I get you?"

"A couple of beers to start," Emery said, looking disappointed that she didn't remember them. Or maybe disappointed that she hadn't reacted to hearing Trask's name.

"So ya ever see Trask anymore?" Emery asked as she put two drafts down on the bar in front of them.

"I guess you haven't heard. He left town nine years ago," she said, sounding as disinterested as she could. "I haven't heard from anyone who's heard from him."

"I thought he was the love of ya life. I'm sure if he was back around these parts, he'd come see *you*."

"I'm dating Junior Wainwright now, so I really doubt it." She started to turn away.

Emery grabbed her arm. "Listen to me, sweetheart," he said, lowering his voice. "I know he's back and I know ya know it. Tell him I want my money. A thousand dollars. Cash."

She looked down at his hand on her arm, then at him. She also lowered her voice. "Touch me again and I'll break that arm." She jerked free of him as her brother Darby walked up.

"There a problem here?" Darby asked.

"No problem," Emery said. "Just havin' a friendly chat with yer sister."

"Why don't you finish your beers and move on along. My sister's too busy to chat right now."

"No problem," Emery said and picked up his beer and downed it. As he slid off his stool, he met Lillie's gaze. "We'll finish this some other time when yer not so busy."

The large man with him chugged his beer and the two left.

"Wasn't that Trask's stepbrother? Emery or something like that?" Darby asked. "I recognized that other one too."

She shrugged. "I handled it, but thanks for being there for me."

"Always." She could feel her brother eyeing her. "Odd, them turning up after all this time."

Lillie said nothing as she picked up their dirty beer glasses and went back to work, her heart in her throat. They knew Trask was back. For some reason they thought he owed them money? How long before they went to the sheriff?

TRASK DROVE TO the spot where he was to meet Johnny even though it was early. Fear for Lillie had him drained. He sat back in his pickup seat and closed his eyes, hoping to rest. So much had happened since he'd been home. Home. He smiled to himself.

Gilt Edge wasn't home yet, but it would be once he

proved he didn't kill Gordon. He knew Lillie didn't trust that he would be staying. She was thinking of the old Trask, who'd had his reasons for not wanting to spend the rest of his life in this town where everyone knew his business.

That Trask had grown up. He'd seen worse since he'd left Gilt Edge. Every family had their skeletons in the closet, their dark secrets, their screwups, he'd realized. He wasn't unique. Nor was his family.

He must have fallen asleep. He checked the time. Johnny was late. He told himself that he shouldn't have been surprised. Whatever was going on with his friend, the man didn't want to share it.

Still he'd expected his friend to come if only to tell him it was none of his business. Or maybe something had come up. But he couldn't help worrying. The Johnny who'd come up the mountain with groceries for him was the old Johnny he'd kept in touch with the past nine years. The one he'd grown up with.

The one he'd seen in the man's new split-level house was running scared. And not just of his father. That had Trask more than a little worried.

As he started to leave, he saw the flash of metal through the trees. Johnny pulled his shiny new car in and cut the engine before climbing out.

From the defeated look on his face, it was clear that Johnny hadn't wanted to come. Trask said as much as he got out to greet him.

"You have no idea what kind of pressure I've been under, still am," Johnny said as he stood shifting on his feet. "The house, the car I drive, the big diamond on my fiancée with a champagne appetite… Not to mention the pressure my father puts on me with his… demands of me."

"You sound like a man about to crack and break, Johnny."

His friend let out a bitter laugh. "I'm way beyond that."

"I know Gordon's death is tied in to whatever was going on at the construction company nine years ago," Trask said. "I'm going to find out the truth. I'd rather hear it from my best friend."

Johnny looked away for a moment. When his gaze came back to Trask, there were tears in his eyes. "I knew when you called to say you'd come back that nothing would stop you."

"Is that why you encouraged me to stay away all these years?" His friend didn't have to answer. "Johnny, how deep are you in this mess? I know you were stealing materials, but I'm guessing it went much deeper than that."

Johnny sighed and sat down on a log near the creek as if his legs no longer held him. He put his head in his hands for a minute. When he looked up, there was even more defeat in his expression.

"Nine years ago Gordon found out that someone had been embezzling money from the company," Johnny said, his voice cracking. "Not me," he added quickly with a shake of his head. "My father."

Trask stared at him, too shocked to speak for a moment. "What happened when Gordon found out?"

Johnny looked away again. "He threatened to have my father arrested if he didn't pay back every dime of it, plus interest. Dad had financial problems I was completely unaware of, everyone was, including my mother. In order to raise that kind of money he would have had to sell everything including our house and still would have come up short. It wasn't good enough for Gordon." He sighed. "I couldn't let Gordon turn him in. Skip was willing to work with a repayment plan, but Gordon…"

Trask swore and stepped back from his friend, half-afraid of what he might do if he didn't. "If you're going to tell me that you killed Gordon—"

"No, of course not. But I did go out to the ranch that night to try to talk some sense into him. I'm the one Brittany heard arguing with Gordon, the one she saw leaving the stables that night, but I swear to you, Gordon was alive when I left."

Trask shook his head. Brittany? Gordon's daughter was the eyewitness? "But you didn't come forward when the sheriff was looking for that man—a man that you knew wasn't me."

Johnny looked as if he might break down. "I couldn't. I wanted to. But my father—"

"Screw your father," he snapped. "Your father is a thief. He turned you into a thief. That's why you were stealing the material off the jobs." Johnny hung his head. "You sold me out to protect your father? How do you know that your father didn't go see Gordon himself and kill him after you left?"

His friend slowly raised his head. "My father may be a thief, but he's not a murderer."

"Are you sure about that?" He could see that Johnny wasn't. "You have to go to the sheriff and tell him what you've just told me. Johnny, you owe me that."

He nodded, his throat moving as he swallowed. "I've tried to. But it will destroy not just my father, but my mother, my…fiancée. My entire family. Not to mention what it will do to the construction company. We are just coming back from the recession. This kind of publicity…"

Trask had always known the kind of hold Johnny's father had on him. What he hadn't seen before was the kind of man it had turned his friend into. "Stop lying. *You're* the only one you're protecting. I knew you were a thief, but I never thought you were a coward." He turned and started toward his pickup.

"It's easy for you," Johnny called after him. "No one had any expectations for you or your family."

Trask didn't turn. He felt sick inside for Johnny. As for expectations, he'd learned that he was the only one who could change the situation he'd been born into. Johnny unfortunately hadn't learned that.

AFTER FINDING JENNA HOLLOWAY'S CAR, Flint called in the state crime techs to search the Holloway farm. They were able to get a unit out that afternoon.

By now everyone in the county was debating not about whether Anvil had killed his wife, but where he might have buried her body.

He thought of the case where a woman who killed her husband told everyone he left her and later hired a backhoe operator to cover up what she said was a new septic tank beside the house.

Murderers often did something telling like rent a jackhammer to dig up the concrete floor in their basement. Or buy new carpet for the bedroom. Or suddenly take up flower gardening in their backyards.

But Anvil hadn't rented a backhoe or a jackhammer. Or bought chemicals that dissolved body parts at one of the local stores.

He had mopped the kitchen floor, though. Preliminary tests of the traces of blood in the cracks in the linoleum hadn't been of a sufficient amount to indicate a murder had taken place in the kitchen.

Still, it was time to step up the search. More and more, he feared that Jenna was dead and possibly buried somewhere on the farm.

Flint was determined to take one more shot at the farmer that afternoon, hoping he could appeal to Anvil's cheapness if nothing else.

He led the DCI team out to the farm and found Anvil working on an old tractor at the edge of a plowed field when they drove up. The farmer glanced up but then continued with what he was doing.

Getting out of the patrol SUV, Flint walked out to the tractor. The day was hot for this early in the spring, the sky looking faded above the new green of the grass of the foothills.

"Don't mean to keep you from your work," Flint said as he leaned against one large nearly bare treaded tire. "I have a warrant here. These state crime scene techs are going to be searching your house, outbuildings, your farm. Got to do it, you know, but if they don't find her, then they will expand their search here in the county. Hate to see that. Could take weeks. Going to cost the state a pretty penny. Seems a shame."

Anvil had been listening, but now he stopped, wrench in hand, to look at the sheriff. "She isn't here. I already told you that. Waste of time looking. She's run off with some man, I'm telling you."

"Maybe so, Anvil, but it's out of my hands. You haven't heard from her. No one has. At this point, we have to consider foul play was involved."

Anvil took off one of his gloves to rub a hand over his face.

"This won't end until she's found, one way or the other," Flint said. "If there is anything else that you can think of that might help…"

Anvil shook his head. "No matter what happens now everyone is going to believe I killed her. I've seen the way people look at me. Women avoid me in the grocery store. People I've known all my life have nothing to say to me. I pray you do find her, not that things will ever be the same."

He went back to work and Flint left him at it. A

fly buzzed noisily next to his ear as he walked back to his patrol SUV. In the distance, he could see a crime scene tech leading a dog into a stand of trees by the creek.

WHEN JUNIOR WAINWRIGHT called again to say what a great time he'd had and suggested another date, Lillie knew she had to quit ducking his calls and be truthful with him.

Trask had dropped back into her life. If things had been different... But they weren't. She loved Trask. No matter how this turned out, she would always love Trask.

"I just don't want you to get the wrong idea."

"That you like me, that we're just friends, that you had a good time the other night? Or that the kiss was anything more than a thank-you?"

She laughed. "Okay, you have the right idea."

"So go out with me again."

She was smiling. She actually liked Junior. For years it had only been Trask. She hadn't let herself even consider that there might be someone else for her.

But Trask had her heart and every waking thought. Junior might have been what she needed—had Trask not come back. He was kind, considerate, loyal... She realized she could be talking about a dog.

Junior was fun and...stable. She could count on him being around tomorrow. Junior was...safe. And right now safe sounded wonderful.

"I can't." Nor could she tell him why, that Trask was back. "It's complicated."

He laughed. "It's Trask. Okay. You're still waiting. But, Lillie, I can't wait any longer."

"You shouldn't." She felt sad. "Thanks, Junior. I really did have a good time." She hung up, angry with herself. She really had been waiting for Trask all those years. He was the only man for her.

But unless they found out who killed Gordon before word got out that Trask was back in town...

CHAPTER SEVENTEEN

FLINT WAS GOING to be late for his date if he didn't hurry. He swore under his breath as he quickly finished dressing, excited about tonight, excited about seeing Maggie.

He'd gotten Ethel at the café to set him up with a dinner for his date. It was warming in the oven. Now it was just a matter of picking up Maggie.

His cell phone rang. For a moment, he considered not answering it. Until he saw that it was his undersheriff calling.

"Sheriff, I'm sorry to bother you after you specifically said you didn't want any calls tonight, but we have a situation down here."

"Mark, I'm sure you can handle it." Flint trusted his undersheriff, Mark Ramirez. If it had been Harp calling, that would have been a different story.

"It's Celeste Duma."

"What?" He couldn't believe this.

"She called on a domestic dispute. I'm holding Wayne. He swears he never touched her and is threatening to sue the department. The mayor's down here.

And now Celeste isn't sure she wants to file charges of physical abuse against him."

"Wait a minute. She said he physically abused her?" Wayne Duma was an arrogant prick. But an abuser?

"She has a black eye and a split lip. The doctor is with her now. He thinks her ribs might be cracked."

Holy hell. "And she swears Duma did this to her?"

"She did. That's why I hauled them in. They were having a hell of a fight when I got there. He swears she's making it all up."

"She's making up a black eye, a split lip and cracked ribs? Who does he say did that to her?"

"He doesn't know. He just swears it wasn't him. He says she's a psychopath."

Flint thought of the woman he'd been married to for the short time before she'd left him for Wayne Duma. He swore under his breath as he saw the time. He was supposed to pick up Maggie in twenty minutes. "I'll be right down."

It was still early when Gordon Quinn's daughter, Brittany, came into the Stagecoach Saloon dressed as if she'd been at a rodeo. She sidled up to the bar with a group of her friends. "Beer," she ordered loudly, slapping her hand on the bar, and laughed. Her friends laughed with her.

Brittany was a few years younger than Lillie, but they'd gone to school together. There'd been no love lost between them. Brittany had been a bully, too cute for her own good and spoiled, since she came from what Gilt Edge considered a rich family. Gordon had come from money, then started the construction company, bought the ranch and done well for himself.

Lillie and Brittany had coexisted well enough in the small community, until Brittany made a play for Trask not long before her father's murder—and Trask's exit.

"I was just thinking about you," Lillie said.

"Really?" Brittany seemed pleased to hear it.

"Is your mother back from her trip to Denver?"

"You mean my stepmother, Caroline?" The young woman made a face, slurring her words a little. "She's back. Why do you care?"

"I wanted to talk to her about your father's murder."

Brittany's blue eyes widened in surprise. Or was that alarm? "Why in the world would you want to do that after all these years?"

"Because the killer was never caught."

"Don't you mean your boyfriend was never caught?"

"Trask didn't kill Gordon."

Brittany smiled. "You just keep telling yourself that." She sighed, clearly bored with the conversation. "I said *beer*. Beer for everyone," she said, motioning to her friends she'd brought in with her. "And one for my horse." That got another laugh.

"I think you've had enough," Lillie said.

Brittany reared back. "Did you hear that?" she demanded of her friends and then leaned in, her eyes narrowing. "You listen to me, Little Lillie."

Darby was suddenly at Lillie's elbow. "I have this," he said under his breath. He must have seen the fire in Lillie's eyes because he gave her a little push toward the other end of the bar. Then he smiled at Brittany and said, "So what's up, Brit?"

Brittany stuck out her lower lip. "Your sister won't give me a drink."

Darby rubbed his hand along his jaw as if giving that some thought. "I'll tell you what. We have a little game we play here. Consider it a challenge." Brittany was always up for a challenge. "If you and your friends can walk the board..." He pointed to a board that had been nailed to a baseboard and painted white. It measured two inches by eight feet. "...without falling off the entire length, I'll be happy to pour you a cold one."

For a moment Brittany looked as if she wanted to argue, but one of her friends cheered her on. "Go, Brit. You can do it, Brit."

Darby came around the bar to pull the apparatus out onto the open floor. Lillie watched with disgust, but at the same time, with a grudging respect for her brother's way of handling it. She'd been ready to throw Ms. Quinn out on her butt—after a fight, of course. But she'd been looking for a fight with the young woman for a long time.

Brittany tossed her cowboy hat on the bar and

pretended to get ready for her stunt. Everyone was watching, including the regulars at the bar. Walking the plank, as it had become known, always drew a crowd. Lillie figured most everyone was hoping Brittany fell on her ass. Or maybe it was just her.

The intoxicated Ms. Quinn stepped up on the two-inch-wide board. It had been Darby's idea to put it in the bar.

"We have to be careful that we don't serve anyone who's already drunk," he'd said. "This way, it makes it fun but gets our point across. A cop pulling them over leaving our bar isn't going to make it so much fun if they are too drunk to drive. Here, they fail, we pull their keys and get them a sober designated driver." He'd shrugged and Lillie had loved the idea.

Brittany teetered, took a step, then another and fell off. "Not fair. I get more than one chance." She tried again and failed. Her friends were losing interest quickly. Brittany was no longer the center of attention.

"How about some burgers?" Darby suggested.

Brittany's friends decided they would forgo the plank for burgers. Several of them put an arm around Brittany and led her to a large table away from the bar. Darby gave them all colas, then turned to Kendall. "Mind watching the bar for a moment?" He motioned for Lillie to follow him to the kitchen.

As he took burgers from the refrigerator and tossed a half dozen onto the grill to cook, Lillie joined him. "You're really good at this," she said.

"Ah, it's nothing. They're just burgers."

"You know that's not what I mean. I'm impressed with the way you handled that in there."

He looked up from where he was cooking on the grill. It was one of their usually slow times. He'd already sent Billie Dee home. "I've always wanted to impress you, little sis, because you blow me away. This place was your idea. You called it and it's been good for us. I'm going to close up after this bunch leaves. Why don't you go on up. I can handle Brittany and her friends."

"She's like putty in your hands because she likes you."

He grinned. "What's not to like?"

"You have a point. You sure you and Kendall can handle it?"

"Easy peasy. Get some rest."

HAVING GOTTEN OFF work early, Lillie had been too restless to stay home. She knew that sleep wasn't what she needed. She called Trask, but his phone went to voice mail. She didn't leave a message. Wherever he was, whatever he was doing, he didn't need to hear about Emery and Vernon. He would know soon enough, she feared.

The last time they'd talked was on the mountain after the cabin he'd been staying in had exploded in flames.

I don't want you helping me anymore, he'd said.

It's too dangerous. I need you to stay close to home where you're safe.

She'd tried to argue, but he'd pushed her into her pickup and told her to go home. She had.

But she wasn't about to stop. They were too close. If he didn't want to run, then they would stay and find the killer and fast. The memory of the cabin exploding, though, still had her shaken. Someone had blown it up believing Trask was inside. Or that she was inside with him?

But how had the killer found them?

Lillie realized with a groan that she *must* have been followed. She'd been so sure as she left town that no one had been tailing her. Obviously, she'd been wrong and it had almost cost them their lives.

A shudder rattled through her. Whoever had destroyed the cabin had wanted them dead. She could think of only one reason. All her questions about Gordon's murder had gotten too close to the real killer.

Her thrill of excitement was quickly extinguished by how far that killer would go to remain hidden. They had to find the killer before he found them again, no matter what Trask said.

Lillie thought about the suspects. Any one of them could have bombed the cabin, not to mention the two crazies Emery and Vernon. But those two wanted money from Trask. Killing her and Trask got them nothing.

No, it had to be someone else. She went over the

list in her head. Skip Fairchild and J.T. Burrows were at the top of her list. But there was also Caroline Quinn. Maybe it was time to pay her a visit.

As she drove away from the Stagecoach Saloon, she noticed someone watching her leave from the front window.

Brittany. The woman glared at her as she drove past.

MAGGIE KNEW IT was bad news the moment she saw it was Flint calling.

"I'm so sorry. I have a situation at the office."

She felt her heart drop but tried to be understanding. "How long do you think it will take?"

"I have no idea. I'm going to have to cancel our date. I can't tell you how sorry I am."

Another cancellation. She told herself that was what happened when you were dating the sheriff. "I understand. It's work."

"I have to go. I promise I'll make it up to you."

She'd heard that before. "Go. Maybe some other time." But he'd already hung up.

She sat for a long time with the phone in her hand, her disappointment a knife to her heart. She had been so excited about this night. She wanted this, needed this. It felt as if something was always going to come up to stop them from finally making love.

Maggie knew she was being silly. Flint took his job seriously. She loved that about him because she was the same way. But his work wasn't like hers.

When someone called with a hair emergency, it usually wasn't a real emergency and could be put off until normal working hours.

She told herself that it must be a real emergency for Flint to break their date, knowing how important it was tonight. If they were supposed to be together, it would happen. Unfortunately, that didn't relieve her mind. If she and Flint did get together, there would be other nights like this. Could she handle having a man who was always on call?

Yes, she thought, if that man was Flint.

Maggie put her disappointment aside and looked around her small house. She'd spend the night cleaning. That would keep her mind off what might have been. But first she had to get out of the new dress she'd put on for her date.

But as she took off the pretty blue dress, she wondered if she'd jinxed her date with Flint by buying it after running into Celeste. She told herself that was crazy thinking. Celeste didn't have that kind of control over their lives.

But she couldn't help being scared she was wrong about that.

LILLIE DROVE AWAY from the Stagecoach Saloon shaken by the venom she'd seen in Brittany's gaze. She tried to shake it off as she drove out to Caroline Quinn's house. She wasn't looking forward to the visit with the wife of the dead man, unsure of what kind of reception she would get.

A few miles down the road, she pulled over, dug her gun from under the seat, where she'd returned it after the day she'd first seen Trask again. Then she exchanged it for the crowbar in her purse and drove on out to the scene of the murder—Gordon and Caroline Quinn's ranch.

An eerie silence fell over the place as she parked and got out. The night seemed to be holding its breath. Not even a breeze rustled the nearby pine trees, standing black against the evening sky. Even the horses had stopped in the pasture to stare at her.

She walked up to the well-lit house, across the front porch, and knocked. The sound echoed under the porch roof. She knocked again. Out of the corner of her eye she saw the stable door close. She turned to stare at it, sure it had been open when she'd driven up. The wind? Except the air was lifeless, not a breath of breeze.

The huge yard light seemed blinding as she made her way to the stables. Dust rose in small puffs under her boots. "Caroline?" she called a few yards from the stables. She looked back at the house. Caroline's SUV was parked out front, but she hadn't answered the door. Maybe that had been her who'd closed the stable's door. Lillie thought it possible that the woman hadn't seen or heard her drive up because inside the stables she could hear horses moving around in their stalls.

She pressed a hand against the stable's door. It was still warm to the touch from the day's sunlight. She pushed. The door creaked open. Stepping from the bright yard light into the cool darkness of the stables, she was momentarily blinded. Dust motes hung in the air just inside the door. She stopped to listen and give her eyes a chance to adjust to the dim light.

It was cooler in there. The air smelled of horseflesh, hay and fresh manure. Several of the horses moved restlessly in their stalls but then fell silent. "Caroline?" she called, her voice sounded strange to her ears as it echoed back at her.

She heard movement at the other end of the stables and started in that direction. After driving all that way, she didn't want to leave without talking to Caroline. Lillie felt as if a clock was ticking. It was only a matter of time before Emery or Vernon or someone who just happened to see Trask told Flint that he was back.

Before that, though, the killer could get to him. Or to her, she realized with a chill.

A furtive movement at the other end of the stables caught her attention. A shadowed figure ducked into the tack room. "Caroline?" she called again, her voice sounding weaker. The woman had to have heard her.

She walked along the stalls to the rustle of horses toward the tack room at the end. The cool darkness of the stables made it hard to see, even harder to hear what was going on. She heard what sounded like a fan rotating loudly. No wonder Caroline hadn't been able to hear her.

Lillie tried to relax. Something had spooked her. A feeling within her? Or something in the air? She tried to shake it off. She was almost to the tack room when a dark figure with a pitchfork rose up from one of the stalls next to her. The figure made a sound like a wounded animal might make.

She lurched away from it, stumbled into an adjacent stall door and fell hard. She'd scraped her arm against the stall door when she'd fallen. Her elbow was on fire as she scrambled to her feet.

The horrible keening sound stopped as abruptly as it had started. She pressed her back against the stall door, preparing to run, when the figure began to laugh.

She froze as she saw the face laughing at her from the shadow of the hooded sweatshirt he wore. Patrick Quinn. Gordon's son.

He was nine years older than he'd been the last time she'd seen him, which made him twenty. He was tall, broad-shouldered, thick across the middle, his once angelic face pudgy, but his hands holding the pitchfork looked strong. Her gaze went to his eyes. They were the pale green of vast bottomless seas.

As a boy, he'd scared her. There had always been something creepy about him. Something not quite right.

"Scared you," he said and chuckled as he lowered his hood with his free hand.

"I was looking for your mother," she said, surprised that her voice sounded almost normal. Her heart was still pounding, her legs still weak, her elbow still burning from where she'd hit it.

"Good luck with that," he said and sneered. "My *mother*. Don't you mean my *stepmother*?" He laughed again and stepped out of the stall.

Unconsciously, Lillie pressed harder against the stall door at her back. For a moment he loomed over her before he turned and walked toward the tack room.

She stood for a moment, trying to catch her breath. She'd let her imagination run away with her. But she knew it was more than that. Patrick had enjoyed scaring her. Patrick, Gordon's strange son.

"Lillie?"

She turned to find Caroline standing just inside the door to the stables. "I was out in the garden. I happened to see your pickup out front…" Her gaze moved past Lillie to where rock music was now coming from the tack room. An odd look crossed her face. She was as uncomfortable in the stables with Patrick as Lillie was. As uncomfortable about her stepson as Lillie was, as well.

"Did you need to see me?" Caroline asked.

"I did." Lillie tried not to hurry toward the stable door, but her step quickened. Behind her, rock music blared. A horse whinnied and then the stables fell deathly silent.

CHAPTER EIGHTEEN

FLINT COULDN'T HELP HIMSELF. He winced at the sight of Celeste, bruised and bloodied. He was filled with an urge to go to Wayne Duma's cell and do the same to him.

Tears filled his ex-wife's eyes as she looked up. "I'm so sorry," Celeste said. "I never wanted you to know."

He sat down, motioning to the deputy to turn on the video recorder. "I need to record this, Celeste. You understand?" She nodded, looking like a broken doll. "Tell me what happened."

She took a breath, flinched and held a hand over her taped ribs.

"Are you sure you're up to this?" he asked.

Celeste put on a brave face. "Where do you want me to start?"

"I understand you and Wayne had an argument?"

She nodded. "He came home in a bad mood. I know to stay out of his way when he's like that, but he was looking for a fight, so I tried to leave. He grabbed me and shoved me back into the house. I fell hard. I don't remember much after that. I woke up on the floor hurting all over. That's when I heard him coming back." She began to cry softly.

"That's when you called 9-1-1?"

"I never wanted it to come to this, but I was afraid he was going to kill me."

"Are you saying this isn't the first time he's hit you?"

She hung her head.

"I'm going to need you to file charges against him. I'll have the deputy give you the paperwork—"

Her head came up. "I can't do that."

"Celeste—"

"You don't understand."

"I do understand. I have a woman missing right now whose husband hit her supposedly only once and now we're looking for her body." He'd raised his voice, making her cringe and curl up tightly in the chair. "Celeste, next time he might kill you," he said more calmly. "Is that what you want?"

"Maybe I deserve it after what I did to you."

"You're talking nonsense. This has nothing to do with us."

She met his gaze, her eyes shimmering in tears. "He's so jealous of you. If he thought I still cared…" She began to cry harder.

He got up and turned off the video. "I can't help you if you don't file charges, Celeste."

"I can't."

"I'm going to go talk to him."

"No," she cried. "You will only make it worse."

"The only way it could be worse is if you're dead. Celeste, you have to press charges against him."

She shook her head stubbornly. "I remember now. We were arguing. Gordon shoved me, but I didn't fall. As he stormed out, I turned and lost my footing. I must have fallen down the stairs."

Flint stared at her in disbelief. "What the hell are you doing, Celeste?"

"Saving my marriage," she announced defiantly. "It was an accident. I'm so sorry I bothered you with this." Celeste began to cry.

He remembered when the sight of her tears turned him inside out. Flint turned and opened the door. "Deputy, would you please see that Mr. and Mrs. Duma get home safely." With that, he turned and walked out.

GORDON'S WIDOW WAS tall and slim with a face like a porcelain doll. She had been fourteen years younger than her husband, a trophy wife if there ever was one. She'd been thirty-nine when her fifty-three-year-old husband had died. Now hugging fifty herself, the grieving widow looked as if she'd weathered the past nine years fine.

"Please, sit down," Caroline said as they entered the living room of the ranch house.

Lillie had been in this room only a couple of times when Trask had been one of the ranch hands working there. Back then it was all dark leather, antler lamps, wagon wheel tables. That had all been replaced with pretty pale colors, warm lighting and a few carefully chosen antiques.

"I'm not surprised to see you," Caroline said once they were seated. She'd taken a corner of the over-stuffed couch. Lillie had taken a wingback chair in the same fabric.

As Lillie studied the woman, she wondered if Caroline had killed her husband. "Why aren't you surprised?" she asked, since no one knew she was driving out here.

The older woman laughed. "I've been expecting you for nine years. You're here about your boyfriend, Trask, right?"

"He didn't kill your husband."

Caroline laughed. "That is exactly what I thought you'd say." She settled into the couch, kicking off her shoes and tucking her feet up under her. "So if he didn't, who did?"

"I was just thinking that you might have."

The woman's laugh wasn't quite as bright this time. "Me? Well, I suppose I can see where you might think that. I'm sure you heard that I was in the process of filing for divorce when he was killed. Would I be so stupid as to do that when I knew I was going to kill him?"

"It could have been a crime of passion."

That got a bitter laugh out of Caroline. "Passion? Honey, there was no passion. At least not for me. All Gordon cared about was making money. When it went his way, he was generous. That's the best I

can say for him. When it didn't go his way, he was..."
Her cinnamon-brown eyes darkened. "Let's just say
he wasn't nice. But I have to ask, why now? Why
come out here professing your lover's innocence after
all these years?"

"I want to clear his name."

The woman nodded slowly. "Okay, how do you
intend to do that?"

"I need to know what happened."

Caroline looked surprised. "Your brother didn't
tell you the gory details? All right. Gordon was apparently struck from behind. A shovel was found
next to him. But what killed him was the pitchfork
protruding out of his back."

Lillie shuddered. "Surely there were fingerprints
on the—"

Caroline shook her head. "The killer must have
been wearing gloves."

She thought for a moment. "Who was on the ranch
that night?"

"I can only guess, since I wasn't here, remember? I was in Billings shopping—and visiting my
divorce lawyer."

Convenient, Lillie thought. "Right, you got back
in time to see the man you thought was Trask leaving the stables before you found your husband dead."

The woman smiled. "You think I'm the eyewitness?" She shook her head. "All I saw when I returned were cop cars, coroners and crime scene

tape." She suddenly stood up. "Can I get you a drink?"

"No, I'm fine," Lillie said as she watched the woman go to a built-in bar.

She poured herself a drink and returned to the couch. "Brittany's the one who saw Trask." She met Lillie's surprised gaze and smiled. "My lovely step-daughter found her father's body after seeing a cowboy she swore was Trask leaving the stables."

Brittany. Lillie couldn't believe what she was hearing. Brittany? The woman who'd gone after Trask only to have him turn her down flat? The woman who'd been glaring at her from the front window of the Stagecoach Saloon earlier?

"She's lying," Lillie said before she could stop herself.

"Probably," Caroline said and took a gulp of her drink. She wiped her mouth with the back of her hand. Lillie realized this wasn't the woman's first drink. She also realized that stepmother and step-daughter weren't close.

"Did you tell the sheriff this?" Lillie demanded.

"Tell him that Brittany lies?" She shook her head. "I figure it will come out at the trial. By then Brittany will have set her sights on some other man. Right now it's Junior Wainwright. Poor sucker."

Junior? "I didn't know they were dating."

"Dating?" Caroline chuckled. "Is that what you call it?"

"So Brittany was here that night. Who else?" Lillie asked, her head swimming with all this information.

The woman seemed to think for a moment. "Her brother, Patrick." Caroline's tone alone told Lillie what she thought of Patrick. "And Gordon, obviously."

"No other ranch hands?"

"The cattle had been sold, so Trask was the only one we needed. Oh, didn't you know? Gordon was... liquidating, as he called it. Selling the ranch, lock, stock and barrel."

Another surprise. "I knew he was talking about getting out of the construction company, but selling the ranch? How did you feel about that?"

"I figured I would get my share and buy my own ranch after the divorce."

Lillie thought for a minute. "What about Brittany and Patrick?"

"They can buy their own ranches."

"I mean, how did they feel about him selling the home where they'd grown up?" Caroline had been Gordon's second wife. When he'd divorced his first wife, he'd kept the ranch and the kids. Apparently, that had been fine with her.

"Brittany threw a fit, but she throws a fit when we're out of cereal," Caroline continued. "Patrick? Who knows? Shallow, dark waters, you know?" She chuckled at her joke.

Lillie felt a shiver roll up her spine at the memory of him in the stables. Both Brittany and Patrick had been so young at the time of their father's death.

She couldn't help but wonder what finding her father murdered might have done to Brittany, let alone Patrick losing his father at such a young age.

"What about his partners in the construction company? I talked to them and got the impression they had something to hide."

Caroline sat up a little straighter as if becoming wary now. "I never knew anything about Gordon's other business ventures."

"But surely you would know, since you were divorcing him and would get a percentage of everything, right?"

"Smart girl." The woman eyed her with amusement and perhaps admiration. "The construction company was in trouble. Someone had been dipping too heavily into the pot. Gordon wanted out."

She thought of the file folders Trask had found. Gordon had already been testing the waters with his own projects. She wondered how his two business partners, J.T. Burrows and Skip Fairchild, had taken that. "Who was stealing the money?" she asked, thinking about what Trask had told her about Johnny.

Caroline looked as if she'd already said too much. She shrugged.

Skip Fairchild, Lillie thought. "You were close to one of the partners. Not that I think you would resort to blackmail, but you could have had the leverage to get him to do anything you wanted. Including kill your husband."

Caroline carefully put down her glass. "It's late.

While this has been...entertaining, I think it's time for you to go."

"I'm going to find out who killed your husband." The threat hung in the air as the woman showed her to the door.

FLINT SAT ON Maggie's couch, hat in hand dangling between his knees, the weight of the world pressing down on his shoulders. She might have felt sorry for him if she wasn't so angry. She had a theory and if she was right...

Maggie said nothing for a long time after he apologized for ruining their date again, but he couldn't tell her about sheriff's business.

"Just tell me one thing," she said, surprised how calm she sounded given how angry she was. "The reason you had to cancel our date again... Was it because of another of Celeste's stunts?"

He groaned. "Maggie—"

She held up a hand as she got to her feet. He thought she was simply jealous of Celeste. "Just tell me. You don't have to tell me any specifics. One simple question. Was it because of Celeste?"

"It isn't what you think."

"Really? What is it you think I think? That Celeste ruined another of our dates on purpose? That whenever she calls, you go running? That you're not over her?"

He said nothing, just hung his head.

Maggie let out a laugh that felt closer to a sob. "So

it was her, just as I thought." She shook her head. She couldn't believe this—not that Celeste had done it again, but that Flint didn't see through the woman. "Can't you see that she will do anything for your attention?"

"I told you, it wasn't like that." He looked up, pain in his eyes. For a moment she almost weakened.

"I don't want to do this anymore." The words were out before she could stop them. It hurt too bad. She would have put up a fight for Flint if the playing field had been even. But Celeste had a hold on the man that Maggie feared he'd never be able to shake off.

"Maggie, you may not like her, but—"

"Flint, don't you dare defend her to me."

"I'm not. It's just that you can't believe she's so manipulative that..."

"She's more than manipulative. The call the other night about the ladder leaning against her shed. Yes, she told me about it when I ran into her at the grocery store."

"I'm sure she told you she felt foolish."

"See, that's the problem, Flint. You still don't see through her and because of that you will go running whenever she crooks her little finger."

"That's not true."

"Did I mention that I saw Celeste earlier at the dress shop? She knew about our date, Flint." Maggie scowled at him. "Two dates, both ruined by your ex. I can't even imagine what she'll pull next time. Except there isn't going to be a next time."

He looked up, his gray eyes filled with hurt. "What are you saying?"

"That if we tried to date again, I would be waiting for your phone to ring and of course it would be Celeste with something that required your help."

"Maggie, you're talking nonsense. Look at all the other dates we went on that Celeste didn't interrupt."

She smiled and nodded. "But once she saw you getting a little serious, look what happened. Oh, she'll tell you she feels terrible that she spoiled what you and I had, but, Flint, get a clue. The woman is never going to let you go."

With that, she walked to the door. "As long as Celeste is in your life, I can't be. I'm sorry." She opened the door.

He slowly got to his feet. "You have no reason to be jealous—"

"Tell yourself that's all it is. Just me being jealous. Just me overreacting. Me being irrational." Maggie shook her head. "Your ex is dangerous. Maybe one day you'll see that before it's too late." He said nothing as he walked out.

"I WENT OUT to the Lazy G Bar Q and talked to Caroline."

Trask couldn't believe what he was hearing on the other end of the phone. He'd turned off his cell earlier and had just turned it back on to call Lillie to check on her and tell her what he'd learned from Johnny. Earlier, he'd told her not to do any more investigating. She knew how dangerous it was. What had she been thinking?

"Lillie, are you crazy? After what happened earlier at the cabin, don't you realize how dangerous this is? If Caroline killed her husband—"

"She isn't going to risk killing me. Everyone believes you killed Gordon. A murder now would look rather suspicious, don't you think?"

He let out an exasperated breath. "Where are you now?"

"I'm headed back home." The winding road followed the spring creek, a famous trout stream. A sliver of moon high over the pines peeked in and out of the clouds. "I have a new theory I wanted to share with you. Caroline told me that someone had been stealing money from the construction company. If it was Skip Fairchild, she could have used that information to blackmail him into killing Gordon."

"It wasn't Skip. Johnny just confessed to me that it was his father."

"So Caroline either didn't know or she wasn't telling," Lillie said. "Still, I think I hit a nerve."

"Yes, accusing someone of first having an affair, then blackmailing her lover into killing her husband could hit a nerve. Lillie, I told you—"

"Also, I found out who Flint's eyewitness is. I hope you're sitting down. It was Brittany."

Trask cursed under his breath. "I know who Brittany really saw. Johnny. He swears Gordon was alive when he left."

Lillie let out a surprised sound. "But soon after, Brittany found her father murdered."

"I know. I think J.T. might have been involved, but still there is no proof."

"And from what I was able to find out, there was little forensic evidence. According to Caroline, Gordon was hit from behind with a shovel, then, when he was down, stabbed with a pitchfork. But there were no fingerprints on either weapon. But once Johnny tells Flint what he told you..."

Trask didn't have the heart to tell her that he didn't expect that to happen. "Lillie, I don't want you doing this. I told you. It's too dangerous." Lillie didn't answer. "Did I lose you?" Cell phone coverage was sketchy across most of Montana except right in town.

"I'm still here. There's a vehicle with its high beams on coming up behind me. The idiot is driving way too fast for this road."

His stomach dropped. "Lillie, pull over and let him pass. Lillie, did you hear me?"

"It's a pickup. I hit my brakes, but the fool driver didn't get the hint to dim his headlights. He's right on my butt."

Trask's throat went dry. "Lillie, listen to me. Pull over, let him pass, maybe that's all he wants." But he had a bad feeling that wasn't the case at all.

He heard the crunch of metal. Then Lillie's gasp. "He just ran into the back of my truck!" There was more crunching metal and Lillie's scream. The phone went dead.

Hurriedly, he dialed 9-1-1. Even after he'd reported the accident, not leaving his name, even as he raced toward the canyon where Lillie had been driving, he knew the sheriff would get there before he could.

Lillie. What had he gotten her into? He prayed that she was all right as he raced out of the mountains.

Mentally, he kicked himself for coming back. None of this would be happening if he'd stayed away. But even as he thought it, he knew that he'd had no choice but to come back.

FLINT WALKED AWAY from the best thing that had happened to him in a very long time. He desperately wanted to go back, to hold Maggie, to convince her that she was wrong. Yes, Celeste had spoiled two of their dates, but that was no reason to call off their relationship.

He started to go back to try to reason with her, but he was exhausted. Maybe tomorrow when Maggie was thinking more clearly. When he had some sleep.

Did he believe that his ex had hurt herself to keep him from making love to Maggie? That would make her a psychopath. Just as her new husband had accused her.

Celeste was…demanding, spoiled rotten and, yes, manipulative, but to hurt herself?

And if she had done exactly what Maggie suspected? Then dating Maggie would put her in danger.

That thought had come out of left field. It made

his blood turn to slush. If Celeste was capable of doing such a thing, then hurting someone else would come too easy to her.

Fear paralyzed him as he drove away. At the same time, his heart ached. He'd found someone he could love. Someone who could love him back. Was he going to let a woman unhappy with her own life keep him from finding happiness?

He felt as if he'd been in a three-ring bout and had lost. He was about to head home to his empty house when he checked his phone. With a curse, he realized he'd turned it off during his visit with Maggie. He had a call from the sheriff's department dispatcher marked urgent.

"The caller wouldn't leave his name, but he said that your sister, Lillie, had been run off the road by someone driving a pickup." The dispatcher gave him the directions on where the caller had thought the accident had happened. "He said he'd been on the phone with her when it happened. I just talked to Harp, who took the call. He said the EMTs have taken her to the hospital."

Flint hurriedly called the hospital. Lillie had just been admitted. She was scratched and bruised but had no other apparent injuries. The doctor was keeping her overnight for observation, though.

Being closer to where Lillie had been allegedly forced off the road by the driver of a pickup, he headed in that direction first.

As he came around a bend in the road, he spotted

Lillie's pickup upside down in the creek, its head-lights shooting a beam back up at the road. Harp was still there taking photos and measurements in the headlights of his patrol SUV.

Flint could see the skid marks on the highway. Several bushes had been wiped out as Lillie's pickup had left the road and rolled, only to come to rest in the middle of the stream.

"Does it appear she was forced off the road?" Flint asked his deputy.

"Sure looks that way to me," Harp agreed. "There are other skid marks up the highway and broken glass from her taillights as well as another vehicle's headlights."

"Get photos of all of it, then have her pickup taken to the evidence garage. I want to know about any paint or damages that might show up from the truck that ran her off the road."

When the doctor finally let him go into her hospital room, Flint found Lillie sitting up in bed.

"Brittany? Brittany Quinn is your eyewitness?" his sister demanded.

It took him a moment to figure out what she was talking about. He'd thought this was about her accident. But no, it was about Trask and the murder.

"Who told you that?" he asked as he pulled up a chair next to her bed.

"Caroline."

"So that's what you were doing on that road tonight." Flint sighed. "What do you think you're doing?"

"Trying to find out who really murdered Gordon Quinn. And the fact that someone ran me off the road proves that I'm onto something."

He groaned. "Or that the person behind the wheel of the pickup that hit you was drunk." He didn't believe this any more than she did. He wished it had been a drunk. Instead, it was probably a killer.

"The driver wasn't drunk. He or she crashed into the back of my truck and then forced me off the road and into the creek. When you find that truck and driver, you'll have your killer."

If only it was that simple. "The 9-1-1 dispatcher said that a man called in the accident. You probably wouldn't know anything about that."

"I was upside down in the creek, so no, I don't. Probably just some driver who came by and saw me hanging there."

"Right, except that the dispatcher said the mysterious caller told her that he was on the phone with you when you were forced off the road."

She said nothing.

"Isn't it time you tell me the truth?"

His sister crossed her arms over her chest. "The person Brittany saw leaving the stables—if she saw anyone—was Johnny Burrows. His father, J.T., had been embezzling money from the construction company and Gordon had found out and was going to come to you with the information. Gordon pulling out of the company would have bankrupted it. And it can't be a coincidence that after I talked to Caroline Quinn, I was run off the road and almost killed."

Flint stared at Lillie. He shouldn't have been surprised that her stirring all this up again had turned up evidence he hadn't gotten nine years ago.

What surprised him was that he'd been so sure Trask Beaumont had killed Gordon, that he hadn't done as thorough a job as he should have, he realized now. He'd been blinded by fear that his sister was involved with a dangerous man from the wrong side of the tracks. He'd wanted Trask Beaumont out of her life. So it had been easy to believe the man guilty after he'd run.

"That's pretty impressive," Flint said, realizing something else. "How long have you been in contact with Trask?"

She turned her gaze toward the window, her face closing over with Cahill stubbornness.

"Lillie," he said with a groan. "Isn't it possible that you're blinded by your feelings for this man, who ran away nine years ago and ran out on you, as well?"

"You don't understand," Lillie cried. "He ran because he was scared—and rightly so, given the way you felt about him."

"You might be right about that."

"You couldn't possibly understand how I feel about him. He's the only man I have ever loved. The only man I *will* ever love."

"You think I'm incapable of loving someone like that?"

"Please, don't compare how I feel about Trask to how you felt about Celeste. Or is it *feel*? Are you trying to tell me that you're still in love with her?" She sounded horrified.

"No. I wasn't thinking of her."

She rubbed her temples as if her head hurt. "Wait, did you just admit that maybe you were wrong about Trask?"

Flint nodded. "I might have rushed to judgment on him, yes. But he's still a suspect, Lillie. If he killed Gordon, he's going to prison."

"He didn't."

Her faith in the man she loved made him wince. Lillie would do anything for Trask. She'd been ready to leave with him nine years ago, leave everything behind.

He thought of Maggie. He'd let Celeste come between them. He didn't blame Maggie for not trusting him. No woman wanted a man who dropped everything and ran to his ex whenever she called. He'd told himself that he was the sheriff, he had to go when he got calls from the office like he had the other night.

But he could have let his undersheriff handle it, although he now suspected that Celeste would have escalated the situation until he came down there.

"You're lucky," he said to his sister.

"Lucky?" She looked ready to fight, as if she thought he was mocking her.

"Yes, lucky. There is no question about what you want and what you will do to get it."

She waited as if expecting a *but*.

"I've made a mess of my love life." He saw his sister's surprise. "You actually inspire me."

She laughed nervously at that. He'd never opened up to her like that and he could tell it made her uncomfortable. "What would you do if Trask came back?" she asked without looking at him.

He felt his heartbeat jump. So that was what all of this was about. "I would take him in for questioning, along with a lot of others. If he's innocent—"

"He is."

Flint nodded. "Then he would go free."

"Then you have to find the pickup that ran me off the road and you'll have the killer."

"I have deputies looking for it as we speak."

"Can't you track down paint chips or something?"

"Or something." Flint got to his feet. "I'd ask if you were all right, but the way you're giving orders, I'd say you're fine."

"I'm fine."

He shook his head. "I'd like to believe that, but clearly you've broken open a hornet's nest. At least you should be safe here, since the doctor is keeping you overnight."

Lillie started to get out of bed.

"Wait, where do you think you're going?"

"Home. I told you, I'm fine. I don't need to stay overnight." She groaned as the doctor came in and ordered her back into the bed. "Please, I need to get out of here."

"To find a killer," her brother said.

"Exactly."

"Not tonight." He raked a hand through his hair as he studied her adorable face. "So where is Trask? I'd still like to talk to him."

She clamped her lips together as he cursed the Cahill stubborn gene. His own included.

CHAPTER NINETEEN

TRASK TRIED LILLIE'S cell phone. It went straight to voice mail. He wondered if she even had it or if it had been lost in the wreck. He'd arrived at the creek in time to see Lillie being taken by stretcher to the ambulance. His heart was in his throat until he saw that she was sitting up and arguing with the EMTs. Relief had made him weak as he'd driven on past. If he stopped, he would be arrested or at least detained for questioning, since he saw sheriff's department personnel everywhere.

As he drove toward Gilt Edge, he passed a vehicle he recognized. Skip Fairchild's sports car. He slowed, waited until Fairchild's fancy taillights disappeared around a curve, then flipped a U-turn in the middle of the road and followed. It was late. He couldn't help but wonder where Fairchild was going on this road. When he turned onto the highway toward Grass Range, Trask followed.

He hadn't gone far when he saw brake lights ahead. Fairchild turned into the Lazy G Bar Q Ranch. Apparently, he and Caroline were still seeing each other. Fairchild didn't use his blinker as he turned into the ranch.

Trask drove on past the turnoff until he knew Fairchild could no longer see him before he turned around and drove back.

There was no traffic on the road this late. Hell, there was hardly any traffic on this road most of the time. He switched off his headlights as he approached the turnoff and swung in.

Ahead, he saw Fairchild's headlights blink off. A moment later, the porch light flashed on, then quickly went out. In those few moments, he'd seen all he needed to.

But it wasn't Caroline caught in the porch light opening the door and rushing into Skip's arms. It was *Brittany*.

He called the hospital to check on Lillie. When he told the nurse he was her brother, she told him that Lillie was being kept overnight for observation. He loved small towns.

LILLIE COULDN'T BELIEVE she was trapped here in the hospital. She kept seeing the headlights, hearing the crunch of metal, feeling her pickup spinning out of control. Her pickup. Darby was right. She'd loved that pickup.

But right now she was more worried about Trask. She'd lost her phone in the accident and couldn't remember Trask's number from the burner phone he'd given her. He'd be worried about her.

Given what had happened to her, she feared he wasn't safe, either.

What surprised her the most was her brother Flint's change of heart. Well, not exactly a change of heart, but at least a start. He was now willing to admit that maybe Trask wasn't guilty.

She'd been run off the road after visiting Caroline Quinn. That couldn't be a coincidence. But now her brother knew. He would be checking the Lazy G Bar Q. Not that the killer would probably take the pickup back there.

But who had been driving it? Caroline? Or her boyfriend, Skip? Not that she couldn't have been followed to Caroline's by someone else. J.T. Burrows. Or even Johnny.

She hoped Trask's once best friend wasn't that deep in all this.

At the sound of her hospital door creaking open, she looked up to see Trask slip in quietly, closing the door behind him.

"You shouldn't be here," Lillie cried as Trask moved toward the bed.

He grinned. "I couldn't stay away. Are you all right?"

She nodded and reached for him. His arms came around her. He'd been so worried about her. He held her gently, sensing that she was sore from her accident.

As he pulled back, he said, "I was so worried about you."

She nodded. "Flint was here earlier. He's starting to believe you're innocent."

"That's good." He told her about Skip and Brittany.

"I thought he was after her stepmother."

Trask shrugged. "I'm just glad you're in here. Lillie, this is getting way too dangerous. We've started something and I'm afraid of how it will end."

"I don't care about any of that right now," she said, cupping his face in her hands. "I'm just so glad to see you."

He leaned down and kissed her, feeling the spark of passion she ignited in him with just the brush of her lips. "I want to be with you so badly without all of this hanging over our heads," he said when the kiss ended.

"Just stay safe. Promise me you'll hide out so no one can find you for the next day or so. Flint is trying to find the truck that ran me off the road. Once he does…"

Trask kissed her again, wishing he could climb into the bed beside her.

At a sound in the hallway, they both started.

"You should get out of here before you're caught," she said. He could tell she didn't want him to leave any more than he did, but he nodded.

"I'll see you tomorrow."

"So much for hiding out."

He smiled. "I've stayed away from you for the past nine years. I can't do it anymore."

With that, he gave her one more long kiss and left.

"DID YOU HEAR? It's all over town this morning." The woman in Maggie's chair, Shirley Barnes, squirmed as if about to bust if she didn't tell. It was early and Maggie was tired. She'd cleaned her house until very late last night, half hoping Flint would come back. He hadn't.

She hated the way they'd left things. But maybe it was for the best. As long as Celeste was—

Maggie realized that Shirley had just said Celeste's name.

"Wayne Duma was taken down to the sheriff's office last night and almost arrested for domestic abuse," Shirley was saying.

Wayne Duma. Maggie couldn't hide her shock. Was it true?

"I heard he beat the hell out of her," Karen Matthews said from the next chair. "A friend of mine who works at the hospital saw her when she was brought in. Probably got what she deserved."

"No woman deserves to be beaten," Daisy said, and Maggie agreed, although she'd wanted to punch Celeste on more than one occasion.

"Huge deal down at the sheriff's office. I heard the mayor was even down there because Wayne's lawyer was threatening to sue the city."

"On what grounds?" Daisy demanded.

"Wayne swears he never touched her and that she's lying," Shirley said.

"Then who beat her up?" Karen said.

"That's just it, once she got down to the sheriff's

office, she said she was having trouble remembering. At first Celeste said he'd hit her, then she said he'd pushed her down the stairs, then she remembered that she'd slipped and fell."

"What?" All eyes turned to Maggie, who shrugged. Apparently, they all thought that Flint told her everything. This was the first she'd heard about it. But now she knew why her date had been canceled. Celeste strikes again. She cringed at her uncharitable thought.

"She said she and Wayne were arguing, he pushed her and that's the last she could remember," Shirley said. "She'd found herself on the floor, hurt, and called the sheriff's office."

Maggie wondered how Shirley knew so much about it. A leak at the sheriff's office? Or was it possible she'd heard this from Celeste?

"What does Wayne say about that?" Karen wanted to know.

"He swears he left the house after their argument and that she was fine."

"He's lying," Daisy said with such anger that Maggie wondered if the girl had been in an abusive relationship in her past.

"Well, I guess the sheriff is trying to sort it out. What a mess. And with Jenna Holloway still missing. I saw Anvil at the clothing store the other day buying himself a pair of jeans. I've never seen the man in anything but overalls. Don't you think it's suspicious he was buying jeans?"

Maggie was still thinking about Celeste. Was it

just a coincidence that she and her husband had argued that particular night? Did she really believe that Celeste had gotten herself beaten up to keep Flint from making their date?

The thought made her sick to her stomach. When had she become that woman? She felt for Celeste, no matter what had happened that night. The woman was unhappy. Maggie felt sorry for her and felt even worse for the way she'd treated Flint now that she knew what he'd had to deal with.

"Stay at my house tonight," Flint said as he drove Lillie away from the hospital later that evening. He'd asked the doctor to keep her as long as he could. Tied up with a series of emergencies, the doctor couldn't sign her out until that evening.

Flint had found her pacing in her room when he arrived.

"Was this your doing?" she'd demanded, narrow-eyed, when she'd seen him.

"You are so suspicious," he said. The X-rays hadn't shown any fractures and, pressed by his sister, the doctor had finally had to release her.

"I'm exhausted," Lillie said, lying back against his patrol SUV seat. "I want to sleep in my own bed, but thanks for the offer." She shot him a look. "Isn't Maggie staying over?"

He shook his head. He wasn't about to tell her that he and Maggie hadn't gotten that far in their relationship. If he knew Lillie, she'd demand why not. "We aren't seeing each other anymore."

"Oh." She leaned back again and closed her eyes. "I'm sorry to hear that. I like her."

"Me too."

Flint drove in silence the rest of the way to the Stagecoach Saloon. He'd called Darby earlier to ask him if he would keep an eye on their sister tonight. He didn't want her to be alone. Darby had readily agreed. Of course, when Lillie found out, she'd be furious.

"What did you do?" Lillie asked, sounding half-asleep.

"What?" He glanced over at her. Did she know about him asking Darby to stay tonight?

"Maggie. What did you do to make her break it off?"

He stared at her for a moment before going back to his driving. "First off, what makes you think she's the one who broke it off?" No answer. "Second, I didn't do anything but my job."

"Huh."

He groaned. "It's Celeste."

Lillie opened her eyes and looked over at him as they neared the saloon. "Do. Not. Tell. Me. You're. Still. In. Love. With. Her."

Flint shook his head. "Of course not. She's married to Wayne Duma."

"Right. But you must have done something stupid."

"Thanks for the vote of confidence," he said as he pulled up behind the saloon. "I defended Celeste."

Lillie groaned. "I thought you were smarter than that."

"Apparently not." He didn't want to talk about it. "I'll walk you up."

"Don't be ridiculous. I'm not an invalid. I can get upstairs just fine." She got out, slammed the door and walked around to tap on his window. "Thanks for the ride, though. And whatever you did, fix it. Maggie's worth hanging on to." With that, she headed for her apartment.

FLINT SWORE UNDER his breath as he left. Lillie was right. He needed to fix it. But first he needed to straighten something out. He headed for the Duma house.

Wayne answered the door. He looked as if he'd been put through the wringer. "Did she call you again?" he demanded, sounding scared. "I don't know what's wrong with her. Sometimes..." The man raked a hand through his graying hair. "I just don't understand her. To let everyone think I struck her..."

"She didn't call me." He could hear Celeste cursing and throwing things in another room. Something broke. "I need to talk to her."

Wayne stepped back to let him in. "Help yourself. I have something I have to do at my office." He headed out the door, closing it behind him.

At the sound of the door slamming, Celeste came

storming into the room as if looking for a fight. Flint remembered before their divorce when they'd fought. She would never let him walk away so he could give them a break in their argument. No, Celeste liked fighting to the death.

That was the look on her face as she stormed into the room. But when she saw that Wayne was gone and it was Flint standing in her foyer, she quickly checked her expression.

"If you came to see about me, I'm fine," she said, leaving enough doubt in her voice to make someone worry she wasn't.

"I'm not here to check on you. You're not my responsibility anymore."

Celeste raised a brow. "You're angry with me for spoiling another one of your dates with Maggie. I feel—"

"Terrible. Right. Except I don't believe you, Celeste. I think you delight in making my life miserable."

She looked coy. "Are you miserable, Flint?"

"Not since I'm no longer with you."

"That's a mean thing to say, especially in my condition." She sat down, wincing as she cradled her ribs in her arms.

"Yes, your condition. Celeste, I'm not sure how sick you are. But if you hurt yourself just to ruin my date, then you're emotionally disturbed and you need professional help."

"Oh, I did ruin your date. I knew it. Now I feel worse."

He shook his head, hating that Maggie might be right. "Celeste, you divorced me. Why can't you leave me alone? Especially now that I'm finally getting over you?"

She looked amused. "You really think you're getting over me?"

Flint stared at her. How could he not have seen this? "Get some help, Celeste. You're sick. And stay away from Maggie."

She looked up at him with those big doe eyes. "So this is about Maggie," she said, anger edging her voice. "And here I thought you were worried about *me*. Well, she'll never make you happy. She'll bore you to death. You need passion." She smiled. "Remember how it was with you and me? Especially after an argument."

"You feed on drama," he said, realizing how true it was. "Our marriage was a roller-coaster ride. I never knew who I was coming home to. I don't miss it, Celeste. I would never go back there, ever. Whatever is going on with this marriage of yours, I don't give a damn. Don't try to involve me again."

Her laugh was like broken glass shards. "Nice speech. But pathetic Maggie could never take my place and we both know it."

He felt fear form a hard knot in his stomach. "Maggie and I broke up. She doesn't want you in her life and she thinks I can't keep coming to your rescue."

Celeste leaned back, clearly unable to hide her

pleasure. He thought again of all the things Maggie had said. He'd argued that she was wrong because he desperately wanted to believe she was. So much easier to believe that Maggie was simply jealous of Celeste.

"Maggie's wrong, though. I'm done with you." With that, he turned and walked toward the door.

"I know you don't mean that," she called after him. "You'll be back."

LILLIE STEPPED INSIDE the back door of the bar and leaned against the wall until she heard Flint drive away. She hurt all over from the wreck, but she hadn't wanted her brother to know how much.

At the sound of a vehicle, she smiled to herself and stepped back outside. Trask.

Moonlight flickered through the pines. She stood breathing in the fresh air, anxious to see him. But after a moment she realized whoever had pulled up on the side of the building had cut his engine. She hadn't heard him get out. Odd.

Maybe it hadn't been Trask. She froze, thinking of the driver in the pickup earlier. He hadn't been trying to scare her. He'd been trying to silence her.

Her gun was in her purse—somewhere in her wrecked pickup. She looked around for a weapon, realizing she'd never be able to reach the door and get it locked before—

A shadow fell across her. Lillie spun around expecting to come face-to-face with a killer. She clutched her chest. "Darby, you just scared the life out of me."

"You didn't used to be so jumpy living here," her brother said as he stepped closer. "Now you're like a long-tailed cat in a room full of rockers." It was something her grandmother used to say when she'd caught them doing something they weren't supposed to do.

"What are you doing here?"

"What do you think?"

"Is something wrong?"

Darby laughed. "That would be my question, Lillie, and this time you aren't going to put me off. Let's step inside."

She'd asked Flint not to mention what had happened to her to her brothers. She hadn't been up to them visiting her at the hospital to lecture her. "You heard about my accident. Look, it's late. I'm really not up to—"

"He's back, isn't he?"

Her brother's words stopped her cold.

"What?" Her voice was barely a whisper.

"He's been here, hasn't he? That means you're jeopardizing your future as well as mine. Either you tell me—"

"Fine," she said, too exhausted by all of this to argue with him. She'd hated keeping this from him anyway. Also, she wasn't worried about him telling Flint, who already suspected Trask was back in town. "I'll tell you everything."

He eyed her in the ambient light coming from the security light out front as if trying to gauge if he could trust her.

"Darby," she said impatiently. "You can trust me."

"I have to wonder about that, little sis."

She pushed open the door and started to go upstairs, but her brother stopped her.

"Let's talk in the bar." He sounded so disappointed in her that she felt like crying. She knew it was a culmination of everything that had finally caught up with her.

TRASK DROVE BY the saloon and saw Flint drop Lillie off. He was going to circle around and come back when Darby showed up. As much as he wanted to see Lillie, he was glad Darby was there. At least she wasn't alone.

He'd done what she asked, stayed in the mountains as long as he could. The more he'd thought about everything, though, the more he'd known he couldn't keep hiding out.

They'd stirred things up and now the killer was running scared. Why else bomb the cabin? Run Lillie off the road in an attempt to scare her. Or kill her? Either way, there was no going back now. They must be getting close to the truth.

Now that he knew Lillie was safe, he drove by Skip Fairchild's house. If Johnny didn't kill Gordon and his father didn't, then that left the other partner.

Fairchild's sports car wasn't out front in the circular driveway. Nor did it appear to be in the three-car garage.

On impulse, Trask drove out to the construction site. The little red sports car was parked in front of the office.

He could see that a piece of plywood had been tacked over the window Johnny had shattered to make his break-in look real.

That he was still covering tracks for his thieving father was beyond Trask. But then again he'd never had a good relationship with his own father. Nor had his father taken that kind of interest in him.

Parking outside the mangled gate, he got out and slipped through the fence. He knew he was taking a chance confronting Skip Fairchild, but he'd already decided to turn himself in to Flint.

Lillie was determined to help him find the killer, and after what had happened earlier, he knew he had to do something to stop her.

At this time of day, Trask figured Fairchild wouldn't have bothered to lock the office door. He was right. When he turned the knob, the door swung in.

Fairchild sat behind his desk in his office. He glanced up, fear instantly tightening the features of his boyish face. He quickly reached for his phone.

"You might want to put that phone down," Trask said as he entered the office and pulled up a chair in front of Fairchild's desk. "I know about you and Brittany."

Fairchild's hand froze, the phone in it. "What are you talking about?"

"The little thing you have going on with mother—and daughter."

The man let out a laugh. "You don't know what you're talking about." But he slowly put the phone back in its cradle. "What do you want?"

"I need to know if you killed Gordon."

He let out a snort. "Of course not. Why would I?"

"For obvious reasons. You wanted his wife. And his daughter apparently."

He shook his head. "You have things so wrong. Caroline was divorcing Gordon. If I wanted her, I didn't have to kill her husband to get her."

"And Brittany?"

Skip took a deep breath as he looked toward the door before shifting his gaze back to Trask. "I don't know what you've found out, but I'm certainly not having an affair with Brittany. She's my *daughter*."

Trask stared at him. "What?"

The man laughed, clearly delighted to have surprised him. "Gordon's first wife, Clare…" He shrugged. "She quickly tired of Gordon as did his second wife."

"Did Gordon know about Brittany?"

Again Skip drew his gaze away. "He'd suspected that Brittany wasn't his, just Patrick, and that was enough to make Gordon bad tempered. Brittany was bright and beautiful. Patrick was, well, Patrick, weird and rather disturbing."

"So other than possibly Brittany's paternity, was

there another reason Gordon was leaving the construction company?"

Skip leaned back in his chair. "I'm sure you've already heard that J.T. was stealing money from the construction company?"

Trask nodded. "Gordon found out and was going to call the sheriff. It would have destroyed your business. You both had good reason to kill Gordon."

"True enough. He was a miserable human being. He made everyone around him unhappy, but the man knew how to make money," Fairchild said wistfully. "Sorry, but you're barking up the wrong tree. J.T. and I certainly aren't sorry Gordon is dead, but neither of us had what it would take to kill him. If anyone murdered Gordon, it was you." He reached for the phone and Trask stood.

"One more question, why didn't you turn J.T. in for embezzling the money?" he asked.

"Ever heard the expression you can't get money out of a turnip? I wanted to recoup what I could out of him." He shrugged. "But sometimes you have to cut your losses."

For the first time, he noticed the boxes half-packed around the office. Skip was closing up shop. "Call the sheriff. While you're at it, tell him about all your secrets, because if you don't, I will."

DARBY PULLED OUT a chair for Lillie at one of the tables in the center of the bar and, turning another chair, flipped it backward and straddled it. He leaned his elbows on the back and stared at her as she sat down across from him.

"How long has Trask been back?" he asked.

Her throat felt dry as dust. She swallowed. "How did you find out?"

He gave his head a slight shake and waited for her to answer his question.

"A few days."

"The day you said you saw the bear out back." He didn't wait for her to confirm it. "What does he want?"

"Want? He's come back to clear his name."

"Clear his name," Darby repeated.

"He didn't kill Gordon Quinn."

"And you know that, how?"

She could see where this was headed. "He didn't do it. Why would he come back knowing that he's a wanted man if he had done it?"

His voice remained conversational. But she knew he was furious with her. "What does he want with you?"

Lillie looked away. "He wants me back."

Her brother shook his head as he gave her a pitying look. "Lillie, don't you think I've seen the change in you. You're late for work. You always show up looking like you did when you'd been making out in the backseat of a car. You're often flushed, your eyes too bright. It's been a while, but I know the look. You've fallen for him again. What has he gotten you involved in this time?"

"It isn't like that. I love him. I'm helping him find Gordon's killer."

"Oh, Lillie," Darby said and swore. "You're scaring the hell out of me right now."

"Trask didn't do it." She felt tears leak out of the corners of her eyes. "If I call Flint, he'll find him, and if one of his fool deputies doesn't kill Trask, he'll lock him up."

Her brother shook his head. "You're exhausted from all this. You're not thinking clearly. If he's innocent, Flint will prove it. He is better equipped than you are. Surely you realize that."

Darby sounded so sensible, so reasonable, so grown-up. He pulled his cell phone from his pocket and then met her gaze.

"I'll do it," she said, her throat constricting with unshed tears as she took the phone from him. "I'm sorry I lied to you." After everything that had happened, she figured the safest place Trask could be right now was in jail.

Lillie dialed the number.

Flint answered on the second ring. "What's wrong?"

She rolled her eyes. She called him so little that when he saw it was from her he instantly thought something was wrong? She took a breath. "Trask is back in town."

Silence. Then Flint said, "I know. He's standing right in front of me."

It took her a moment to shake off her surprise.

"Then do your job. Arrest him." She disconnected and looked at Darby. "Trask had already turned himself in."

Her brother nodded and stood. "You should get some rest."

She couldn't imagine, even as exhausted as she was, how she would be able to sleep. She was in too much pain, both physical and emotional. What would happen to Trask now if the real killer wasn't caught?

"I'm staying down here tonight." She started to argue, but he stopped her. "I'm staying. Period. I'll get my stuff from my truck."

It hurt her physically to have her twin mad at her. They'd always been so close. "Please, I can't bear us not being best friends."

He looked at her in surprise. "Lillie, nothing could change that. I'm scared for you and sad. I know you love him. I was just worried how far you would go to be with him."

She said nothing around the lump in her throat.

FLINT HAD JUST gotten home when there was a knock at his door. He'd been half hoping it was Maggie. It wasn't. He'd opened the door and stared at Trask Beaumont, telling himself he shouldn't have been surprised, but he was. Just then Lillie had called.

After disconnecting from his sister, he looked at the young man who'd stolen her heart.

"I heard you've been looking for me," Trask said. "We need to talk."

Flint nodded slowly, his mind reeling as he stepped aside to let the man in. "I didn't kill Gordon. I came back to clear my name. Lillie—"

"I know she's been helping you. I suppose you wouldn't know anything about her pickup being run off the road yesterday."

"I was on the phone with her when it happened. That's why I'm here. I doubt you can stop Lillie any more than I can, so I suggest you find Gordon's killer and fast. Lillie's in danger."

Flint swore under his breath. "Whose fault is that?"

"Mine. Which is the reason I can't be behind bars right now. I have to keep your sister safe. I've hired a lawyer. I need to make bail right away."

"On a murder case?"

"If the sheriff has faith that I won't skip town…"

Flint studied the man his sister had fallen so desperately in love with. "How do I know you won't leave again?"

"Because I'm not that kid anymore. Also, I love your sister. I'm never leaving her again. And why would I turn myself in if I plan to run? I could have just stayed gone."

"Turning yourself in will go a long way with the judge," Flint said. "I'll do what I can for you, but the two of you have to stop your investigation."

"I hope you can convince Lillie of that."

Flint thought about how his sister was going to

take the news if he arrested Trask. If anything, she would be more determined to clear this cowboy.

"She isn't going to stop looking for Gordon's killer," Trask said. "I think you know that. It's getting more dangerous."

"She's going around town accusing people of murder and she didn't realize how badly this could go?"

"She loves me and I love her."

Flint groaned. "She wants me to arrest you. I think she's hoping you'll be safer in jail."

Trask shook his head. "You know I have a better chance of protecting her in this than you. You can't be with her 24/7. I can."

"You're the reason people are trying to kill her."

"That's why I have to be out. We're getting close to finding the killer."

"That's my job," Flint snapped.

Trask just looked at him.

"Johnny Burrows called earlier. He told me everything, including that he was the man Brittany saw leaving the stables that night—not you. So apparently she was mistaken."

"Or lying."

"Either way, I don't have enough evidence to arrest you."

LILLIE WATCHED HER twin disappear into the dark before she headed upstairs. She couldn't stand the disappointment in her brother's eyes. At least in her apartment she could be alone. She desperately wanted to talk to Trask. Tomorrow she would visit the jail. She would see about hiring him a good lawyer.

She felt bereft. Darby was right. She would have given up everything nine years ago and run away with Trask. Worse, she would have done it now if Trask had wanted to run again. What would she do now if he went to prison?

Pushing open her apartment door, she froze. For a moment she felt disoriented. She was sure she'd locked her door. Just as she was sure she'd left a light on. Had the power gone off?

She started to look behind her to see if the security light in the kitchen was on. She caught only a glimpse of the light glowing below her when she remembered that she hadn't used her key downstairs, either. The door had been open.

Terror coursed through her an instant before her arm was grabbed and she was jerked into her apartment. She caught a rank smell, heard movement both behind and in front of her.

A hand clamped over her mouth. An arm wrapped around her waist and she was slammed into a body that smelled both bad—and familiar.

"Make a peep and I'm gonna hurt ya," Emery Perkins said next to her ear.

"Your brother still down there?" Emery asked.

She managed to shake her head, suddenly terrified for Darby.

"You lyin' to me? Won't do ya no good. Vernon's down there. He'll take care a him if he don't leave."

She shook her head again and tried to cry out—
until she felt the cold biting blade of Emery's knife.
Her skin burned red-hot where he'd nicked her skin.

"Ya make another sound and I'll cut ya bad, ya
hear?"

There was nothing she could do. She just prayed
that Vernon didn't hurt Darby badly.

"Okay, now yer goin' to call Trask."

Lillie's mind raced. Trask had turned himself in to
Flint. They were probably on their way to the sheriff's office right now.

"Ya hear me?" he demanded.

She nodded.

He sighed as she heard heavy footfalls on the
steps. Vernon appeared in the ambient light from
downstairs.

"You take care of the problem?" Emery asked.

"He's sleeping like a baby."

Lillie felt a wave of relief that made her knees go
weak. At least Vernon hadn't killed Darby.

"I'm goin' to take my hand off yer mouth. Ya start
screamin' or ya lie to me and I'm goin' to hurt ya."

She gagged at the stench of him and wiped her
mouth the moment he removed his hand. "I don't
know where he is."

Emery swore. "Yer lyin'." He slapped her with his
free hand, making her cheek burn as if on fire and
her head snap back.

"I'm not."

"Betcha ya can call 'im. Don't pretend ya don't know his number."

"I need a phone."

"She's needs a phone," Emery said, mocking her. "Like you don't own a cell phone."

"I was in an accident yesterday. I lost my phone. I'll have to use the landline on the kitchen wall." She started to move toward the stairs when Emery stopped her.

"We'll all go."

Vernon had stepped into her still dark apartment. She heard him trip over something and begin to hop around from the sound of it, mewing like a kitten in his pain.

"Turn on the damned light," Emery snapped.

"Why don't you let me get it," she told Emery as she put a little distance between them to turn on the light. Vernon had stopped hopping on his good leg and was now holding his hurt knee.

Emery swore but motioned for her to start down the stairs. She quickly considered her options. Making a run for it wasn't one of them.

Going for her gun in her bedroom was also not an option. She could feel Emery watching her, waiting for her to try something. He was small and fast and mean.

She led the way downstairs to the small kitchen and started to reach for the phone when Emery snatched it out of her hands.

"Ya call him. I'll do the talkin'," he said, handing her back the phone.

Trask might already be in jail. She hoped that he was still at Flint's house. She dialed the number. Flint answered on the first ring.

"Lillie?" Flint asked.

"Trask, Emery—" Before she could finish, Emery grabbed the phone.

"Trask? I have somethin' ya might want," Emery said into the phone. "Think ya might want to renegotiate to get 'er back?"

She heard a sound behind her. A moment later, Vernon dropped a large burlap bag over her head. She hadn't been watching the other man. She screamed and tried to fight him off her. The blow to her head made everything go black.

TRASK GRIPPED THE phone as he listened to Emery's demands. Emery didn't really expect him to come up with that kind of money tonight, did he? His gaze was on Flint. The sheriff was watching him after motioning for him to take the extension. "If you hurt her—"

"Yer in no position to be makin' no demands. Ya just listen up. Meet us at the pond. Ya know which one. Come alone and bring the ten grand or yer girlfriend is goin' to pay in ways I know ya don't even want to think about." The line went dead.

"I take it you know the caller?" Flint demanded.

"Emery Perkins and a man named Vernon."

"I remember Emery." Flint swore. "I'll take care of this."

"I know these two. They'll hurt her just for the fun of it if they see you. You have to let me handle this."

The sheriff shook his head. "Lillie is my sister and I'm the damned sheriff."

Trask met his gaze and held it. "Lillie is the only woman I've ever loved. I will die for her if it comes to that." The two men stood staring at each other for a few moments.

"Then let's go," Flint said.

Clouds hung low over the city as Trask drove his pickup out of town. The sheriff sat in the passenger seat. Neither spoke, each no doubt praying as they fought to keep faith that Lillie would be all right, Trask thought.

"You shouldn't have run," Flint said, sounding angry.

"I know. But I was scared I'd get railroaded if I stayed. I knew how you felt about me." Flint looked over at him. "I thought you'd do anything to keep me away from your sister."

"I'm not that kind of sheriff. But I'll admit I wasn't sure you were the right man for her. I might have been blinded by that."

Trask nodded without looking at him. "I wasn't the right man for her back then. I am now."

"We'll see."

The pond was on an old homestead five miles out of town. He and Emery had swum in it a few times on hot summer days. It was surrounded by pine trees and just far enough off the road that it was isolated.

Trask slowed to a stop as he reached the turnoff. "Let me go in and see what the situation is. I'll take care of it, if I can. Give me time."

Flint nodded and opened his door. They could see the pine trees around the pond in the distance. "Be careful."

"You too."

Flint closed the door. Trask took a breath and drove toward the pond. He hadn't gone far when his headlights flickered over the dark pines, picking up the dusty gleam of an old van's taillights.

Emery had parked in the trees, where it was impossible to see who was in the van.

Trask brought the truck to a stop a good distance from the van, shut off the engine and lights, and sat for a moment to let his eyes adjust to the darkness. Also to calm down. He needed to be cool. He couldn't let Emery get to him. Mostly, he couldn't be the old Trask who went into things with his head down at full speed like a damned bull.

Moonlight painted a silver path across the pond but quickly disappeared as the clouds shrouded it again. He saw nothing move along the shore. Heard nothing beyond the pounding of his heart. Emery had Lillie and Emery couldn't be trusted.

Trask opened his pickup door, wondering where Flint was now as he got out. He closed the door with a soft click.

"Emery?"

No answer.

He called a little louder, still using the pickup as a shield. Emery wanted money, but he also wanted revenge for every injustice he felt someone owed him. That someone right now was Trask.

Still no answer. He had no choice. Walking slowly, he moved toward the trees and the van sitting silently in them.

"Lillie?" he called, just as afraid she wouldn't answer.

He heard a sound like a groan and felt his blood quicken. If Emery hurt her… Trask moved with more purpose. If Emery wanted a fight, he was about to get one. But not until Lillie was safe.

He'd almost reached the van when he saw something on the ground on the other side of the van. He could make out what looked like boots and part of a leg.

For a moment, his heart seemed to stop. His breath caught in his throat and his feet refused to move.

He heard movement on the other side of the van. Stepping quickly, he reached the van, keeping low as he edged along the side to the back.

He recognized the boots first. Emery's and then Vernon's. Both were still attached to their feet. Neither man moved. In a sudden splash of moonlight from between the clouds, he saw the blood and dark neat cuts at their throats.

He heard the shuffle of boots in the grass near

the front of the van. Bending down, he looked under the vehicle, but it was too dark to see anything more than shadows.

Rising, he moved toward the front and stopped. "Let me see, Lillie, or I'm out of here."

The laugh he heard froze his blood even before Patrick Quinn stepped from the side of the van. He held a bloody knife to Lillie's throat.

LILLIE TOOK SHALLOW breaths and tried not to panic. She'd awakened when they'd jostled her into the back of the van. The weave of the burlap bag wasn't enough to keep out light. She sat up enough to look out the back window of the van and see headlights behind them.

Her thoughts had rushed past like a freight train on a runaway track. When they arrived at the pond, Emery had said he was going for a swim while they waited.

"Get her out, but make sure she doesn't run off," Emery said as he climbed out from behind the wheel and started toward the open water of the pond.

Vernon opened his door and, taking her arm, pulled her from the van and tugged off the burlap bag. They both looked after Emery, who'd stripped down. He waded out into the pond, the water silvery gray in the cloudy night. There was a splash and a few moments later he came out.

Emery pulled on his jeans and boots and walked

bare-chested back toward them. "We should have some fun while we're waitin', don't ya think?"

She'd heard a vehicle engine in the distance earlier when Emery had been in the water. Then she'd thought she'd heard a twig snap nearby. Once they'd turned onto the pond road, the headlights she'd seen behind them had disappeared.

She'd given up hope. But at Emery's words a cold horror filled her. She'd fight him to the death before she'd let him rape her.

He started toward them when a figure materialized out of the darkness.

The attack had happened so quickly that Emery hadn't seen it coming. The figure grabbed Emery and cut his throat in one quick motion as if it was something the killer did every day.

Blood gushed from the cut and ran down his chest. His eyes widened in alarm and shock, but he'd been unable to do a thing but fall to his knees, then keel over face-first into the dirt and dried pine needles.

The figure then turned toward her and Vernon, and in a slice of moonlight, Lillie saw his blond hair under the dark hood. She hadn't realized that she'd been holding her breath until she'd heard the whoosh of air escape her mouth.

Vernon took a step back, bumping against her as he'd tried to run. But he hadn't gone but a few steps when the man leaped onto his back and drove the knife blade into Vernon's neck.

Lillie finally found her feet and stumbled back a

step, then another toward the pond, her mind screaming *run*, but her legs felt like deep stumps beneath
her.

She hadn't gone but a few yards when Brittany
stepped out, the moonlight gleaming off the shotgun in her hands. "Go ahead and run. Wanna bet
I'll shoot you?"

Before Lillie could react, Patrick tackled her from
behind and put the knife to her throat. Realization
had sunk in slowly because few people could imagine a sixteen-year-old and an eleven-year-old mur-
dering anyone—let alone a parent.

"Why did you do it?" Lillie cried. "He was your
father."

Patrick laughed. "That was enough reason. We
used to watch him beat our mother until she couldn't
take it anymore and left. She wanted to take us with
her, but he wasn't having any of that."

"Stop," Brittany ordered. "It's none of her business."

Her brother shrugged. "It isn't like she's going to
tell anyone. She'll be dead."

"Still."

Lillie felt their shame. The story she'd heard was
that their mother had died before they moved to
town, before Gordon married Caroline.

"But why that day?" Lillie pushed. She was stalling for time—not that it would do any good. Trask
thought she'd been taken by Emery and Vernon. She
was on her own with two psychopaths, one with a

bloody knife and the other with a shotgun. Lillie could see no way this would have a happy ending.

She thought of Trask. They deserved a second chance. They'd already been through so much. Didn't they deserve to be together?

"Your boyfriend made it too easy," Brittany said, as if needing to finally tell someone. "We overheard the argument. When Trask hit him and knocked him down, it was all we could do not to cheer."

"But he got up and was worse than even before," Patrick said. "We knew he would kill our horse before the night was over."

"So you killed him first." It made a kind of sense that two kids from an abusive home would understand.

"It wasn't that easy," Brittany said. "I thought one good blow with a shovel, but it only dazed him. He took it away from me, swung at my head, then tossed it aside. He would have killed me, but I managed to duck out of the way and grab the shovel up again. He was going after Patrick. I swung the shovel, harder this time, and caught him in the back of the head. He went down and Patrick grabbed the pitchfork and finished him off."

Lillie felt sick. "Why didn't you tell the sheriff that? You were just trying to protect yourselves."

Brittany laughed. "You seem to have forgotten the part where I hit him first with the shovel."

"You were afraid of him. Your mother would have testified that he was dangerous. You wouldn't have gone to jail," Lillie said, as if she could re-write history.

"And the whole world would have known about our family," Brittany said with a shake of her head. "I'd think you of all people would know what it's like to have that kind of shame attached to your name. Your father thinks he was abducted by aliens."

"My father was," Lillie said stubbornly and re-membered she still had a knife to her throat.

Brittany and Patrick both laughed.

"Still," Brittany said, "it's not the same. People look at us funny. They want to know if he beat us or, worse, if he molested us. They think just because he's a bully he's probably a pervert. Even if we tell them he never tried anything with us, they don't believe us. Even if they believe that our father is abusive, they don't do anything but give us a card and tell us to call the next time we need help, and then they have a talk with our father." She wagged her head. "You think that won't get me the beating of my life? So we rip up the card and keep our mouths shut."

Lillie heard the pain in her voice. Brittany had cried out for help only for the system to make her situation worse. "How old were you when you first tried to get help?"

"Ten," Patrick said. "I was five." He pulled the pressure of the knife away from her throat to rub his arm for a second. She saw the long gash of an old scar and felt sick to her stomach.

"You won't get away with killing me," Lillie said.

"Of course we will," Patrick said. "We got away with killing our father."

"You should have stayed out of it," Brittany said. "But you believed your lover and look where it's gotten you. Everyone will believe that he killed you along with your friends."

That's when they heard Trask's pickup coming up the road.

Now Lillie watched heartbroken as Trask walked toward her. He'd come out there thinking he would be dealing with two blackmailers, not two cold-blooded killers.

TRASK FELT HIS insides turn to mush. Patrick had the knife to her throat. But what was even more terrifying was the smile on his face and the look in his eye. The bloodlust hadn't been satisfied by killing Emery and Vernon. Trask could tell that Patrick couldn't wait to feel the knife slice across Lillie's throat. To feel the hot gush of blood run onto his hand. To smell death.

He'd been eleven when his father had been murdered in the stables—run through with a pitchfork. No one had suspected him, not an angelic strong boy with watery-green eyes. If anything, they felt sorry for him and his sister. Brittany was sixteen the night Gordon died. A wisp of a girl, pretty, but definitely not sweet, Trask knew from experience.

Still he hadn't thought either of them was capable of murder. His mistake.

"Let Lillie go. Your argument is with me."

Brittany laughed. "You think this is about you turning me down for a date? Really, Trask, get over yourself."

"I think you framed me for murder and now you plan to kill me before the truth comes out," Trask said.

"You shouldn't have come back," Patrick said in a singsong voice that sent a chill creeping up Trask's spine.

"I keep hearing that." He was surprised how calm, how rational he sounded when all he could think about was getting Lillie away from that madman.

"Caroline told us that Lillie was asking all kinds of questions about that night, including where the two of us were," Patrick said. "With you gone, everyone had forgotten about our father's death."

"Not everyone," Trask said. "I hadn't forgotten and I doubt the sheriff had."

"You coming back here stirring things up is a problem," Patrick continued as if Trask hadn't spoken. "Now we have to take care of the mess you made." He didn't sound that sorry about killing people.

"You won't get away with this," Trask said.

"Why do people say that?" Brittany demanded. "We've gotten away with it for nine years. No one suspected us, the unfortunate children of Gordon Quinn, the most reviled man in the county. No one would have cared if you had left well enough alone.

Now your friends are dead." She tsked. "All your fault."

"They weren't my friends," Trask said.

"Well, they're dead and you and Lillie are going to join them."

"So you can both spend the rest of your lives in prison?" he asked, stalling for an opening. As long as Patrick had a knife to Lillie's throat, there was nothing he could do. Patrick would love nothing better than for him to make a move.

"Prison?" Brittany laughed again. "We'll be heroes. Imagine the publicity we'll get for finding all of you dead out here. First you killed your friends. I would imagine they called you to come out here, so the call will be on your phone. From what I gathered, they were blackmailing you, using your girlfriend as bait. You kill them, but now you have a problem. Lillie, sweet girl that she is, is shocked and horrified by what you've done. She tries to get away, but you chase her down and cut her throat, as well. We show up and fortunately I have a gun."

Brittany leveled the shotgun at him. "I shoot you, but not before you've killed three people. It was so gruesome," she said, sounding close to tears, as if before a television camera. She brightened. "I'm just bummed that we couldn't have gotten here sooner and at least saved Lillie. Poor Lillie. I would imagine your brothers will hold some kind of reception for you at your crummy bar. Right now I'm dating

Junior Wainwright, but when I'm through with him, I'm going after Darby. I figure he's easy pickings."

Trask saw Lillie's eyes flash with anger and terror. He shot her a look to stay calm as he wondered again where Flint was. Like him, the sheriff didn't dare make a move. He hated to think that if he hadn't gone to the sheriff, these two might have pulled off their plan. Now he had to give himself and Flint both an opening.

"Not a bad plan, Brittany. I'm assuming it was yours," he said. "Unfortunately, Lillie doesn't look like she made a run for it," he pointed out as he saw Patrick getting itchy to cut her throat.

"Good point," Brittany acknowledged with a nod of her head. "Let her go, Patrick. You should be able to catch her without any trouble. Let her run toward the lake. You can kill her when you catch her."

At first Trask thought Patrick was going to argue, but then he laughed, apparently realizing that the idea appealed to him. Trask gave Lillie a nod. Her gray eyes were wide in the moonlight, but he saw determination in them.

"Run, Lillie!" Trask said, giving her a knowing look.

Patrick laughed. "Good luck, Lillie." He released her, giving her a shove toward the pond.

"Run, Lillie!" Trask cried. *"Run!"*

She did. Patrick gave her a head start, sporting young man that he was. Then he took off after her in the moonlight.

Trask prayed the sheriff had heard all of that and was ready. Brittany held the shotgun on him, but she didn't want to miss the fun, so she was watching her brother out of the corner of her eye. He knew she wasn't inattentive. He had to time this right or...

Patrick seemed to stumble after a half-dozen yards, as if one of his legs had gone out from under him. He heard Patrick swear. Lillie was faster than Patrick had thought and it was dark.

The sound of the gunshot startled them all, even Trask, who'd been praying for it. The first shot made Patrick stumble again. The second sent him sprawling. He fell awkwardly, the knife still in his hand. He let out an animal cry as he fell on the blade.

Brittany screamed and instinctively took a step toward her brother. Trask made his move, closing the space between them and grabbing the shotgun. She was strong. He'd heard that crazy people were often abnormally strong. She fought hard, but he was bigger, stronger and even more determined. He finally tore the gun from her fingers.

She rushed at him, all nails and wild eyes, and he dropped her with one punch.

WHEN LILLIE HEARD the gunshots, she stopped running to cry out, thinking that Brittany had shot Trask. She spun around, terrified she would see Brittany standing over Trask lying dead on the ground. Terrified that Patrick would be right behind her with the knife.

What she saw shocked her. She looked back in confusion. Trask had taken the shotgun from Brittany and was standing over her on the ground. Her brother Flint was leaning over Patrick, who was screaming in pain on the ground only yards behind her. She saw at once that if her brother hadn't shot him, he would have caught her, he would have...

She shuddered and stumbled toward her brother, never so happy to see anyone. He finished handcuffing Patrick, gave her a quick hug and hurried over to slip restraints on Brittany.

"You're all going to regret this," Brittany screamed as she rubbed her jaw. "I'll sue. I'll have your jobs, your bar. I'll have your ass. You have no idea who I am. My father—"

"Skip Fairchild isn't going to help you," Trask said. "You did him a favor by killing Gordon, but do you really think he will ever admit it? He'll deny he's related to you. He'll distance himself from you. I was just at his office earlier. He was cleaning it out. He's skipping town, so to speak. Like you, he's afraid a lot of truths will come out. Want to bet you'll never see him again? If you try to implicate him, it will be your word against his."

Brittany glared at him in the moonlight. He saw the change in her features, from fury to coy in an instant. "You should have gone out with me. Now you'll never know what you missed."

Trask shook his head as he stepped to Lillie and took her in his arms.

TRASK TOLD HIMSELF that it was over, and yet he wasn't about to let Lillie out of his sight. After the coroner and several deputies arrived, Flint took Lillie's statement and told them they could go home.

Home. He loved the sound of that. With Lillie curled against him in the front seat of his pickup, he drove her to the home she'd made for herself. Once inside the apartment, she stepped into his arms.

"Just hold me, Trask," she whispered against his chest.

He held her, kissing the top of her head as she clung to him.

"I never thought it would be Brittany and Patrick," she said, sounding close to tears. "They were so young. How could they do something like that?"

He didn't know. When he closed his eyes, he could still see the excitement on their faces, the bloodlust. It terrified him to think how close he'd come to losing Lillie. He understood how angry she'd been with him the night at the construction company office.

The bond between them was so strong, always had been, even when they'd been apart. She'd waited for him. Not just that night sitting on the back stoop of the Stagecoach Saloon, but all nine years. She'd known he'd come back for her. He held her tighter, choked up with gratitude that she was alive and in his arms.

After a while, he stripped off her soiled clothing and his own and led her into the shower. Under the warm spray, he gently soaped her beautiful body, careful to avoid the bruised and bandaged areas. Rinsing them both off, he wrapped her in a towel and carried her to the bed.

"You saved my life," she whispered as she met his gaze.

He chuckled, smiling down at her. "You saved mine years ago when you fell in love with me." He leaned down to gently kiss her.

Her lips turned up in a smile beneath his. "You came home."

"Yes, I came home. To you. And I'm never going to leave you again."

Exhaustion tugged at her eyelids. He lay down next to her, pulling her into the curve of his body. She snuggled against him with a sigh as she let go of the nightmare events and fell asleep in his arms.

As Lillie walked in the back door of the Stagecoach Saloon before noon the next day, a wave of nostalgia washed over her. She stopped to take in the familiar rich scents coming from the stove. Billie Dee was singing about yellow roses and Texas. Past her, the gentle clink of bar glasses seemed to pick up the beat of the country song playing on the jukebox in the other part of the building.

She could hear the murmured voices of the regulars already cozied up to the bar.

"Made my famous chili," Billie Dee said when she saw Lillie standing there taking it all in. "You want a bowl?" She blinked and seemed to focus more intently on her and the small bandage covering the cut in her neck. "You're looking a mite peaked. Feeling okay?"

Lillie nodded and managed a smile as she fought tears. She'd come so close to losing this. To losing everything she loved.

"I am," she said, realizing that she'd never felt more alive. That was what almost being killed did to you. The day seemed brighter, every emotion felt more powerful, every breath a gift. That morning she'd awakened in Trask's arms, the only place she'd ever wanted to be.

They'd made love, slowly as if they had all the time in the world. They did, she thought.

"I need to take care of some business, but I'll be back soon," he'd said as he dressed. "Are you going to be all right until I come back?"

She'd stretched, breathing in the morning air coming in the window, feeling the sunshine warming the bedroom, and smiled. "Hurry back."

Trask had laughed and come to the bed to kiss her. "I'd say goodbye, but I'm never going to say that to you again. See you soon."

"I might have some later, thanks," Lillie said to Billie Dee now, smiling to herself at the memory of her and Trask this morning as she moved through the building she and her brother had saved.

Darby was behind the bar. He looked up when she walked in. His expression made it hard to hold back the tears that welled in her eyes.

Without a word, he stepped around the bar to pull her into his arms. He held her so tightly for a moment that she could hardly breathe. She laid her head against his shoulder and said, "I'm all right."

"You sure are," he said, his voice thick with emotion.

"What about you?" she asked, pulling back to look at her brother. "How is your head?"

"Fine," he said, smiling. "You know how hard-headed I am. I'm just glad it's over and you're safe."

"Buy that woman a drink," someone called from down the bar.

It didn't surprise her that everyone had heard about what had happened last night. Word traveled fast in a small town.

She smiled and pulled back from her brother's hug to look at the loyal regulars at the bar. They'd been coming since the Stagecoach Saloon had opened and had always been supportive of whatever was going on at the bar. Lillie didn't think she'd appreciated them enough before now. Almost dying seemed to bring everything into sharp focus. She'd never take any of this for granted again.

"Just coffee," she said as her brother stepped back behind the bar to pour her a cup. She climbed up onto a stool next to a local rancher. He patted her arm and then quickly changed the subject to the weather. This was Montana, where the weather mattered.

Darby set the cup of coffee in front of her. He still looked worried about her. She gave him what she hoped was a reassuring smile before she took a sip. It tasted amazing.

In the kitchen, Billie Dee began to sing "Amazing Grace" as Cyrus and Hawk came rushing into the bar and headed straight for Lillie. Apparently, they'd just heard the news. From their expressions, they didn't like being the last to hear. But it was the concern in their faces that made her eyes blur with tears.

"Easy," Darby said as the two brothers began to fire questions at her. "You'll hear all about it. Just give her a little breathing room."

Hawk, once he was sure she wasn't injured, dragged Lillie off the bar stool, the two sandwiching her in a bear hug.

"I said let her breathe," Darby ordered, only half joking as he put two draft beers on the bar for them.

Lillie appreciated their show of affection. Neither of them was good at expressing emotions, especially love, but it was clear how much they cared. She'd never doubted their love. But had never felt how deeply it ran until now.

Past them, she saw her father. Ely had stopped just inside the door. She'd never seen him so emotional as he walked toward her. Like Darby, he said nothing as he pulled her to him. He hugged her for a long time, until someone at the end of the bar insisted on buying them all a drink.

"It's a little early for me," Ely joked as he let go of her and took a stool. Everyone laughed. "Make it whiskey. Straight up. I think we need to celebrate."

The bar had that kind of feel today.

"Where's Trask?" Darby asked.

"He'll be back." She met her brother's eyes. "He saved my life."

Her brother nodded. "Flint told me."

"Where is Flint?" Hawk asked. "He should be here."

"I would imagine he has his hands full down at the sheriff's office," Darby said.

"We should have a picnic," Ely announced, holding up his shot glass of whiskey. "A picnic to celebrate before I go back up into the mountains."

Lillie and Darby shared a look. "A picnic sounds like a great idea," her brother said. Lillie agreed.

Kendall came in then, as always early for her bartending shift. "Lillie, I just heard." She rushed to her to give her a hug. "I'm so glad you're all right."

Lillie nodded. "Thank you."

Darby cleared his throat and looked at his watch as if he thought Lillie needed her space.

"I better get ready for my shift," Kendall said, shooting Darby a grin.

Lillie noticed the way her brother's gaze followed the young woman.

"Something going on with you and Kendall?" Lillie asked quietly of her brother.

Darby chuckled. "Nope, just thinking about who I have on the schedule to work the Chokecherry Festival."

"Darby—"

"Stop trying to marry me off, little sis. If I ever meet a woman who makes me hear wedding bells, I'll let you know."

The front door opened. Everyone turned as Trask Beaumont stepped in.

TRASK DIDN'T KNOW what kind of reception he would get as he pushed open the Stagecoach Saloon door. He stopped just inside.

Everyone turned, but it was Darby who came around from behind the bar to walk toward him. Trask wouldn't have been surprised if Lillie's twin punched him. He knew he had it coming. He'd hurt her. He'd almost gotten her killed.

But it wasn't the man's fist he held out. It was his hand. "Welcome back," Darby said, and Trask shook his hand. He saw her other brothers slide off their stools and head toward him and braced himself.

But to his surprise, they too were welcoming, if though a little grudgingly. Trask knew he'd have to prove himself to Lillie's brothers. He was good with that. He'd come back to make up for the past. He'd spend the rest of his life doing whatever it took to make Lillie happy.

The Cahill brothers parted and Lillie stepped to him. He wrapped his arms around her, breathing in her scent as he buried his face in the side of her neck.

"I think this calls for drinks on the house," Darby announced, and everyone but the two of them moved back to the bar.

"I hate to steal you away from here, but there's something I need to show you," Trask said. "I promise we won't be long."

Lillie cupped his jaw with her palm, looking at him as if memorizing the angles of his face. "I thought I'd never see you again. That feeling was worse than the thought of dying."

"I know. But we're together now and no one is going to come between us if they know what is good for them."

She laughed. He could tell it felt good. It certainly sounded good to hear.

"We'll be back in a minute," she called to her brothers.

Darby still looked worried but seemed to be trying to hide it. Trask knew that he worried about what would happen next. Her brothers had little faith in him sticking to anything. He'd have to show them what kind of man he'd become thanks to their sister.

He'd come back. He'd cleared his name with her help. But now what?

It was the question that seemed to chase them out of the bar.

Trask's pickup was parked outside. He opened the passenger-side door and she slid in. As he climbed behind the wheel, he said, "It's a short drive."

The spring day sparkled like the rare jewel it was. Before long a squall would blow through, bringing rain, possibly even hail and often wind that whipped the pines and kicked up dust for miles.

But right now, it was beautiful, a day that promised new beginnings.

LILLIE LOOKED OVER at Trask as he drove. For so long there had been tension in the lines of his face. Now, though, a peacefulness had taken over his features, softening the hard lines, making him even more handsome.

They hadn't gone far when Trask pulled over to the side of the dirt road. "What I have to show you is a surprise." He pulled out a bandanna from the glove box. "I'm going to have to blindfold you."

Lillie smiled over at him. "What are you up to, Mr. Beaumont?"

"You'll see." He tied the bandanna around her eyes, making sure it was tight enough but not too tight. "No peeking." He shifted the pickup into gear. "The smartest thing I ever did was fall in love with you. If it wasn't for you, well, I might be in prison right now."

The pickup bumped along the road, made a few turns. Lillie lost track, too excited to concentrate on where exactly they were going. She could feel Trask's excitement, as well. Whatever the surprise, it was something he'd planned for some time.

"Can I see now?"

"Not yet. You have no patience."

"I never had. You should know that."

He chuckled as he braked and brought the pickup to a stop, climbed out and opened her door. She felt his hand on her arm. He pulled her out of the pickup and into his embrace. "Okay, you can take it off now."

With trembling fingers, Lillie reached up and pulled down the bandanna. She stared in surprise at the ranch house on the side of the mountain. "Trask?" she asked in a whisper.

"I bought the old Chandler place. The house isn't much, but we can build the house of our dreams over on that hill."

She couldn't take it all in. "You bought a *ranch*?"

"Lock, stock and barrel. It's all ours under the company L.T. Enterprises."

"L.T.?"

"Lillie and Trask. I told you I worked hard those nine years, saved every penny I could. I dreamed of coming back to you, but not as the saddle tramp who'd left here. I wanted to make you proud. I thought we'd start by running a few hundred head of cattle. I know you'll still want to work at the Stagecoach Saloon with your brother, but I was hoping down the road some maybe we could have a baby or two or three?"

She looked over at him, tears blurring her vision. "Oh, Trask." Her voice broke.

"I couldn't tell you about the ranch until I knew I wasn't headed for prison. I know you love your apartment. Tell me you wouldn't mind living here with me and making a family of our own."

"Mind?" She laughed. "Oh, Trask" was all she could get out without crying. She threw her arms around his neck and kissed him.

"There is one more thing," he said as he held her at arm's length for a moment before he got down on one knee, reached into his pocket and pulled out a small velvet box.

Her eyes widened as she looked at him, at the box, back at him.

"I told you that nine years ago I was putting money down on an engagement ring for you?"

She nodded, unable to speak.

"Well, John T. Marshall down at the jewelry store let me keep paying on it. Marry me?"

Lillie couldn't believe this was happening. For so long she thought Trask was lost to her. Even when he returned, she didn't see how they could ever have a happy ending.

"Be my bride?" he asked again, looking a little worried.

Married. They were going to be married.

Tears filled her eyes. She made a swipe at them as she smiled and nodded vigorously, her heart lodged too securely in her throat to speak.

Trask slipped the ring on her finger. She stared at the large diamond. "Is this—"

"The ring I had on layaway for ten years?" he asked with a laugh. "It seemed right somehow, though I remember the diamond being much smaller. I think Mr. Marshall gave us an upgrade."

Lillie laughed and burst into tears as he rose and took her in his arms. "I love you and I don't want to spend another day without you. I suppose you want a big wedding."

She laughed. "You know me better than that. You're all I want or need. But if you don't invite my brothers, there could be hell to pay."

"We don't want that," he agreed as he kissed her.

"I'll call them. Mind if we get married at the stagecoach stop?"

"I'd love it." Trask kissed her.

Lillie melted into his kiss, telling herself there would be a million kisses more in their future. "Oh, there is something I probably should mention," she said when the kiss ended. "How do you feel about starting that family sooner rather than later?"

His eyes widened. "Lillie, you're—"

"Not yet, but with a little luck, soon."

CHAPTER TWENTY

FLINT BEGAN WORKING late at night to avoid going home to his empty house. Since the breakup with Maggie, the place felt hollow. His footsteps seemed to echo as if mocking the loneliness he denied.

He told himself he'd been fine before Maggie. He would be fine again. But he felt as if he hadn't known what he'd been missing before Maggie.

Sometimes he would think he heard her laugh at the grocery store and he'd follow it only to be disappointed when it wasn't her. When the laugh was wrong, when he realized that no one but Maggie could put the right lightness into it.

He missed her smile and her easy manner. He missed kissing her. Holding her. Talking with her.

Amazingly, their paths hadn't crossed even in such a small town. Unfortunately, he'd run into Celeste more than a few times.

She'd attempted conversation, but he'd walked on past as if he hadn't seen her, hadn't heard her call his name, hadn't seen the mixture of sympathy and gloating on her face.

He'd given Celeste the benefit of the doubt for

so many years, it had become natural. He'd had a hard time believing that Celeste gave anything—especially him—that much thought that she would plot against him.

But Maggie believed it. The picture she'd painted of Celeste… He still shuddered at the thought the woman could be that evil. That manipulating. That hateful.

Maggie didn't know the woman he'd fallen in love with, married and had lost. She didn't understand Celeste the way he did. If things had been different, Celeste would now be the mother of their children.

The problem was that Maggie wasn't the jealous type. She wasn't mean or judgmental or controlling.

That was why what she said about Celeste refused to go away. Celeste was spoiled. She was demanding. She was difficult. But psychotic? Dangerous?

He shook his head. Not the woman he'd once promised to love until death did they part.

But in the back of his mind, he couldn't help worrying what Celeste would do if he and Maggie got back together. If they got serious enough to marry. So he concentrated on work. He'd been hearing little things about Anvil Holloway.

I saw Anvil buying jeans at the clothing store the other day. Jeans, a woman told him. *A man who we haven't seen wearing anything but overalls for years, his wife disappears and he starts wearing jeans?* The woman lifted a brow. *You really should look into that, Sheriff.*

Another saw him in town and he was smiling. *Smiling!*

Then Deirdre from the library called to say Anvil had signed up for the beginning computer class she was teaching. *I know you asked about his wife and computers. Just thought I'd let you know.*

Flint knew it wasn't going to do an ounce of good, but he drove out to the Holloway farm. He found Anvil painting his porch. For a moment, he sat in his patrol SUV, merely watching the man paint. Nothing wrong with a man fixing up his place, he told himself. Nothing wrong with him wearing jeans, smiling or taking computer classes. Nothing wrong with him moving on.

He climbed out of his rig. Anvil kept painting. The farmer didn't ask if Flint had any news of his wife. They both knew that wasn't going to happen.

"Still no word from Jenna?" the sheriff had to ask anyway.

Anvil kept painting for a few moments and then put down his brush and turned toward him. "I know this is going to sound crazy," the farmer said. "But didn't your father see something strange out by that missile silo on your ranch the night Jenna left?"

Flint groaned inwardly. "Jenna wasn't abducted by aliens. Anvil, I'm sure she's a lot closer than some distant planet in the solar system."

Anvil glanced toward the sky. "Who knows where she is by now."

Flint shook his head. His father's story about the aliens returning had started it all up again.

Anvil went back to his painting. Flint watched him for a few minutes. The one thing he figured they both knew was that they'd never be seeing Jenna Holloway alive again.

Law enforcement had taught him a lot about people. He'd gone in believing in good and evil, but he now knew there were shades of gray. In those shadows, good people did bad things for often understandable reasons. Gordon Quinn was a mean man who beat horses with two-by-fours. A man despised by everyone around him including his own son and the daughter he suspected wasn't his. He was a cruel man who'd met a cruel end.

Anvil was a simple farmer who worked the earth to feed his family. Jenna Holloway hurt him badly with her lying, stealing and finally cheating. But the last straw was when she told him that she'd never loved him and could walk away without the least bit of remorse.

Because of that, there were now murderers among them. Their acts blurred the lines of justice. The law was simple. The crimes not so much.

"I might never know where your wife is," Flint said quietly as he looked out at the land that stretched to the Snowy Mountains. Anvil stopped painting to look at him. He met the man's gaze. "But that's the thing about dead bodies and secrets. They're hard to keep buried."

Anvil's expression didn't change, but there was a faraway look in his eyes. Flint wondered if he was reliving the night Jenna disappeared or if he'd buried it along with her body.

Settling his Stetson on his head, he walked away from the newly painted porch to his patrol SUV. The sun was high in a sky devoid of clouds. Summer was coming and he was betting it would be a hot one.

MAGGIE'S DAYS BLENDED together in a blur of perms, cuts, dyes and highlights. She smiled, she chuckled, she commiserated, treading through her days like a sleepwalker.

At night when her hands were no longer busy, she let the regrets in, along with the sorrow for what could have been and, ultimately, the ache in her heart that had made her cry herself to sleep more often than she wanted to admit.

Maggie licked her wounds, held her head up high and went on. She did her best to avoid Flint. It was Celeste she didn't dare run into until she'd cooled down. She feared she would strangle the woman with her bare hands if they crossed paths.

The more time she'd had to think about it, the more convinced she was that Celeste had gotten herself beat up that night to ruin Maggie and Flint's date. She knew that sounded crazy.

Just as she knew that when her path crossed with Celeste's, the woman would give her that pitying look, all the time grinning because she'd won. How could Flint not see the pleasure the woman took in hurting him? In hurting Maggie.

But Maggie wasn't one to wallow in misery, so with the light of day, she bucked up. She wasn't about to let anyone know how badly she hurt.

She'd promised herself that the next time she ran into Celeste, she would be nice to her, no matter what the woman said or did. It wouldn't change things between her and Flint. She hadn't heard from him since that night she'd broken up with him.

But he'd been busy. The town was aflutter with the news about Patrick and Brittany. Flint had saved his sister's life with the help of Trask Beaumont. It didn't surprise her that both were being called heroes.

She'd heard from one of her clients that Trask and Lillie were engaged and that Trask had bought the old Chandler ranch and was planning on raising cattle. She couldn't have been more happy for them. She knew Flint must be pleased. She'd almost picked up the phone to call him. Almost.

As one day led into another, she'd been tempted to call Flint, apologize, but she'd had back-to-back appointments and hardly a break. At least that's what she told herself. The truth was she couldn't help thinking that maybe it was for the best that she and Flint weren't together right now.

She wasn't proud of the way she'd acted after their second big date was canceled. She *had* been jealous of Celeste. She'd been scared the woman would come between her and Flint—and Maggie had let her. She didn't know how to fix things, but she was willing to give it some time.

As she stepped out of the shop, she noticed that the clothing store was still open. Maybe if she hurried…

She'd just stepped in when she saw Celeste. Her first instinct was to turn around and leave. But unfortunately the woman had seen her.

"Maggie." Celeste had used makeup to cover her bruises, but it was clear she'd had a black eye and a cut lip not all that long ago. Also, she was moving as if her ribs hurt. Had she really fallen down the stairs? Or had Wayne Duma hurt her? Maggie figured they might never know.

Whatever Celeste's ailments, none of them stopped her, though, as she made her way to Maggie. "I'm so glad to see you. I owe you an apology."

That was the last thing Maggie wanted. "No, I'm—"

"I feel so terrible. Flint told me about your breakup."

She cursed inwardly. Flint had told Celeste about their breakup?

Had he gone right to Celeste the night after their argument? Maggie fought not to show her surprise or hurt, but of course the woman saw it. A smile curved her still rather fat lip.

"I'm so sorry. I feel responsible. I've been so demanding of Flint's time lately."

Maggie felt herself frown and say, "I'm sorry, I'm not sure what you're talking about."

That stopped Celeste. She didn't look so much like the cat who ate the canary and enjoyed every bite. "You and Flint. He told me that he wouldn't be seeing you again."

"Really?" She smiled. "You must have misunderstood him." The lie slipped out so easily, Maggie felt her Catholic upbringing practically smack her with a nun's ruler. "In fact…" Seeing how much pleasure her breakup with Flint gave the woman, she tried to stop herself, but couldn't. "I'm here looking for something special to wear for our next date."

This was definitely not what Celeste wanted to hear. Her expression was priceless. She looked like someone had taken away her sucker. The threat of eternal damnation couldn't stop Maggie now. "Actually, we've decided to take our relationship to the next step."

Celeste appeared too shocked to speak. "But I thought…"

Maggie laughed as if they were two girlfriends sharing a joke in the dress shop. She had stooped to Celeste's level and was mortified by what she'd done. Celeste would have the last laugh when she found out the truth.

Celeste recovered quickly. "I should let you get ready for your date, then." She seemed to brighten. "You've probably already discovered that Flint hates waiting."

The woman always managed to remind her that Flint had been hers first. It wiped away that moment of guilt and regret.

"He's changed a lot, I guess," Maggie said with a

laugh. "Or maybe I don't keep him waiting." It was as if her mouth had taken over. All the things she'd wished she'd said to Celeste were just waiting to come shooting out with no end in sight if she didn't stop this now.

Celeste gave a brittle nod and stepped back as if to leave. But she seemed lost, as if she'd forgotten what had brought her into the shop to begin with. She looked at her diamond-studded watch before giving Maggie a wan smile. "I'm going to have to shop another day. We have people coming over. Just the mayor and a few local dignitaries…"

Who was the woman kidding? The local mayor owned a fertilizer business in town. Maggie couldn't imagine any dignitaries unless she meant some of the people on the city council or the school board. She wanted to laugh, but she was too close to tears to do so. For a while, she'd believed she really did have a special date with Flint. But pretending made it all seem so much sadder and more pathetic.

She watched Celeste leave the store, get into her huge SUV and drive away. Maggie went to the lingerie section of the store to buy more panties—the real reason she'd come in. Normally, she bought the white cotton comfortable ones to work in. She picked up a three-pack, feeling miserable and ashamed. Her gaze shifted to the silky bikini ones in an assortment of beautiful colors.

"May I help you?" the clerk asked disinterestedly,

looking longingly after Celeste, who'd left without buying anything.

"I want these." Maggie hesitated as she picked up the silky bikini ones. "And some of these and a few of the matching bras."

The clerk's eyes lit up a little. "Is there anything else? We just got in some really cute sundresses. Let me show you my favorite."

It was the most service Maggie had ever gotten, so she let the young woman show her the sundresses. She bought two and left, feeling a little better. Too bad Flint would never see her in the sundresses, she thought. Maybe she'd wear one at work.

That thought surprised her. She'd always worn practical clothing, sensible shoes and a simple hairdo at work, while Daisy wore high heels, cute tops and skirts, and often did something fun with her long hair.

Maggie wondered at this change she felt coming over her as she walked to her car with her full shopping bag. But she was smiling. No matter how things turned out with Flint, she was going to be all right.

In the days that followed, Caroline Quinn put the ranch up for sale. She stopped into the Stagecoach Saloon the afternoon after she talked to the Realtor.

"I guess you were right," she said to Lillie as she took a stool at the bar. It was a slow afternoon. A sad country song played on the jukebox. A couple of regulars were shooting pool near the back and

Darby was in the kitchen with Billie Dee making homemade tamales.

"Right?" Lillie asked as she poured Caroline a glass of white wine. "Right about what?"

"You were confident that Trask didn't kill Gordon and you were right."

The memory of that night by the pond still haunted her. Brittany's and Patrick's trials were still months away. She hated to think what would happen to them now. "I never imagined Brittany and Patrick were responsible."

"I wondered," Caroline said after taking a sip of her wine. "A couple of times I saw them with their heads together." She shuddered. "I think they planned to get rid of me next. They both would have inherited under Gordon's will if I was dead and I think they knew it."

Lillie felt a chill skitter up her spine at the thought of what those two might have done if they had gotten away with murder a second time that night at the pond.

"They've turned on each other, I've heard. Brittany admitted hitting Gordon with a shovel but swears Patrick acted alone when he picked up the pitchfork. According to him, Brittany was the one who insisted he finish his father off."

Lillie studied the woman for a moment. "Did you know that Brittany wasn't Gordon's daughter?"

Caroline shook her head. "I also didn't know about Skip and Gordon's first wife, either..." Her smile had an edge to it. "Another reason I'm selling the ranch and leaving."

"Where will you go?" Lillie asked.

"South. Arizona maybe. Maybe even Texas. Billie Dee was trying to get me to check out the Houston area. I might." Her smile was distracted.

"Skip going with you?" Lillie had heard that he had closed down the construction company. He'd also filed a civil suit against J.T. Burrows for the money he'd embezzled. She wondered how long before J.T.'s son, Johnny, got dragged into it.

"I doubt Skip will ever see that money. J.T. is broke. I feel bad about his son, though," Caroline said, thinking also of Johnny. "I assume you've heard."

Lillie hadn't and her expression must have shown it.

"Johnny's fiancée broke it off. I doubt he'll be staying around. Like rats fleeing a sinking ship." Caroline took another drink of her wine. "What about you?"

"No plan to ever leave here," Lillie said almost proudly. "Trask bought the ranch up the road, one he'd always admired when he was a boy.

"Good for him. I always liked him. Did I hear you're engaged?"

Lillie felt her face heat as she lifted her left hand.

"Nice engagement ring," Caroline said. "I predict the two of you will be very happy."

Lillie could only smile. She didn't want to jinx the

future, but they'd been through so much, she thought they deserved some happiness.

Caroline finished her wine, dropped some money on the bar and slid off the stool to leave.

"I hope you find what you're looking for," Lillie said.

"Thank you. I think I'm going to get a plant once I'm settled and see if I can keep it alive. Only then will I consider a relationship with a man." She laughed. "What do you think?"

"I think that's a really good idea."

ELY INSISTED THEY have the picnic at the ranch. They picked a day when the bar was closed. Darby brought the Stagecoach Saloon's big barbecue along with enough pork ribs to feed an army. Billie Dee made sides from there, including jalapeño corn bread and black-eyed pea salad, smoky baked beans and two tubs of two different kinds of potato salad.

Lillie helped as much as Billie Dee would allow her. "You should be with your fiancé, not here in this kitchen working," the cook said, shaking a spatula at her. "Go have some fun with that good-looking cowboy. I've got this covered."

When she and Trask arrived at the ranch, she saw that her family was waiting. She took them all in, thankful for them in ways she couldn't have imagined just days before.

They greeted the two of them, drawing them into the gathering on the large deck that overlooked the creek. Everyone talked at once at first, the sound echoing through the pines and across the babbling water of the stream.

Lillie was content to listen and watch Trask interact with her family. She'd never been happier. The day was beautiful and she and Trask were together. Their future stretched out in front of them like Montana's big sky—seemingly endless.

Trask was excited about the building of their home. They'd spent the morning talking about floor plans and babies and cattle and their wedding. It had been bliss. She couldn't wait to become Lillie Beaumont. Mrs. Trask Beaumont. She felt like a teen again, wanting to just write the name again and again on a notebook.

"You look happy," Flint said, joining her.

"I am."

"I still can't get over what happened," he said, remnants of his fear still in his gaze. "You could have been killed."

Lillie nodded. "But you saved me. You and Trask."

He looked away for a moment. "Brittany and Patrick were just kids when they killed Gordon."

"Didn't you once tell me that murder begins at home?"

Flint chuckled. "I didn't think you ever listened to me."

"More than you think. But you have to quit arresting Dad."

He shook his head. "I'm still the sheriff. He has to quit acting up."

"Well, we're safe for a while. He's anxious to get back into the mountains." She met Flint's gaze. "You aren't still worried about him going, are you?"

He glanced toward their father. "I'll always worry, but no matter what happens, it's where he wants to be. It's where he's happiest. I certainly can't deny him that."

Flint moved away and she joined Trask again. "The hardest part is living down my past," she heard Trask tell her brothers. "Not just my past but my so-called family."

"You got a raw deal, no doubt about it, but you've overcome it. And now you have us for family," Darby said.

"Which means you really are screwed," Cyrus said with a laugh and looked around to make sure Ely wasn't within hearing distance. "At least your old man wasn't abducted by aliens."

"I believe him," Trask said. "Ely isn't one for hyperbole. Nor does he scare easily, but when he talks about that night, I've seen the terror in his eyes."

Darby studied him for a long moment. "You might be the only one who believes him."

Trask shrugged. "I've read about other people from around the world who claim to have been abducted by aliens. Their stories all have a lot in common." He glanced up at the vast, clear blue sky overhead. "I think it is pretty arrogant to think that we are the only beings in our galaxy."

"I didn't realize it before," Hawk said, "but you and Lillie are perfect for each other. You're going to fit right into this family." He raised his beer in a toast. "Welcome. Always room for another nutcase in the Cahill family, right?"

They ate at a large table, devouring the ribs and the sides Billie Dee had made.

"I love this corn bread," Darby said. "We have to serve this with your chili at the bar." The cook beamed at the compliments.

Ely ate with his usual healthy appetite, but Lillie caught him looking toward the mountains longingly. The towering peaks, the rocky cliffs, the stands of cool pines, those were now the loves of his life. But she suspected they were also his escape from whatever haunted him. Aliens or a jungle in Vietnam. They might never know what monsters he had to fear.

But he looked peaceful as he stared at the mountains wistfully. Soon he would be back there again and they wouldn't see him for maybe months—until she got a call from Flint that their father needed to be bailed out of jail.

After they were stuffed as ticks, Hawk picked up his guitar and began to play an old Western ballad. Lillie watched him, seeing how much he loved to make music. He had talent. Not that he'd ever pursued it. He just enjoyed playing his guitar and she loved to hear him play.

She was smiling to herself when a shadow fell over her. Looking up, she saw Trask standing over her. Devilment danced in his blue eyes, making her heart beat a little faster. "Lillie?" He held out his hand. Her heartbeat picked up the beat of the music as she stood and let him pull her out onto an open space on the wide deck.

"Dance with me," he said, the deep tone of his voice sending goose bumps skittering over her.

She smiled. There was no place she loved more than being in his arms, she thought as he pulled her to him. Her body fit perfectly into his. She laid her head on his shoulder and breathed in his masculine scent mixed with the smell of the pines and the creek below.

Lillie told herself that she would always remember this moment in time, being in Trask's arms, her family all around her, Hawk's music filling the spring afternoon air. She closed her eyes, tucking it neatly away in her heart for keeps—just as she had Trask all those years ago.

DARBY STOOD IN the doorway of the Stagecoach Saloon kitchen and watched Kendall Raines working behind the bar. Her blond hair was pulled back into a ponytail that swung as she moved. He watched it brush her slim back as she stopped to talk to one of the regulars. Her blue eyes lit and her full mouth turned up in a near blinding smile.

Everyone loved her. She was the perfect employee. So why wasn't he interested in her?

He shook his head. Maybe Lillie was right and there was something wrong with him.

He walked back into the kitchen, where Billie Dee was making enchiladas.

"Why don't you ask her out?" the cook said without looking at him. "You have something better to do?"

"I don't know what you're talking about."

Billie Dee laughed and shook her head.

"She's not my type."

The cook turned to give him a disbelieving look. "She's *everyone's* type unless…"

He chuckled. "I like women, if that's what you're asking."

"Well, you couldn't tell it by me." She turned fully from her cooking to put her hands on her hips as she considered him. "I haven't seen you date since I got here. What's up with that?"

"I haven't met anyone who…interests me. I like a challenge. Someone who intrigues me."

Billie Dee let out a hoot at that. "Intrigues you, huh?" She shook her head again. "You Cahills, never met such a stubborn, independent bunch. Guess you all want to be bachelors the rest of your lives."

"There's worse things," Darby said and looked back toward the bar. Kendall was laughing with a couple of ranchers at the far end of the bar. She definitely had something about her that drew men, there was no getting around that.

He just wasn't one of them. "Did Lillie tell you she's making me go to the Chokecherry Festival this year?"

"I knew that the saloon sponsored part of the festival," Billie Dee said. "Other than donating money, what else do you have to do?"

"Give a short speech." Just the thought of it made his stomach roil. "And throw Stagecoach Saloon T-shirts to the crowd."

The cook turned to look at him and laughed. "I think you can handle that."

He wished he shared her confidence.

"Maybe you'll meet someone…intriguing there."

Darby rolled his eyes, hating that he'd confided in her. "You and my sister. Always trying to marry me off. Why don't you play matchmaker with my brothers?"

"Because they're hopeless," Billie Dee said, sounding serious. "But you, Darby? You, I have hope for."

* * * * *

Read on for a sneak peek at
OUTLAW'S HONOR,
New York Times *bestselling author B.J. Daniels's*
next CAHILL RANCH NOVEL

DARBY CAHILL ADJUSTED his Stetson as he moved toward the bandstand. The streets of Gilt Edge, Montana, were filled with revelers who'd come to celebrate the yearly chokecherry harvest on this beautiful day. The main street had been blocked off for all the events. People had come from miles around for the celebration of a cherry that was so tart it made your mouth pucker.

Darby figured it just proved that people would celebrate anything as he climbed the steps. Normally, his twin sister, Lillie, attended, but this year she was determined that he should do more of their promotion at these events.

"I hate it as much as you do," she'd assured him. "But believe me. You'll get more attention up there on the stage than me. Just say a few words, throw T-shirts into the crowd, have some fry bread and come home. You can do this." Clearly, she knew his weakness for fry bread as well as his dislike of being the center of attention.

The T-shirts were from the Stagecoach Saloon, the bar and café the two of them owned and operated outside of town. Ever since it opened, the bar had helped sponsor the Chokecherry Festival each year.

He heard his name being announced and sighed as he made his way up the rest of the steps to the microphone to deafening applause. He tipped his hat to the crowd, swallowed the lump in his throat and said, "It's an honor to be here and be part of such a wonderful celebration."

"Are you taking part in the seed-spitting competition?" someone yelled from the crowd, and others joined in. Along with being bitter, chokecherries were mostly seed.

"I'm going to leave that to the professionals," he said and reached for the box of T-shirts, wanting this over with as quickly as possible. He didn't like being in the spotlight any longer than he had to. Also, he hoped that once he started throwing the shirts, everyone would forget about the pit-spitting contest later.

He was in mid-throw when he spotted the woman in the crowd. What had caught his eye was the bright-colored scarf around her dark hair. It fluttered in the breeze, giving him only glimpses of her face.

He let go and the T-shirt sailed through the air as if caught on the breeze. He saw with a curse that it was headed right for the woman's back. Grimacing, he watched the rolled-up T-shirt clip the woman's shoulder.

She looked back, clearly startled. He had the impression of serious dark eyes, full lips. Their gazes locked for an instant and he felt something like lightning pierce his heart. For a moment, he couldn't breathe. Rooted to the spot, all he could hear was the drumming of his heart, the roaring crowd a dull hum in the background.

Someone behind the woman in the crowd scooped up the T-shirt and, scarf fluttering, the woman turned away, disappearing into the throng of people.

What had *that* been about? His heart was still pounding. What had he seen in those bottomless dark eyes that had him…breathless? He knew what Lillie would have said. Love at first sight, something he would have scoffed at—before moments ago.

"Do you want me to help you?" a voice asked at his side.

Darby nodded to the festival volunteer. He threw a T-shirt, looking in the crowd for the woman. She was gone.

Once the box of T-shirts was empty, he hurriedly stepped off the stage into the moving mass. His job was done. His plan had been to have some fry bread and then head back to the saloon. He was happiest behind the bar. Or on the back of a horse. Being Montana born and raised in open country, crowds made him nervous.

The main street had been blocked off and now booths lined both sides of the street all the way up the hill that led out of town. Everywhere he looked, there were chokecherry T-shirts and hats, dish towels and coffee mugs. Most chokecherries found their way into wine or syrup or jelly, but today he could have purchased the berries in lemonade or pastries or even barbecue sauce. He passed stands of fresh fruit and vegetables, crafts of all kinds and every type of food.

As he moved through the swarm of bodies now filling the downtown street, the scent of fry bread in the air, he couldn't help searching for the woman. That had been the strangest experience he'd ever had. He told himself it could have been heatstroke had the day been hotter. Also, he felt perfectly fine now.

He didn't want to make more of it than it was, and yet he'd give anything to see her again. As crazy as it sounded, he couldn't throw off the memory of that sharp, hard shot to his heart when their gazes had met.

As he worked his way through the crowd, following the smell of fry bread, he watched for the colorful scarf the woman had been wearing. He needed to know what that was about earlier. He told himself he was being ridiculous, but if he got a chance to see her again…

Someone in the crowd stumbled against his back. He caught what smelled like lemons in the air as a figure started to brush by him. Out of the corner of his eye, he saw the colorful scarf wrapped around her head of dark hair.

Like a man sleepwalking, he grabbed for the end of the scarf as it fluttered in the breeze. His fingers closed on the silken fabric, but only for a second.

She was moving fast enough that his fingers lost purchase and dropped to her arm.

In midstep, she half turned toward him, his sudden touch slowing her. In those few seconds, he saw her face, saw her startled expression. He had the bizarre thought that this woman was in trouble. Without realizing it, he tightened his grip on her arm.

Her eyes widened in alarm. It all happened in a matter of seconds. As she tried to pull away, his hand slid down the silky smooth skin of her forearm until it caught on the wide bracelet she was wearing on her right wrist.

Something fell from her hand as she jerked free of his hold. He heard a snap and her bracelet came off in his hand. His gaze went to the *thump* of whatever she'd dropped as it hit the ground. Looking down, he saw what she'd dropped. *His wallet?*

Astonishment rocketed through him as he realized that when she'd bumped into him from behind, she'd picked his pocket! Feeling like a fool, he bent to retrieve his wallet. Jostled by the meandering throng, he quickly rose and tried to find her, although he wasn't sure what exactly he planned to do when he did. Music blared from a Western band over the roar of voices.

He stood holding the woman's bracelet in one hand and his wallet in the other, looking for the bright scarf in the mass of gyrating festivalgoers.

She was gone.

Darby stared down at his wallet, then at the

strange large gold-tinted cuff bracelet and laughed at his own foolishness. His moment of love at first sight had been with a *thief*? A two-bit pickpocket? Wouldn't his family love this!

Just his luck, he thought as he pocketed his wallet and considered what to do with what appeared to be heavy, cheap costume jewelry. He'd been lucky. He'd gotten off easy in more ways than one. His first thought was to chuck the bracelet in the nearest trash can and put the whole episode behind him.

But he couldn't quite shake off the feeling he'd gotten when he'd looked into her eyes—or when he'd realized the woman was a thief. Telling himself it wouldn't hurt to keep a reminder of his close call, he slipped the bracelet into his jacket pocket.

MARIAH AYERS GRABBED her bare wrist, the heat of the man's touch still tingling there. What wasn't there was her prized bracelet, she realized with a start. Her heart dropped. She hadn't taken the bracelet off since her grandmother had put it on her, making her promise never to take it off.

"This will keep you safe and bring you luck," her grandmother Loveridge had promised on her deathbed. "Be true to who you are."

She fought the urge to turn around in the surging throng of people, go find him and demand he give it back. But she knew she couldn't do that for fear of being arrested. Or worse. So much for the bracelet bringing her luck, she thought, heart heavy. She had no choice but to continue moving as she was swept up in the flowing crowd. Maybe she could find a high perch where she could spot her mark. And then what?

Mariah figured she'd cross that bridge when she came to it. Pulling off her bright-colored scarf, she shoved it into her pocket. It was a great device for misdirection—normally, but now it would be a dead giveaway.

Ahead, she spotted stairs and quickly climbed a half-dozen steps at the front of a bank to stop and look back.

The street was a sea of cowboy hats. One cowboy looked like another to her. How would she ever be able to find him—let alone get her bracelet back given that by now he would know what she'd been up to? She hadn't even gotten a good look at him. Shaken and disheartened, she told herself she would do whatever it took. She desperately needed that bracelet back—and not just for luck or sentimental reasons. It was her ace in the hole.

Two teenagers passed, arguing over which one of them got the free T-shirt they'd scored. She thought of the cowboy she'd seen earlier up on the stage, the one throwing the T-shirts. He'd looked right at her. Their gazes had met and she'd felt as if he had seen into her dark heart—if not her soul.

No wonder she'd blown a simple pick. She was rusty at this, clearly, but there had been a time when she could recall each of her marks with clarity. She closed her eyes. Nothing. Squeezing them tighter, she concentrated.

With a start, she recalled that his cowboy hat had been a light gray. She focused on her mark's other physical attributes. Long legs clad in denim, slim hips, muscular thighs, broad shoulders. A very nice behind. She shook off that image. A jean jacket over a pale blue checked shirt. Her pickpocketing might not be up to par, but at least there was nothing wrong with her memory, she thought as she opened her eyes and again scanned the crowd. Her uncle had taught her well.

But she needed more. She closed her eyes again. She'd gotten only a glimpse of his face when he'd grabbed first her scarf and then her arm. Her eyes flew open as she had a thought. He must have been onto her immediately. Had she botched the pick that badly? She really *was* out of practice.

She closed her eyes again and tried to concentrate over the sound of the two teens still arguing over the T-shirt. Yes, she'd seen his face. A handsome, rugged face and pale eyes. Not blue. No. Gray? Yes, with a start she realized where she'd seen him before. It was the same man as the one from the bandstand, the one who'd thrown the T-shirt and hit her. She was sure of it.

"Excuse me, I'll buy that T-shirt from you," she said, catching up to the two teens as they took their squabble off toward a burger stand.

They both turned to look at her in surprise. "It's not for sale," said the one.

The other asked, "How much?"

"Ten bucks."

"No way."

"You got it *free*," Mariah pointed out, only to have both girls' faces freeze in stubborn determination. "Fine, twenty."

"Make it thirty," the greedier of the two said.

She shook her head as she dug out the money. Her grandmother would have given them the evil eye. Or threatened to put some kind of curse on them. "You're thieves, you know that?" she said as she grabbed the T-shirt before they could take off with it *and* her money.

Escaping down one of the side streets, she finally got a good look at what was printed across the front of the T-shirt. *Stagecoach Saloon, Gilt Edge, Montana.*

LILLIE CAHILL HESITATED at the back door of the Stage-coach Saloon. It had been a stagecoach stop back in the 1800s when gold had been coming out of the mine at Gilt Edge. Each stone, like the old wooden floorboards inside, had a story. She'd often wished the building could talk.

When the old stagecoach stop had come on the market, she had jumped at purchasing it, determined to save the historical two-story stone building. It had been her twin's idea to open a bar and café. She'd been skeptical at first but trusted Darby's instincts. The place had taken off.

Lately, she felt sad just looking at the place.

Until recently, she'd lived upstairs in the remodeled apartment from the time they'd bought the old building. She'd made it hers by collecting a mix of furnishings from garage sales and junk shops. This had not just been her home. It was her heart, she thought, eyes misting as she remembered the day she'd moved out.

Since her engagement and the completion of the home on the ranch with her fiancé, Trask Beaumont, she'd given up her apartment to her twin, Darby. He had been living in a cabin not far from the bar, but he'd jumped at the chance to live upstairs.

Now she glanced toward the back window. She'd left the curtains. One of them flapped in the wind. Darby must have left the window open. She hadn't been up there to see what he'd done with the place. She wasn't sure she wanted to know, since she'd moved most everything out, leaving it pretty much a blank slate. She thought it might still be a blank slate, knowing her brother.

Pushing open the back door into the bar kitchen, she was met with the most wonderful of familiar scents. Fortunately, not everything had changed in her life, she thought, her mood picking up some as she entered the warm café kitchen.

"Tell me those are your famous enchiladas," she

said to Billie Dee, their heavyset fiftysomething
Texas cook.

"You know it, sugar," the cook said with a laugh.
"You want me to dish you up a plate? I've got homemade pintos and some Spanish rice like you've never
tasted."

"You mean *hotter* than I've ever tasted."

"Oh, you Montanans. I'll toughen you up yet."

Lillie laughed. "I'd love a plate." She pulled out
a chair at the table where the staff usually ate in the
kitchen and watched Billie Dee fill two plates.

"So how are the wedding plans coming along?"
the cook asked as she joined her at the table.

"I thought a simple wedding here with family and
friends would be a cinch," Lillie said and took a bite
of the enchilada. She closed her eyes for a moment,
savoring the sweet, hot sauce before all the other fla-
vors hit her. She groaned softly. "These are the best
you've ever made."

"Bless your heart," Billie Dee said, smiling. "I
take it the wedding has gotten more complicated?"

"I can't get married without my father and who
knows when he'll be coming out of the mountains."
Their father, Ely Cahill, was a true mountain man
now who spent most of the year deep up in the mountains either panning for gold or living off the land.
He'd given up ranching after their mother had died
and had turned the business over to her brothers
Hawk and Cyrus.

Their oldest brother, Tucker, had taken off at eighteen. They hadn't seen or heard from him since. Their father was the only one who wasn't worried about him.

"Tuck needs space. He's gone off to find himself. He'll come home when he's ready," Ely had said.

The rest of the family hadn't been so convinced. But if Tuck was anything like their father, they would have heard something from the cops. Ely had a bad habit of coming out of the mountains thirsty for whiskey—and ending up in their brother Sheriff Flint Cahill's jail. Apparently, Tuck had avoided getting arrested, wherever he was. Lillie didn't worry about him. She had four other brothers to deal with right here in Gilt Edge.

"I can see somethin's botherin' you," Billie Dee said now.

Lillie nodded. "Trask insists we wait to get married, since he hopes to have the finishing touches on the house so we can have the reception there."

Trask, the only man she'd ever loved, had come back into her life after so many years that she'd thought she'd never see him again. But they'd found their way back together and now he was building a house for them on the ranch he'd bought not far from the bar.

"Waitin' sounds reasonable," the cook said between bites.

"I wish we'd eloped."

"Something tells me the wedding isn't the problem," Billie Dee said, using her fork to punctuate her words.

"I'll admit, it's been hard giving up my apartment upstairs. I put so much love into it."

"Darby will take good care of it."

She couldn't help shooting a disbelieving look at Billie Dee. "He'll probably just throw down a bedroll and call it home. You know how he is. Have you seen what he's moved in so far?"

Billie Dee gave her a sympathetic look. "I know it was your baby, but once you took out your things, it didn't feel so much like yours, right?"

Lillie nodded. "Still, it was my home for so long. I thought maybe Darby might need my help decorating it."

The cook laughed. "I'd say 'decorating' is probably the last thing on his mind. So how is the new home?"

"Beautiful. Trask is great about letting me do whatever I want. But it still isn't like my apartment. I put so much of myself into that place. I miss it."

"And you will put so much of yourself into your home with Trask. It's going to take time. How long did it take you to get the apartment upstairs to your liking?"

"Years."

"Exactly." Billie Dee studied her for a moment. "You aren't gettin' cold feet about the weddin' and marryin' Trask, are you?"

"No." Lillie shook her head adamantly. "Never."

She thought of the day when she and Trask would have a family and she wouldn't even be working at the bar anymore, but pushed that away. "I guess change is hard for me. I feel like I'm giving up the bar even though I'll still be half owner and still work until the babies come."

"Babies?"

"I'm not pregnant yet, but Trask and I want a big family."

"So who is coming to your wedding? I'm still waiting for you to introduce me to some big, strong Montana cowboy," Billie Dee joked as she had often before. "I want one like Trask."

"Who doesn't?" Lillie said with a laugh. Trask was handsome as the devil, sweet, loving, wonderful. "Guess I'll have to rope you up one."

"I can do my own ropin', thank you very much. Just point me at one."

"You have someone in mind?"

"Might. Ain't tellin'." She gave Lillie a knowing wink.

"By the way, speaking of handsome cowboys, where is Darby? I thought he'd be back by now from the festival." She'd barely gotten the words out when they heard a vehicle pull up under the tree next to the building where Darby always parked. A few moments later, her brother came in the back door, took a whiff and said, "Billie Dee's famous enchiladas."

She and the cook both laughed. "Don't worry. We left plenty for you and our customers tonight."

Darby tossed his hat onto the hook by the back door and hung up his keys on the board along with the extra keys to the bar and the upstairs apartment. Not that Lillie would need to use the spare key. She still had an apartment key on her key chain. She just hadn't used it.

"I was just asking Billie Dee if she'd seen what you did with the apartment," Lillie said.

Her twin brother scoffed. "If you're so curious, go on up. But I warn you, you won't like it."

"Why?"

"Because I'm a firm believer in less is more."

She groaned. "You haven't done anything."

"I wouldn't say that. I have a bed, chest of drawers, the lamps and rug you left me, the television you left me and a chair I bought for myself."

"That's it?"

"That's all I need, little sis." As he took off his jean jacket and hung it, Lillie heard something make a clinking sound in one of the pockets. He heard it too and reached into the pocket to pull out his cell phone and shove whatever had "clinked" deeper into the pocket.

He really was handsome, she thought as she studied her brother. A real catch for some woman. The problem wasn't Darby. She got the feeling he was open to a relationship, but that he hadn't found a woman who was interested.

The cook motioned toward the stove. "Help yourself. But I thought you would have eaten at the festival."

"Wasn't hungry," he said, his back to them as he pocketed his phone and went to the stove to fill a plate.

Both women looked at him in stunned silence, then at each other. Darby was *always* hungry. He stayed too busy to gain weight, but there was never anything wrong with his appetite.

"You didn't even have any fry bread?" Lillie asked. "That doesn't sound like you."

He shrugged, still not looking at them.

She felt a stab of guilt for making him go to the festival. In truth, she could have covered it. But she thought he ought to start doing it, since she didn't know how long she would be able to. She and Trask were planning to start a family right away.

"That was the only thing I *was* looking forward to," he said. "But the line was too long." He looked away.

Lillie wondered what her brother was leaving out. He never missed a chance to have fry bread. "But otherwise everything went all right?"

"I said a few words. Tossed the T-shirts into the crowd and got out of there before I had to take part in the pit-spitting contest," he said and stabbed a bite of enchilada. He mugged a face at her. "Did you know they were going to try to rope me into the pit spitting?"

She laughed. "No, but I would have paid money

to see that." Still, as she studied her twin, she got the feeling something had happened to upset her usually unflappable brother. She and Darby had always been close. They'd shared the same womb together. But she couldn't put her finger on what it was about him that made her think he wasn't telling her everything.

"Did you run into our brothers while you were there?" she asked.

"Didn't see Hawk or Cyrus, but Flint was walking around looking like a Western lawman," Darby said.

"He *is* a Western lawman," Lillie said of her brother Sheriff Flint Cahill, the black sheep of the family. Flint had always played by the rules. Now he followed the letter of the law, while the rest of them had never minded bending the rules or the law. Needless to say, they often butted heads over it—especially when he arrested their father on those occasions when Ely came out of the mountains and had too much to drink.

"Hawk and Cyrus stopped by earlier," Billie Dee said as she got up to put her plate in the dishwasher. "They said they were moving cattle today and skipping the festival and all that craziness. I asked if they were going to the dance tonight. No surprise, they weren't."

"They are going to stay old crotchety bachelors forever at this rate," Lillie said and saw that her brother had stopped eating. He was picking at the spicy pinto beans distractedly, frowning as if his mind was miles away. Or maybe just back downtown where the festival was still going strong.

Lillie felt worse about making him take care of their promotion at the Chokecherry Festival. Now something was bothering him that hadn't been this morning before he'd left.

"Is everything all right?" she asked, bringing him out of his trance.

Darby smiled, complimented Billie Dee on the food and dug back into his meal before he said, "Couldn't be better."

But she sensed that wasn't true. Something was definitely different about him.

Since he and Lillie had traded shifts today, Darby had the rest of the day off. He almost wished he was working, though. At least that would help keep his mind off the woman at the festival.

"Thanks for dinner," he said to Billie Dee as he put his plate into the dishwasher. "You sure you can handle it tonight without me?" he asked his sister.

"It will be slow with everyone at the festival and street dance," she said. "I'll probably close early, but thanks for the offer. What are you going to do the rest of the day?"

He shrugged. "Probably just take it easy." Retrieving his Stetson and jacket, he headed upstairs, glad his sister hadn't asked to see what he'd done with her old apartment. As he unlocked the door and looked around, he admitted there wasn't much to see.

When it had been Lillie's, the place had such a

homey feel. Now it was anything but. He'd bought a bed, taken his chest of drawers from his room at the ranch complete with the stickers from his youth on the front and found an old leather recliner at a garage sale.

Other than that, the apartment was pretty sparse. Fortunately, Lillie had left the rug on the living room floor and a couple of lamps, along with a television. The place was definitely nicer than where he'd been living in an old cabin, so it was just fine with him. More than fine. He'd never needed much for creature comforts.

As he closed the door behind him, he felt bad, though. He'd have to be a complete fool not to know that Lillie was dying to help him "decorate." He cringed at the thought. She'd fuss and bring in plants he'd forget to water, a bunch of pillows he didn't have a place for and knickknacks he'd end up breaking. No, she had her big house on the ranch to do her magic. He wouldn't bother her. At least that would be his excuse.

He hung up his hat and was about to do the same with his jean jacket when he remembered the bracelet. Taking it out, he turned it in his fingers. It was fancy enough looking. Heavier than it appeared too, the surface buffed to a rich patina. He brushed his fingertip over the round black stone on one side of the wide cuff bracelet. Probably plastic. The whole bracelet was no doubt made out of some cheap metal and not worth anything. Otherwise, why would the woman have to resort to stealing?

As he started to put it down, he noticed that the clasp was broken. It must have happened when he'd pulled it from her arm. With a start, he remembered the tan line on her wrist, a wide white patch of skin where her bracelet had been as she was hurrying into the crowd. Surprised, he realized this was a piece of jewelry she wore all the time. If it was nothing but cheap costume jewelry, then it must have sentimental value. He frowned, as curious about the bracelet as he was about the woman who'd worn it.

His mind whirling, he looked at his phone to check the time. The local jewelry store was still open. If he went the back way and entered the store from the rear, he could avoid the crowds still on the main street.

There was, of course, a temptation to look again for the woman. But he told himself that she wouldn't have hung around. After what happened, wouldn't she be worried that he'd alerted the sheriff about her?

Now that he thought of it, why hadn't he? What if she'd been picking pockets all day at the festival? He let out a groan, realizing that he'd been so captivated by her that he hadn't even thought about reporting her.

Maybe it was enough, he told himself to relieve some of his guilt, that she would think the sheriff was searching for her after her botched pickpocketing with him and leave. If he was right, there would be no reason to look for her in the crowd.

Darby knew what he was really looking for—something that would tell him about the woman who'd worn the bracelet. He was still curious. Still shaken by the effect she'd had on him for that second when their eyes had met.

The piece looked unusual enough, he told himself. The fact that it must have been a favorite of hers piqued his interest even more. He stuffed the bracelet back into his jacket pocket and, Stetson on his head, headed for the door.

THE ELDERLY JEWELER put the loupe to his eye and slowly studied the bracelet Darby had handed him. "You say you picked it up at a garage sale?"

He wished now that he'd come up with a better story. "In Billings."

"Interesting."

Darby waited as jeweler John T. Marshall went over every square inch of the bracelet. "It's just costume jewelry, right, John?" No answer. The piece couldn't be *that* interesting, he thought.

John finally put the bracelet down along with the loupe. He shook his head, seeming unable to take his eyes off the piece. "It's not costume jewelry. It's 14-karat yellow gold."

That explained why it was so heavy. With a start, Darby realized it could be worth more than just sentimental value to the woman. "So what can you tell me about it?"

"The gold alone in weight is worth several thousand dollars, but its real worth is that it is a rare piece of vintage Gypsy jewelry."

"Gypsy jewelry?"

The jeweler nodded. "I've only read about it. This type of cuff was once made for the whole family, including men and children, and was usually worn in pairs, one on each wrist. This bracelet is definitely rare."

"You're saying it's *old*?"

"In this country, most surviving pieces date from 1900 to 1930." He picked up the loupe again to look at the black round stone at the center. "Gypsies almost always used synthetic stones because of difficulties in verifying a gemstone's authenticity unlike real gold that cannot be faked easily."

"So the stone is what? Plastic?"

"In this rare case, a precious gemstone, onyx. This is an amazing find. I've never seen any original Gypsy jewelry before. It's quite remarkable." He picked up the bracelet again and began to point out the designs on it.

"Look at this profiled face of a beautiful woman, possibly a Roma queen.

"Roma. The word *Gypsy* is a misnomer. They were called Gypsies because they were believed to have come from Egypt. But they were actually part of an ethnic group whose ancestors left India a thousand years ago. Many of them still call themselves Gypsies, though some consider it a derogatory term."

Darby thought of the woman he'd seen at the festival. Was she Roma?

The jeweler was still inspecting the bracelet with a kind of awe. "Flowers and stars are common, along with a horseshoe for luck. It is always worn with the horseshoe up so the luck doesn't spill out." He traced a finger over one of the designs. "The wirework or filigree is so delicate." He met Darby's gaze. "I'd say this bracelet is worth from ten to twenty thousand dollars."

Darby was taken aback. He'd almost thrown the piece away. Worse, he hadn't picked it up at a garage sale—he'd torn if off a woman's wrist. Admittedly, she was trying to pick his pocket at the time, but still…

"And you say you paid fifty cents for it? The person who sold it must not have known its real worth." John shook his head. "If you're interested in selling this piece—"

"No," he said quickly. "If it's that rare, I think I'd like to keep it. But I do want to get the clasp fixed."

The jeweler nodded. "I don't blame you. It will only take a minute."

Darby stepped to the back of the shop to watch as John worked. He couldn't believe this. He'd really thought the jeweler would tell him it was nothing but junk. He thought about the woman who'd been wearing it and found himself even more intrigued.

"It's a shame how much of this jewelry has been lost," the jeweler was saying as he worked. "Much of it was melted down in the Great Depression. For the wearer, the jewelry was like a portable bank account. With the price of gold up like it has been, people have been melting it down again to sell."

So why hadn't the woman sold it if her situation was dire enough that she had to steal? Or was it possible, like him, she'd underestimated its value, since maybe she'd stolen it herself?

"You are wise to keep this," John was saying. "According to superstition, Gypsy jewelry is very good luck to have, but bad luck to sell. You wouldn't want to sell off your good fortune now, would you?"

Don't miss
OUTLAW'S HONOR by B.J. Daniels,
available June 2017 wherever
HQN books and ebooks are sold.
www.HQNBooks.com

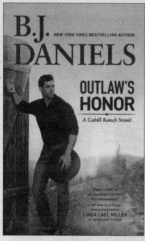

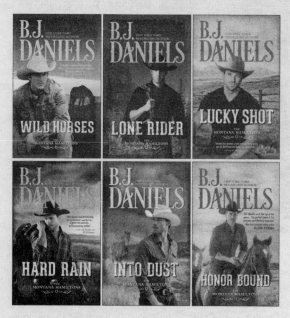

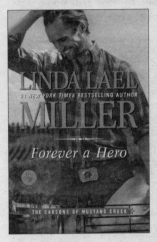

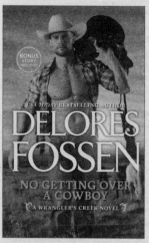

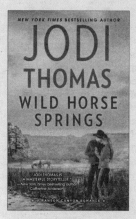

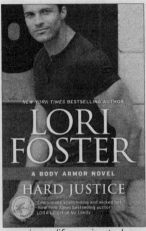

Turn your love of reading into rewards you'll love with
Harlequin My Rewards